THE CREEK

A BERRY SPRINGS NOVEL

AMANDA MCKINNEY

HH TISEVICH

Paperback ISBN 978-1-7324635-4-7
eBook ISBN 978-1-7324635-3-0

Editor(s): Nancy Brown
Jennifer Graybeal

https://www.amandamckinneyauthor.com

DEDICATION

For Mama

ALSO BY AMANDA

THRILLER NOVELS:

The Stone Secret - A Thriller Novel

A Marriage of Lies - A Thriller Novel

The Widow of Weeping Pines

The Raven's Wife

The Lie Between Us

The Keeper's Closet

The Mad Women - A Box Set

ROMANCE SUSPENSE/THRILLER NOVELS:

THE ANTI-HERO COLLECTION:

Mine

His

ON THE EDGE SERIES:

Buried Deception

Trail of Deception

BESTSELLING STEELE SHADOWS SERIES:

Cabin 1 (Steele Shadows Security)

Cabin 2 (Steele Shadows Security)

Cabin 3 (Steele Shadows Security)

Phoenix (Steele Shadows Rising)

Jagger (Steele Shadows Investigations)

Ryder (Steele Shadows Investigations)

Her Mercenary (Steele Shadows Mercenaries)

BESTSELLING DARK ROMANTIC SUSPENSE SERIES:

Rattlesnake Road

Redemption Road

AWARD-WINNING ROMANTIC SUSPENSE SERIES:

The Woods (A Berry Springs Novel)

The Lake (A Berry Springs Novel)

The Storm (A Berry Springs Novel)

The Fog (A Berry Springs Novel)

The Creek (A Berry Springs Novel)

The Shadow (A Berry Springs Novel)

The Cave (A Berry Springs Novel)

The Viper

Devil's Gold (A Black Rose Mystery, Book 1)

Hatchet Hollow (A Black Rose Mystery, Book 2)

Tomb's Tale (A Black Rose Mystery Book 3)

Evil Eye (A Black Rose Mystery Book 4)

Sinister Secrets (A Black Rose Mystery Book 5)

And many more to come...

LET'S CONNECT!

Text **AMANDABOOKS to 66866** to sign up
for Amanda's Newsletter and get the latest
on new releases, promos, and freebies! Or, sign up below.

https://www.amandamckinneyauthor.com

THE CREEK

When DNA evidence links Lieutenant Quinn Colson's brother to the scene of a grisly murder, Quinn realizes he'll do anything to keep his brother from returning to prison, even if it costs him his job... and the woman who's stolen his heart.

Shooting range owner by day, yoga instructor by night, Bobbi Cross is as ironic as her two businesses—she's an independent, tough-as-nails woman, except when she's meditating away the discontentment she feels inside. But no amount of Zen can help her when she finds her business partner bludgeoned to death in a burning house. The scene is something straight out of a horror movie, excluding the smothering hot Police Lieutenant who saves her from the flames.

Quinn Colson accepted a position at the police department in the small, southern town of Berry Springs for one reason —to keep an eye on his little brother, newly released from prison. He couldn't care less that the locals eye him like the plague, until he meets a green-eyed stunner at the scene of his first big case. Bobbi Cross is nothing like anyone he's ever met, and when they team up to solve her friend's murder, it becomes evident that no woman in town is safe from the ruthless killer, including Bobbi.

With a mountain of evidence that doesn't appear to link together, the case is as confusing as his growing feelings for the town's sweetheart... until a DNA test connects his brother to the scene of the crime. In an instant, Quinn's world is turned upside down, and he realizes he'll do anything to keep his brother from returning to prison, even if it costs him his job... and the woman who's stolen his heart.

PROLOGUE

HE RAN HIS calloused fingers over the bright red silk, then lifted the teeny straps to his nose and inhaled. A smile spread as he imagined her warm skin against the fabric.

Another deep inhale, and this time, his pulse picked up.

He wanted her *so bad.*

He squeezed the thong in his hand, imagining the thin lace hugging low on her hips. And the silk, sliding in between...

Heat flushed below. His pants began to tighten.

Not now. *Not yet.*

He fingered the rest of the racy lingerie folded neatly in the drawer, the bright colors standing out against the darkness of the room. The woman took pride in her underwear.

A rush of jealousy caught him. How many men had seen these provocative little numbers? How many men had seen her naked? How many men had she been with?

A snarl lifted his lip. When was the last time Hannah had seen that asshole she'd been talking to lately? A lowlife loser. Had they had sex?

He wasn't naive, he knew she was no virgin, but how long ago was the last time? Was he about to be where some other bastard, someone unworthy, had just had their dick? If so, had she enjoyed it?

Anger had his jaw clenching. It was the anger that no amount of anti-depressants, anxiety meds or booze could control. And after the accident, things had only gotten worse. He'd added pain pills to the mix, giving him a new appreciation for drugs. But, not even those horse pills slowed him down. He'd never had a jealous streak, until he met Hannah. The beautiful, alluring, hypnotizing Hannah. It made him insane to imagine her with another man.

He inhaled through his nose and shook his head. It didn't matter. It didn't fucking matter because she was going to be his from now on. Starting tonight, no other man would lay their hands on that ivory, smooth skin. It was going to be his body now. She was going to be his.

The night was black as ink—ideal for his impromptu visit, or break-in, more like. He hadn't planned to break-in. It was just supposed to be a visit to profess his love, but the door had been unlocked. Fate? No doubt about it.

But, to his surprise, she wasn't home, so he helped himself to a tour of her cute, little house, and her panty drawer had quickly become his favorite spot.

His gaze shifted to the woods that surrounded the house. He squinted, barely able to make out the spot just beyond the tree line where he'd hidden exactly thirteen times in the last two weeks. It would've been fourteen times if it weren't for a damn appointment he'd had one evening. It was a perfect spot, nestled between two pine trees behind a thicket of bushes, with an unobstructed view into her bedroom. He was surprised the grass hadn't died—or hell, thrived—around it. He'd dumped enough semen to leave a mark. It had become his little spot. His little spot carved out of the woods to watch the woman that had completely captivated him.

It had started out as a small crush that quickly turned into an obsession. That obsession turned into an unrelenting desire. The first time he'd jacked off to her picture—one that he'd taken from his spot—he'd had the most intense orgasm of his life. He'd almost taken a picture of the load he'd blown all over his bathroom floor. Years and years of emptiness finally being released in a dizzying explosion. He *felt,* for what seemed like the first time in his life. It was a euphoria that was instantly addictive. Like a drug. And that's when it began. Hannah was the one, he knew it.

Over the course of the last month, the obsession took a turn, into all-consuming thoughts about being intimate with her. In every different position imaginable, in every possible crevasse of her body. It was all he could think about.

Since that turning point, it had become a daily ritual to jack off to her picture every day, sometimes twice a day. His life had totally changed. He finally had something to focus on that made him happy. Truly happy. Before her, it took everything he had just to get out of bed in the mornings. He hated his life. His dark, boring, disgusting life. But now, he found himself actually waking up before his alarm clock, excited to jump in the shower and rub himself, thinking of her, until he climaxed. He'd even purchased a strawberry scented body wash to use while he stroked himself, imagining it was her hand. He'd spend the days thinking of her, wondering what she was doing, counting down the hours until he could take his evening shower and visit her again, in his head—and on it, for that matter. During times that he felt particularly restless, he'd bring in props. A heated jar of jelly took his imagination to the next level.

He'd fantasized about tying her up while doing things to her body that was so taboo, people only whispered about it behind dark shadows. Things that could get him thrown into jail. He loved it all. He wanted to do it all. He wanted her submissive underneath him, a true sign of love. He wanted her to touch every part of his body, her fingers, her tongue, use toys on him, and then take it when he wanted to do it back to her. His new sexual obsession had taken his porn watching to new levels. He'd found videos on the dark web that made his heart pound so hard that his ears rang. He never knew he had a thing for S&M. But there was something about the look of fear in someone's eyes, the submissiveness. The dominance, the control. He wanted to control her. He was going to be her master.

God, he *wanted* her.

She'd become like a magnet to him. An exquisite, kind, soft woman that seemed to exude beauty from the inside out. Women like that never showed him attention. They either ignored him, or looked down on him like the trash he was. She was nice to him, cared about him. Maybe the only woman to care about him in his life.

He had to have her. He'd waited long enough. And tonight was the night. Tonight, he would confess his feelings to her and they would finally—*finally*—be together. Take their relationship to the next level.

He licked his lips as he looked at her bed. Would it happen there? Would tonight finally be the night? Excitement shot through him, funneling between his legs. The urge to touch himself made his fingers tingle, but, no. He wanted to be on top-of-his-game for her. He'd even refrained from masturbating the last forty-eight hours, just to be ready for tonight.

He reached into his pocket and fingered the condom. He'd never wanted anyone so badly in his life. Never wanted to touch, to feel, to be inside someone like he did with her. And he wanted it reciprocated. He wanted it all, and he wanted it with her.

Right now.

Where was she?

He flexed his fingers and began pacing her bedroom.

What was she doing?

He glanced at his watch—8:34 p.m. He knew she had been home recently because a lamp was on in the living room. Hannah wasn't the type to leave the lights on all day. She was an earth-lover, after all.

Impatience and nerves had his heart pumping double time.

Was he sure he wanted to do this?

Don't puss out, you fucking coward.

What did he have to lose?

His neck snapped toward a sound outside. A zing of panic shot through him as he jogged on his tiptoes to the window, doubts racing into his mind. What the *hell* was he doing? He shouldn't have let himself inside, *Jesus!*

Would she be mad at him?

His eyes darted around the woods, an almost-full moon stretching shadows across the lawn. There was nothing. His nerves were getting the best of him. Dammit, he had *not* thought this through. She'd freak when she saw him in her house. He needed to get out, now.

As he turned away from the window, he heard the front door open.

Fuck, fuck, fuck!

She must've parked along the far side of the house.

Stupid, stupid, stupid!

He froze, paralyzed with panic. The door closed and he heard her voice.

Was she with someone?

His heart skipped wildly in his chest as he listened to her voice—her voice only. She was on the phone. Next, he heard the thud of her purse hitting the floor.

Oh my God, oh my God.

He turned back to the window, flipped the locks, and pushed. The damn thing wouldn't budge.

Footsteps down the hall.

Shit!

He jumped into the closet and crawled to the corner. He curled into a ball, and pulled her long dresses over him.

"Okay girl, talk later, bye."

The sledgehammer in his chest thudded at heart-attack speed as Hannah passed by the teeny closet and tossed her phone on the bed. She turned on a lamp and he silently shifted, moving his foot out of the light now spilling into the closet. His eyes widened as she stepped into his view.

With her side facing him, she kicked out of her furry boots and tossed her jacket on the floor. Her skin-tight spandex told him she'd been at the gym. She pulled the black tank top over her head, revealing a hot-pink sports bra and spilling cleavage.

He swallowed the knot in his throat as goosebumps flew over his skin. A strip tease just for him.

She grabbed the top of the bra and tugged. His jaw slacked open, his eyeballs bulging as she wrestled her way out of the bra, her pink nipples peaked from the chill in the air.

The blood rushed between his legs.

Hannah turned, sat on the bed—her plump breasts bouncing—and yanked the leggings off. His eyes swept over her body, awestruck at the beauty. It was exactly as he'd imagined. No, it was better. Much better.

Saliva filled his mouth, his thoughts clouded. *So much better than the pictures.* He reminded himself to take a breath, very aware that he could quite possibly die of a heart attack right there in her closet.

Then, she stood and slid out of the black lace panties, revealing a thin trail of brown hair between her legs.

His mouth dropped, the throbbing between his legs intensifying. She turned, her back to him now. Her ass was perfect. Freaking perfect.

She swooped down and picked up her clothes from the floor, her cheeks spreading and he thought he was going to faint.

Almost instinctively, he reached down and touched himself through his jeans, his erection so hard, so sensitive, he almost jumped at the touch. She stepped out of his view and he had to fight from running after her.

He listened to her footsteps across the room, the clanking of something in the bathroom, and then the creak of the faucet turning on.

The shower.

He blinked.

The *shower.*

It was *fate.*

His mind began to race, a frantic frenzy of half-thoughts jumbling together in his haze of shock. Shock that he was hiding in her closet. Shock that he'd finally seen her naked. The fact that she hadn't known he was watching added to the excitement.

He heard the break in water as she stepped inside the

shower. He closed his eyes imagining the water sluicing over her body, cascading over her round, full breasts. Snaking down her soft, springy pad of hair.

He felt the wetness of his tip through his jeans. The throbbing was almost painful now.

Listening to the water splashing on the porcelain sides, he unzipped and folded himself out of his jeans. The skin-on-skin touch of his hand was like a volt of electricity through his body. He gripped, squeezed.

He spit in his hands, closed his eyes and began to stroke. He released an exhale as the purest pleasure waved over him, a lightheadedness taking him to his happy place.

His strokes picked up, imagining the soap sliding over her body, over her ass, her soft folds.

And then the smell hit his nose.

Strawberries.

His eyes shot open, his cock pulsating in his hand.

He sniffed, smelling the scent of *her.*

That was it—he had to have her.

Blinded, clouded by the primal need for sex that over-took him, he released and tucked himself back into his jeans, but left himself unzipped and unbuttoned. Determi-nation clenched his jaw.

This was it. He was going to have her.

Driven by a confidence he'd never felt, he stepped out of the closet and into the bedroom.

The smell was stronger, the steam rolling out of the shower like a siren slowly beaconing him, motioning him to her.

He was coming. Oh yes, he was coming.

He had the power. Everything was in his hands. He reached down and touched the swollen gorge between his legs.

He was good for her. Rock hard. Tonight was the night.

With his hand on himself, he stepped in front of the shower hidden by a paisley-print curtain.

He slowly pulled the fabric to the side.

The shrill scream pierced his ears.

1

"*N*OW, INHALE—*ONE... TWO... three*—and exhale—*one... two, three.*" Bobbi took a deep breath, leading her students through the last few minutes of her hot yoga class. Hot was an understatement. The temperature of the room had climbed to ninety-five, and combined with the humidifier she had going, they might as well have been in the Amazon. Exactly the way she liked it. The lights were off, the last of the day's sun streaming in through the haze of humidity and incense burning in the room. Candlelight danced along the walls, flicking across her body as she lay flat on her back, eyes closed, soaked in sweat at the head of the class.

She continued, "Now let your attention expand to include the entire body as a whole." She spoke slowly, her voice low and soothing—as it should be after the hellish class she'd just led them through. They'd held challenging poses until even *her* muscles started to shake. A few had given up in the middle, dropping like flies onto their mats. That was fine with her. Just being there was the first step, pushing yourself through the heat and pain was the second.

No pain without gain, her brother always told her. A fitting mantra for the former Special Ops Marine. It had been drilled into their heads as children by their father, a former lieutenant commander in the navy. Pushing herself to the max and committing fully was just part of Bobbi's day-to-day.

On the outside, anyway.

"Now inhale, bringing your attention to the top of your head... and exhale... releasing the breath through the body and out the tip of your toes. Imagine the breath moving through your body in waves, cleansing, removing negative energy and leaving you open to receive positivity. Be aware of each part of your body as the breath flows through you. Relax into the rhythm. One more time, inhale..."

The class inhaled and exhaled together. A peaceful rhythm.

"Now, roll onto your right side." She let a minute pass. "And slowly sit up and repeat after me." She pressed her palms together, pressing her thumbs into her sternum, closed her eyes and bowed her head. "The light in me honors the light in you."

"The light in me honors the light in you," the yogis repeated.

"Namaste."

"Namaste."

Bobbi lifted her head and opened her eyes. A moment of silence, stillness, settled in the room. A small smile crossed her lips as she looked at the silhouettes outlined in the darkness of the room, incense swirling around the thick, humid air.

She reached up and turned on the lights, keeping it dim to allow tired, exhausted eyes to adjust.

"Damn." Cheeks flushed, mascara smudging below her bright blue eyes, Payton Chase blew out a breath and wiped

the sweat from her forehead. Her drenched, auburn hair was pulled into a tight bun on the top of her head. She'd come straight from work, as she always did. "Feels like we breached a hundred in here." A journalist at NAR News, Payton had joined Bobbi's yoga class to research a column she was writing about "Millennials and Mindfulness." A tenacious workaholic, Payton was posturing to be the next prime-time anchor at the station. At five-foot two with curves for days, Bobbi was immediately impressed with Payton's natural talent for yoga and her teeth-gritting determination to hold a pose no matter how exhausted she was. Bobbi had respect for women like that. She was like that.

Bobbi pushed to her bare feet and glanced at the thermostat. "Nope. Only ninety-five." She clicked off the humidifier. Sure, it added to the stifling heat, but it also helped muscles stretch. "You guys blew out a lot of hot air today."

She looked around the room at her regulars. The *diehard* yogis, they liked to call themselves.

Wells, a local park ranger, chugged his water, his long, lean limbs glistening with sweat. At just twenty-four, Wells had been practicing yoga since he was a preschooler. Next to him sat Kinsley Harp, the newest member of Bobbi's tribe. The twenty-five year old worked part-time at Bobbi's shooting range—Bobbi's other business—while working on her Doctorate in Environmental Science. Kinsley had a brilliant mind. Another trait Bobbi admired in a woman. Behind her was Grady Messick, born and raised in Berry Springs and a full-time employee at his father's IT firm. Lastly, Alice Moore. A *yogi-for-life*—she proudly labeled herself—Alice was pushing seventy and more fit than anyone who attended Bobbi's classes.

Payton, Kinsley, Wells, Alice and Grady made up her core yogis. Always willing to volunteer and help out where needed. She valued each of them and considered them friends, and would reward them for their loyalty by offering late-evening classes just for them, like she was doing now. They appreciated it because each of her other classes were usually packed to the walls, and she'd just recently started having to turn people away. Not that she minded much. Her little business was thriving.

Wells rested his elbows on his knobby knees. "Who the heck invented hot yoga anyway?"

"India." Bobbi grinned.

"Did you know summers can exceed one hundred twenty degrees in India?" Kinsley, the smarty pants, said.

"Bobbi, you hear that? Dr. Harp wants you to crank it to one-twenty-two next week." Barely sweating, Alice rolled her yoga towel and sent Kinsley a wink.

Kinsley grinned and stared thoughtfully at the ceiling. "*Hmm,* Dr. Harp. I like it. Rolls right off the tongue, doesn't it?"

"Kind of like the river of sweat running down your back. Geez, Harp get a towel." Grady laughed, then turned to Wells. "Toss me that water, will ya?"

Wells launched a bottle across the room.

"Alright, guys, lets talk about the retreat for a minute. We've got five days to get this thing together. Everyone will be arriving around three Friday afternoon." Bobbi grabbed her notebook from the windowsill, and wrinkled her nose at the pages crinkled from the humidity in the room. "Gross." She flipped it open. "Okay, I talked to Pauline at Shadow Creek Resort today and confirmed all seventeen cabins on site will have an added bunk, along with memory foam mattress covers and white linens, as we requested. Oh," she turned to Alice. "Are the Lotus flowers on their way?"

"Yep. Should be here Thursday."

"Perfect."

Grady raised his hand as if they were in a schoolhouse. "Do you really think people won't mind sharing rooms?"

"First, they're cabins. Luxury cabins. Shadow Creek is a five-star resort. People from all over the country vacation there. And the added bunks are part of the experience. Yoga is all about acceptance and opening your heart to what's around you. Helping others. I want them to share together, to bond, and hopefully walk away with a renewed energy, spirit, and lifelong friendships. But, for those total introverts—"

"Like Payton."

Payton rolled her eyes.

Bobbi smirked and continued, "They paid an additional fee for a solo cabin, or a tent."

"*Luxury* tents." Kinsley added.

"Exactly. Have you guys seen the pictures? They literally have hardwood floors and furniture. Beautiful. I'll be staying in one." She looked at Kinsley. "Did you get the charm necklaces ordered?"

"Yep, personalized, and rose gold, just like you asked."

"Perfect." She looked down at her list. "I've asked for extra lights along the hiking path that leads up the mountain to the outlook—"

Wells cut in. "And I'm making sure the trails and paths will be freshly cleared. We're adding decorative stones along the sides, too."

"Great, thanks. And hanging the lanterns from the trees?"

"Will be done, yes. It will look like a magical fairyland, just like you asked. All that's missing is the pixie dust."

"Why don't we just wipe up Kinsley's sweat?" Grady

asked as he turned to her. "Why the hell are you so sparkly anyway?"

She cocked an eyebrow. "It's shimmer. I'm *shimmering.*"

Bobbi grinned at Kinsley. "Seriously, yeah, I noticed it when you walked in. You look like a vampire in sunlight."

"That's only in Twilight. Vampires don't sparkle in sunlight," Wells corrected, almost defensively.

"Well if anyone would know, you would. Good to know Kinsley isn't a blood sucker."

"It's a new lotion, guys. *Geez*. It's supposed to make me glow."

"Hey, I have an idea. We can just hang her from one of the trees instead of the lanterns." Grady said with a wink.

"*Ha. Ha.* You are so funny."

"Okay, guys, back to the subject." Bobbi glanced back at Wells. "Be sure to block off any trails that are too steep or dangerous. The landing on top of Summit Mountain will be open twenty-four-seven for anyone who wants to practice, meditate, or—"

"Make out." Wells wiggled his eyebrows.

Kinsley rolled her eyes. "Speaking of, how many men— *not boys*—" she sent a sidelong glance at Wells, "do we have coming?"

Bobbi flipped a page in her notebook. "Thirty-one."

"*What?*" Payton said, "Wow. How many people have signed up?"

Bobbi blew out a breath and flipped another page. "Ninety-six."

"Are you serious?" Kinsley's mouth dropped.

"Yeah." She smiled, hiding the subtle current of nerves she'd felt since her little retreat had exploded into a full-blown event. Yogis from the surrounding states had signed up, much to her surprise. Word of mouth had spread like fire. She should be proud—and she was—but the whole thing was consuming every second of her spare time, and that was something she didn't have much of to begin with. She would've liked her first retreat to be small and more low-key so she could make the inevitable mistakes and iron out the kinks. Nevertheless, here she was, and now she felt like her reputation was on the line—which was a lot for someone who owned two successful businesses.

Kinsley looked at Payton. "That's a lot of people to interview for your column... and maybe finally get a date, you workaholic." She winked.

"You're one to talk." Payton grinned. "But, yeah, I've already got it all planned out. I'm splitting the story up into multiple pieces." Payton's eyes sparkled and Bobbi smiled. The girl loved her job.

Alice returned to the subject. "How are we on budget, B?"

Bobbi swallowed the knot in her throat. "At eight-nine percent."

Alice tipped her head to the side. "Well, we're not over yet."

"Damn close."

"Hey, what about the mats?" Wells asked. "Did you get the logo printed on them?"

"Yep. I'm going to pick those up tonight." She glanced at the clock. "But I've got to run by the range, first." She closed the notebook and stood. "Let's call it a night, guys. Remember, the quieter you become, the more you can hear. Don't forget to meditate at least once a day."

The group filed out and after a quick mop over the floor to wipe up Kinsley's *shimmer,* then tossing the towels in the laundry, Bobbi hit the lights and followed Grady out the door. She always gave him extra time to stretch after class.

They stepped outside of the small cottage she'd turned into a yoga studio. A mild breeze carrying the fresh scent of budding flowers swept over her sweat-slicked skin. Spring was in full-bloom in the small, southern town of Berry Springs.

She inhaled deeply, glancing at the mountains in the distance, outlined in a deep orange of dusk. Stars were just beginning to twinkle in the sky.

Grady stumbled next to her but caught himself. Her stomach clenched.

"Hey," she reached out. "Let me help you."

He wobbled on his cane down the stone steps, but shook his head. "I'm fine, Bobbi."

She bit her lip and angled herself beside him in case he fell.

He flashed her a sympathetic smile. "You've got to get over it, Bobbi."

Her heart sank and she looked down. Although Grady sat half the class due to his injuries, she was glad he still came. Every day she said a little prayer he'd be able to do just a bit more than the day before.

"I've reminded you a hundred times—it was an accident. I'm fine." He kicked out his cane, decorated with a rainbow of colors, stickers, and signatures, reminding her of a high school football player's cast. "And I get to carry this badass thing around all day."

Bobbi forced a smile.

"Seriously. You need to just let it go. I mean, don't retract my free yoga or anything, but let everything else go." He winked.

They walked down the lighted pebbled path that led from the studio to a small gravel parking lot. Being a nature lover, Bobbi had purchased a small patch of woods that connected to the city park. She carved a spot out of the soaring oak and pine trees to build her cozy, quaint yoga studio. Although it was technically in the middle of town, the building was enclosed with trees and thick vegetation. She'd spent countless hours landscaping, adding stone statues and lights, making it her own fairy wonderland—as Wells would say. It was a perfect spot to escape the day-to-day, release stress, and take a breath. Bobbi came often when she wasn't teaching, just to get in a quick meditation by herself. But that was only when she couldn't escape to the *real* woods, which was her happy place. A close second stress reliever? Shooting a few rounds at her range.

They stepped up to Grady's old, beat-up Subaru, parked next to her Jeep.

"I'm halfway done with the *Thank-You-for-attending-my-badass-retreat* notes," he said.

She cocked her head. "Let's go with something less politically incorrect... how about kickass."

"You got it. I should be done by tomorrow. I'll bring them to Gentle Yoga."

"Sounds good. Thanks, Grady." She went to open the door for him, but stopped. How emasculating. Instead, she smiled and climbed into her Jeep.

Bobbi pulled onto the narrow two-lane road that led through the middle of town. Wind whipped around her, feeling like silk against her skin. In celebration of the warmer weather, she'd taken the top off her Jeep.

She took a deep breath, inhaling the crisp evening air.

Bobbi loved springtime. More yoga outside was always a good thing.

Her mind drifted to all the different outdoor places around town where she could conduct her yoga classes. Little field trips were great for breaking out of routines, and a little free marketing, she'd learned. Berry Springs was a small town nestled deep in the Ozark Mountains. The town embraced the outdoors, with most of its yearly revenue coming from tourists seeking the picturesque hiking trails and campsites that speckled the mountains, as well as boating and fishing on Otter Lake. And, of course, the hunting. Berry Springs was the type of town where people, of all ages, still called each other sir and ma'am and on any given day, you'd see more cowboy hats and boots than baseball caps and sneakers. A bit antiquated and hillbilly some might say. Sure. But the natives of Berry Springs were proud of their little town and wouldn't have it any other way.

She stopped at the single stoplight in the town's square.

"Hey, B!"

A jacked-up Chevy with two wildly excited hound dogs in the back pulled up next to her, windows down.

Bobbi laughed. "Turner, Hooch, hey babies!" She shifted her gaze to Chance Sutton and Clement Murphy, a few of her high school friends that had never left town. "What're you boys out doing?"

"Fixin' to meet Granny Iva at Donny's for dinner." They nodded to the small diner on the square, complete with red leather booths and blue and white checkered curtains hanging from the windows. The diner was a fixture in Berry Springs, legendary for its cheese grits.

She glanced at the clock—7:51 p.m. "A little late for dinner."

Chance shook his head. "Church."

Ah—church. The only thing that kept Berry Springs up and running past eight on week days.

"Give Iva and those doggies a kiss for me. In *that* order."

"Will do, see ya beautiful." Clement blew a kiss from the passenger seat as the grumble of sawed-off pipes drowned out her radio. She shook her head. Southern boys and their trucks.

After making a quick run through the post office to check her box, then a stop at the office-supply store to get a few things she needed, Bobbi was almost to the range when her phone rang.

"Hey, Hannah," she answered. "Missed you tonight."

"Got your top off, huh?"

"What?" Bobbi glanced down at her tank top.

Hannah laughed. "The Jeep. Not your shirt."

Bobbi slowed to ease the wind whipping around the phone. "Oh. Whoops, sorry."

"No worries, it's a beautiful night for it. How was class?"

Bobbi's unofficial business partner at the yoga studio, Hannah Winchester, taught classes when Bobbi was unavailable. Hannah was new to town, but they'd quickly bonded over their single status and their love for yoga.

"Class was good. The usual crew, Kinsley, Payton, Alice, Grady, and Wells."

"Nice. Well, I was calling to let you know I've got the mats for the retreat. Bonnie called a bit ago and had just finished. I just picked them up. They look great."

"Awesome. Mind if I swing by and get them on my way home? I'm going to start taking loads to the resort tomorrow." Bobbi heard the jingle of keys through the phone.

"Just walked in the door now. Come by anytime."

"Perfect. I'm gonna run by the range first, then I'll swing by."

"Okay girl, talk later, bye."

"See you soon."

Click.

Five minutes later she pushed through the front door of B's Bullseye, the indoor shooting range and supplies shop she'd opened exactly three years earlier, to the day. Within the first week, she'd exceeded revenue expectations for the month, and that success had carried through year over year. In a small, redneck town like Berry Springs, she learned she could count on two things: Everyone was loyal to local businesses, and everyone carried a gun—usually more than one. It had become a gold mine for her, especially when her brother, Wesley, began to sell some of his handmade guns. His guns were one-of-a-kind, exclusive to her shop, and expensive. As any good brother would do, he gave her a hefty cut of each sale.

"Well, hey there, Lil' Miss." Butch, Bobbi's assistant manager, waved from behind the counter. With skin that looked like leather, Butch was a sixty-something year old former military man with a penchant for fine guns. Wesley had recommended him for the job.

On the other side of the counter, a tall, thick man in a black hoodie and ball cap glanced over his shoulder. Her stomach dropped to her feet and she froze.

Pop, pop, pop!

The sound of gunfire from the range had her snapping back to attention. She hadn't seen her ex-flame, Lee, in over five months. In a small town, that was nothing less than shocking. They'd dated off and on for a few weeks only to crash and burn when she'd woken up one day and realized she was bored with him. She needed more, and she wasn't getting it from him. That was Bobbi's problem when it came to men. She'd lose interest. Quickly. Work was her number one priority, boys a far second. Bobbi had a canned breakup speech that she could recite while doing long division in her head... with her eyes closed. The guy would be surprised, piss and moan, but that was it. There was no going back.

Then the guilt would set in. Damn the guilt.

It wasn't their fault, it was hers. She truly believed that. However, regardless of her reputation as a heartbreaker, Bobbi was still asked out on dates, which surprised her.

With long, dark hair, feline-like green eyes and a toned body chiseled from hours in the yoga studio, men fell over themselves to talk to Bobbi. And thanks to the aloof, *I-don't-give-a-shit* nature when they'd hit on her, it usually made them want her even more. The thing was, Bobbi never felt like she needed a man. Sex, yes. Dinner and dates, absolutely. She enjoyed being courted, she loved the feeling of a man wanting to take care of her, even though she didn't need it. She just didn't have the time or patience when the relationship hit the inevitable fizzle, and things began to get boring. Bobbi ran two businesses and worked her ass off, she didn't need to work on a relationship, too.

And she sure as hell didn't need to run into one of those fizzles after a long day's work.

She took a silent inhale, squared her shoulders and forced a smile. As she wove her way through the hunting gear and fishing poles, she caught a glimpse of herself in the dressing room mirror, and cringed.

Her sweat-soaked hair was matted to her head—a look that compared to not being washed in a month. The little makeup she'd had on had sweated off, and her cheeks were still flushed. She'd pulled her green headband down around her neck, a contrast against the black tank-top and yoga leggings. Thankfully, she'd grabbed a red flannel button-up from the backseat of her Jeep and tied it around her waist on the way in. Her yoga attire was a bit too revealing for the range. This haphazard look was topped off by her old, stained, fuzzy Uggs that she'd slipped into on the way out of the studio.

Yep, it was one sexy outfit.

Lee turned fully to her, his eyes dropping to her cleavage.

Maybe she should have put *on* the flannel before walking in.

"Long time no see." Her attempt at a light-hearted tone failed miserably.

Butch cleared his throat, pretending to be working on his evening paperwork.

Lee's lips pressed into a thin line. "Just came in to get my brother something for his birthday."

"Ah." She nodded. "Okay, anything I can help with?"

"No, there's definitely nothing you can help with." The disdain for her in his voice made her take a step back.

Damn. Whatever. She didn't have time for this. "Okay, then, maybe Butch can help ya out."

"He was. See I was originally going to go with this flashy M1911 with the American Flag on the handle, but then remembered that flashy isn't always good for the long-term." He narrowed his eyes. "Going to go with dependable this time around."

Her brows slowly tipped up. It had been seven months since their breakup—if you could even call it that—and apparently Lee needed another seven to get over it.

She refused to engage in a tit-for-tat.

She stared at him for a moment—*yeah, Lee, I caught that innuendo*—then forced another smile. "Well, good to see ya, Lee."

Bobbi breezed past her ex and slid behind the counter, feeling his gaze on her like a laser-beam burning holes into her skin.

Butch turned to Lee and quickly picked up the conversation to ease the tension. "Well, Lee, what do you think..." He motioned to the guns.

Bobbi clicked on the computer to take a glance of the day's sales, but couldn't ignore Lee's cranky voice next to her. Her body had tensed, which was the exact opposite that was supposed to happen after an evening of hot yoga. Frustrated now, she ground her teeth and pulled her SIG from behind the counter. Maybe a quick round in the range to close out the day. At least until cranky-pants was gone.

Bobbi slid on a pair of glasses and earmuffs and stepped into the range. She inhaled the scent of gunpowder and an ounce of tension left her shoulders. Target shooting had always had that effect on her. Blame it on being raised in a military family. It was in her blood.

Blasts of gunfire came from the last lane, so she stepped into the first. As she loaded her gun, she glanced at the target in the distance.

The bullseye was destroyed.

No way. She squinted and leaned forward. Not a single shot outside the center.

Geez, when did Wyatt Earp move to town?

Eyebrow cocked, she leaned back, trying to see who was behind the lane. Dark, short hair peeked out from the top of the divider. She guessed it was a man. A very tall man.

Bobbi took another glance at the impressive bullseye, then clipped her target and sent it back. A tickle of competitiveness sent a grin across her face.

Okay, mister Earp, it's go-time.

She raised her SIG, zeroed in on her target, inhaled, and took three shots. One bullseye, two just outside.

This was answered with two shots from Earp. Two more bullseyes.

She ground her teeth—two more shots.

He followed with two more shots of his own.

The corner of her lip curled. They were in a little

impromptu shooting competition. Bobbi narrowed her eyes and fired off four more shots. All bullseyes.

The man moved his target further away—bullseye.

She moved hers a bit further—bullseye.

Grinning now, Bobbi looked around the divider again, wanting to see who her challenger was. No luck. Just then, the lights dimmed. It was closing time.

Dammit, just when she was actually having fun.

She picked up her shells as Earp fired off a few more shots. After taking one more glance at the lane, Bobbi made her way out of the range and into the store.

Butch glanced up from the computer. "I chased Lee off. And charged him five percent more for pestering you."

Bobbi snorted and slid her gun back under the counter. "Hadn't seen him in months." She frowned. "By the looks of it, he would've been happy to go the rest of his life without seeing me again." She sighed and focused on the computer.

"Ah, he'll get over it. You're a rare one, you know."

"A rare one?"

"Yoga and guns. A loaded combination to steal any man's heart. Around these parts, at least."

She paused, thinking about the comment. Her entire life, she'd always felt a little different. Never feminine enough to hang out with the cheerleaders in school, never quite hardcore enough to hang out with the diehard cowgirls. Growing up, her father took her to the shooting range the way a normal father would take their daughter to the ice-cream shop. Her love of yoga was born through her love of the outdoors. She could sit in the middle of the woods for hours, unmoving, listening to the sounds of nature around her, inhaling, exhaling, appreciating the beauty of Mother Nature. Those moments turned into official meditation, which turned into yoga.

Yes, Bobbi was a bit different. On the outside, she was a tough-as-nails, capable, independent woman. But on the inside, she struggled daily with discontentment. Always wanting more, never feeling like she had enough, or was where she was supposed to be. And with her thirtieth birthday right around the corner, she began to look at the future in ways she never had before. That scared the crap out of her. Maybe being little, *never-give-anyone-a-chance* Bobbi Cross wasn't going to give her the life of contentment she so badly wanted.

Bruce elbowed her in the ribs. "You know, if I were thirty years younger, I'd take a pass at you myself, Lil' Miss."

She snapped back to present. "Take a pass? Oh you're so romantic."

He grinned. "My wife sure thinks so."

The phone rang. Bobbi picked it up and took notes about a special gun order. Just as she was about to hang up—

"Nice shooting, Tex. Night."

"Night."

Her head turned toward the deep, smooth voice. Butch turned off the front lights just as a dark silhouette pushed through the front doors. A clean, freshly-showered scent mixed with gunpowder followed him, and every sensor in her body awoke. Her gaze lingered on the mystery man. The broad shoulders, confident stride. She shifted to the window and watched the black truck pull out of the lot.

2

---

*B*OBBI SHIVERED AS she drove down the narrow dirt road, the wind cutting through the flannel she'd slipped on. The temperature had dropped a few degrees while she'd been at the range. She glanced up at the once clear sky, now spotted with clouds. It was a dark, silent night. Eerie, almost.

She clicked on her high beams and scanned the dense woods around her, wishing she hadn't taken the top off the Jeep.

A fox darted out from the ditch, its rust-colored tail flicking in the headlights. She slammed the brakes, missing the innocent little creature by a few inches.

Phew. Bugs she could kill, things with bushy little tails, she could not.

Silence settled around her accompanied by a weird chill running up her spine. Bobbi glanced over her shoulder, then looked from left to right, then the other shoulder.

Why was she so jumpy all of a sudden?

A monster probably wasn't going to climb into her Jeep, but in reality, anything else could, so she accelerated.

9:16 p.m.

She'd stayed at the range longer than she intended, but if luck was on her side, she'd be home with a glass of wine and remote in her hand by ten o'clock.

Bobbi flicked on her turn signal—not that she needed to, not a single person was around—and turned onto a rock driveway lined with painted flower pots that led to a charming little house.

Hannah lived on the base of Summit Mountain, in a small, brick house she'd inherited from her grandmother a year earlier. It was perfect for the earthy, hippie twenty-something just out of college trying to figure out what she wanted to do with her life.

Bobbi rolled to a stop behind Hannah's rusted Volkswagen and turned off the engine. She frowned and leaned forward.

A grey cloud—mist, maybe?—slowly slithered up from the side of the house.

What the hell?

Instinct had her heartbeat picking up as she jumped out of the Jeep. That wasn't mist.

Smoke.

Definitely smoke.

Hannah's house was on fire.

"Hannah?" Bobbi yellowed out as she jogged across the driveway, her eyes darting around the landscape.

"Hannah?" She pushed through the front door. A haze of hot, sour smelling smoke was moving just below the ceiling.

Oh, no.

"Hannah?!"

A flash of movement pulled her attention to the

bedroom door, where a dark silhouette darted out of the room and through the back door.

"Hey!" She called out, running down the hall. The back door popped on its hinge then slammed shut and the silhouette disappeared into the darkness.

To go after him, or not? *Shit,* where was Hannah?

She whipped around. Her heart stopped when she noticed the smoke was coming out of the master bedroom—Hannah's room. She took a quick glance out the kitchen window, still debating on running after whoever the hell that was.

No, she needed to find her friend. Bobbi spun on her heel and every lesson she'd learned in elementary school about fire safety flashed through her head. *Stop, drop, and roll; smoke rises, stay low.* She hunkered down and jogged into the bedroom.

"Hann..." The rest of the name escaped in a breathy whisper.

Her blood turned ice-cold, jaw slacked open.

Smoke swirled around Hannah's pale, naked body lying across her bed. Her arms lay folded neatly on her stomach, her legs crossed at the ankles. Her head, cradled in pillows, lobbed to the side, blood trickling down the white pillow. Her eyes, open, staring blankly at the doorway.

"Hannah!" Bobbi lunged forward, her heart feeling like it was about to explode out of her chest.

"Shit, shit, shit, shit. Oh, my God." Tears welled in her eyes. "Hannah," she whispered as she lightly placed two fingers on her friend's throat. But Hannah was gone. Her stomach rolled as she noticed the bloody, oozing flesh puffed up around the wound on Hannah's head, under wet hair matted with blood.

Panic began to replace the shock. Bobbi straightened

and began frantically looking around the room. Flames flickered in the bathroom, smoke barreled from the closet.

The fire appeared to be only in the bathroom but would undoubtedly spread quickly.

Okay, Bobbi, focus.

She yanked her cell from her pocket and dialed 911.

"Nine-one-one, what's your emergency?"

"I'm..." The words froze in her throat. It was as if her brain was suddenly broken. *"Shit,"* she inhaled to gather herself. *Emotions make you messy, just tell the facts.* "I'm at Hannah Winchester's house. I'm not sure of the address but it's off County Road 3228, around Summit Mountain. She's dead, and the house is on fire."

"Okay ma'am, we're sending someone now. Are you hurt?"

"No, ma'am." Tears rolled down her cheeks.

"Is anyone else in the house?"

"No. But someone was here when I got here. Someone ran out."

"Okay, ma'am, I need you to go outside immediately, do you understand?"

"Okay. Yes." She paused, looking down at Hannah's dead body. "I... *leave* her?" She choked on the last word and began coughing. The phone dropped from her hand, clattering on the hardwood floor.

"Dammit." She looked at her friend's beautiful face. Someone had killed her. Hannah had been *murdered.* Anger flooded her system, adrenaline bursting through her veins. Her mind cleared and sheer determination took over.

"You are not burning to ashes in this freaking house, Hannah," Bobbi promised her deceased friend.

The smoke swirled around her, her vision becoming cloudy.

She swooped down searching for the cell phone she'd dropped. The distant voice of the dispatcher disappeared as she ended the call. Her hand shook as she clicked on the camera. She took two pictures of the body, then quickly, two of the room, then slid the phone into her pocket.

"Alright, let's go."

With strength amplified by adrenaline, Bobbi slipped two arms underneath Hannah's cold body, sucked in a breath, and picked her up.

Cradling her like a baby, Bobbi carefully turned, wobbled a bit at first, then slowly made her way out of the room. Black smoke, thick as a blanket, engulfed her. Her stomach clenched, nausea waving over her body. She wasn't sure if it was from the smell, or the dead body in her arms. She blinked, tears blurring her already hampered vision. Dizziness had her pausing at the hallway.

Sirens blared in the distance, but she didn't hear them.

Bobbi swallowed the bile in her throat, squinted and pressed on. Her knees shook, sweat rolled down her back.

Her toe caught on a rug, sending her stumbling. The rug wrapped her ankles and she flew forward, sending Hannah tumbling out of her arms and Bobbi's head bashing into the corner of a table.

Stars burst in her vision. She heaved, but nothing came out. The pain was excruciating. Waves of queasiness had her feeling like she was on a small fishing boat in the middle of the ocean.

A trickle of warm blood ran down her face. If she didn't get out of there, EMS was going to be removing two bodies.

With a grunt, Bobbi pushed to a squat and rolled Hannah to her. She released a guttural scream as she pushed to a stance with Hannah in her arms.

Chest heaving, she looked down at her friend. Hannah's

head dangled grotesquely backward as if snapped at the neck, swaying back and forth.

Get out, Bobbi. Now.

Shouldn't she be at the front door by now?

Bobbi ground her teeth and focused on one foot in front of the other, until a cool gust of wind separated the smoke. She'd left the door open, thank God. Blue and red lights bounced off the walls. She gasped the clean air as she stumbled over the threshold.

She was outside. She'd made it out. *Alive.*

Wind whipped past her, intensifying the floating sensation she was already feeling.

Holy *shit,* she did *not* feel good.

Bobbi gripped Hannah's body tighter, as if that was going to steady her.

As her vision went in and out, she focused a dark silhouette in uniform sprinting toward her.

"Just give her here, ma'am. Everything's going to be okay."

Her eyes were blurred by tears, so she focused on the deep voice in front of her.

"Here, I've got her." The man repeated, "Let go, ma'am."

Let go.

His voice was calm, strong, with a kind of innate authority that was made exactly for situations like these. There was something to his tone that seemed to melt the panic inside her.

"Ma'am—"

As she felt the weight of Hannah's body lift from her arms, her vision wavered and her knees buckled.

And she was out.

3

*B*OBBI BLINKED, coming to. The first thing that registered were sirens wailing in the distance, not a steady sound but more of a *whomp, whomp, whomp,* as she felt like she was fading in and out of consciousness. Next, a popping and hissing behind her. An angry sound. Menacing.

"Get the ME out here now. I've got a woman deceased, and another in need of medical assistance. And where the hell is the EMT?"

Bobbi focused on the voice vibrating out of the hard chest against her ear. Deep, sexy. Safe.

A *crackle, crackle,* then "10-4, sending now. EMT is almost there, and Hayes should be on location."

"Firetruck ETA?"

Pause. "En route. Approximately a quarter-mile from your location." The voice sounded like it was coming out of a cardboard box.

The siren cut off and was followed by the sound of crunching gravel. Bobbi's brain raced to catch up, but the fog in it was too thick to penetrate. Like she'd had ten tequila shots then run five miles... right into on-coming traffic. The woods zoomed past her, as if she was floating through the air. And then, the faintest scent of soap mixed with the musky scent of man. An incredibly sexy scent that she vaguely remembered.

Her eyes opened fully—she was being carried.

"Hey... *hey.*" She twisted her neck and looked up at the stubble on the sharp jawline attached to a thick neck.

"Welcome back," the man said without looking down.

It was the same voice she'd been fixated on before her world went black. Her gaze trailed to the mouth, the lips full, barely open to let breath escape with each step. He wasn't even breathing heavily.

Cars doors slammed, then heavy footsteps, then—

"Hayes, secure the scene immediately," the man demanded. "Once the truck comes through, no one in or out of the head of the driveway, got it? Don't let a single person set foot close to the body until I approve it."

The body.

Hannah.

She shifted her head so she could see the house, where flames flicked out of the bathroom window.

"Oh, my God. *Hannah.* Is she..." Her voice trailed off. She wasn't sure why she was asking. Maybe she needed to hear it again.

"Yes, ma'am."

"Where is she? Her body? Did I drop—"

"She's secured, ma'am."

Secured.

Her heart started to race.

"I passed out?"

"Yes."

"How long?"

"Seconds."

Okay, that was good. At least this isn't a *what-year-is-it* scenario. "Where are you taking me?"

"Away from the house. Are you hurting anywhere else other than your head?"

Then the pain registered. Her head felt like it connected with a wrecking ball. She did a mental scan of her body.

"No."

"Can you tell me your name?"

"Bobbi Cross."

"And your birthday, Miss Cross?"

"That's one of the top ten questions you're never supposed to ask a lady, Mr..."

He didn't smile. They stopped, and he began to slowly lower her.

"Will you sit, please." He asked, although she didn't have a choice when he placed her firmly on her ass.

More car doors slamming, more shouts.

Her rescuer, who was shouting something else now, had taken her a good thirty feet from the house. She was next to the woods where blue and red lights flashed off the trees.

She watched in awe for a moment as the firemen moved hoses toward the house. The flames looked to be only in one spot. It wasn't a total loss.

Except for Hannah's life.

She looked up at the man who'd taken Hannah from her and then carried her to safety. He stood close to her, hovering above her, almost as if he were protecting her. He yelled orders to a few other men. He was in full uniform—a cop—and he was tall. Massive. Not just his height, but he was built like an ox, or maybe it was just because she was at his feet. She squinted, trying to see his face through the flashing lights.

He looked down at her, and she quickly looked away. Busted.

Jesus, how hard had she fallen?

She felt movement beside her, turned, and was pinned by deep brown eyes, clear and crisp with intensity. He'd kneeled down next to her. His gaze shifted to her forehead and she took that quick second to soak in his face, rugged, strong, all male. *Gorgeous.* She recognized him immediately.

"Are you still dizzy," he asked.

Their eyes connected again. He was only inches from her face, and after a second slid by, she realized he didn't recognize her.

"No, I'm fine." She started to stand, but he placed a firm hand on her shoulder. She caught another whiff of that fresh smell.

"EMT's coming over to check you out." He gently placed his hands on her face and assessed the wound. "You've got a pretty good gash on your head." He began lightly dabbing her skin with something. "I'm assuming you hit it somewhere inside before you passed out."

Thanks for the newsflash, she wanted to say. She glanced away, her cheeks heating. She didn't like being fussed over. It made her feel weak. Being tended to while a real emergency took place embarrassed her almost as much as the fact that she'd passed out in the first place. She'd been called many things in her life, but a baby wasn't one of them.

As if reading her thoughts he said, "You inhaled a good amount of smoke in there. Carbon dioxide decreases the amount of oxygen in your body. You're lucky you didn't pass out inside."

"No, but I fell." *Christ,* she *was* embarrassed—and then she got mad at herself for being embarrassed.

"Smoke makes you dizzy before you pass out. Not your fault." He lightly swept the hair away from her face. "You're going to need stitches."

Bobbi rolled her eyes, feeling completely out of sorts now. "I'm the last person you should be fussing over. Hannah..." her voice trailed off.

Hannah was dead.

She shook her head, still in total disbelief of the last fifteen minutes of her life. "Hannah's body. You need to be looking her over for evidence. *Oh!* I... I took pictures..." She reached into her pocket. "*Shit!* My phone." She tried to surge to her feet but almost threw up. Strong hands wrapped around her and guided her back down.

"*Sit.*" He demanded, his voice less patient now.

Bobbi nudged out of his hold but he kept a hand on her. "Sit." He narrowed his eyes, those smoky, smothering eyes. "Butt on the ground. I'm not going to tell you again, Miss Cross."

Usually, she'd argue—she wasn't one to be told what to do—but the dizziness had crept back along with the new sensation of ants crawling up her skin. So, in an attempt to avoid another embarrassing replay, she put her butt on the ground.

He reached into his pocket, then held out his hand—baseball glove, more like. "This phone?"

She snatched the cell. "Thank, *God.* Where..."

"It fell out of your pocket when you passed out. What pictures?" His attention was then pulled behind her. "*Over here!*"

Just then, a large, leather tote dropped next to her, followed by a pudgy, balding man with wide-rimmed glasses.

"Bobbi Cross. *Geez,* hun, what did you get yourself into tonight?"

"Dr. Buckley." She released an audible sigh, thankful for a familiar face—that recognized her, anyway—and thankful to be pulled away from the man that seemed to be knocking her off balance more than she already was.

Buckley began pulling all sorts of scary looking things out of his bag. He glanced at the cop. "I live right down the road. Heard the commotion, came right over." He looked back at her. "Took a knock to the head, huh?" Buckley clicked on a flashlight that was so bright it could burn a hole through the ground.

She squinted, the light like an ice pick through her eye, and nodded.

The doctor checked her eyes, then lifted the light to her forehead. He pressed around the wound until her stomach balled up.

"You're going to need a few stitches..."

"And she needs to be examined for a concussion."

Buckley cocked a brow and looked up. "I wasn't finished."

Apparently, Buckley wasn't a fan of the guy who'd saved her life.

"As I was saying, Bobbi, you're going to need some stitches and to be examined for a concussion. You're gonna have a heck of a bruise, dear." He dabbed something on her skin that felt like acid. "The hospital is already expecting you."

"The hospital?" She sat up straighter and raised her voice against the blasting water hose beside them. "Buckley, that's ridiculous. I'm fine. It's just a little cut."

"Bobbi." Buckley blew out a sigh and sat back on his heels.

"You've been more stubborn than a dog with a bone since you were a little girl." He held his hand a few feet from the ground. "Since this tall, my dear. But you need to get looked at. Don't want that beautiful face of yours all scarred up, do you?"

Bobbi had plenty of scars. Tomboys usually did. She sighed, knowing that in order to move this night along, she was going to have to concede.

"We'll see, Buckley. Thanks for—"

"She'll see you at the hospital, Doctor."

Her eyebrows tipped up. "Uh, I'm sorry, but that's my decision."

Buckley snorted and shook his head. "EMT'll come over in a sec. I'll be at the hospital in a bit." The doctor pushed to a stance with a grunt, cast a look at the black body bag that was being pulled out of the ambulance, and then looked at Mr. Demanding. "Hell of a way to get your feet wet, Lieutenant Cotter. Hope you're up for it."

"Colson."

"Sorry. Colson."

Lieutenant Colson.

As Buckley strode away, an EMT that she didn't recognize jogged up. Doogie Howser looked to be fresh out of high school. He kneeled down, patchy stubble covering his puppy dog face.

"Ma'am, I'm Jacob Hill, with the Emergency Response Team. How are you feeling?"

As she pushed to her feet—she was *done* looking *up* at men—Lieutenant Colson's hand connected with the small of her back, steadying her, or ready to catch her if she fell. Heat blazed under his touch.

"Thanks," she muttered but pulled away, and addressed Jacob Hill. "It's just a little bump."

The EMT began checking her over, and another officer

jogged up. She smiled—Officer Hayes. A sheen of sweat suggesting he'd been on the front lines of the fire covered his brow, an eager look in his blue eyes. Bobbi had met Hayes at the local rodeo a few years earlier when he was the newest member of the Berry Springs Police department.

"Hayes. What's going on? Is the house—"

"Is the fire contained?" The Lieutenant dismissed her and interrupted.

"Yes, sir. Almost out."

Sir.

Hayes gave a quick "hey" nod at Bobbi, lingering on her forehead for a second before looking back at his boss—apparently.

"It was only in the bathroom and partially in the bedroom. Had just started by the looks of it. Fire Chief's in there now." He frowned and looked back her. "You okay? I mean... not just about the bump on the brain?"

Bobbi opened her mouth to respond but was interrupted again when Lieutenant Colson addressed the EMT.

"Take her to the hospital to get checked out, now."

"Yes, sir." He zipped up his bag. "I'll be right back."

The Lieutenant looked at Hayes. "Are we cleared to go inside?"

"Not yet."

"Push them. We need in there now. And get a crime scene log going. Everyone signs in and out, no matter what."

"Done." There was a tension between the two men that she immediately picked up on.

"Once we get inside, I want you to start checking for prints."

Hayes nodded and disappeared into the darkness.

She turned to the Lieutenant, dark shadows dancing across his face.

"What pictures," he asked.

She frowned.

"You said you'd taken pictures..."

She'd already forgotten. She turned on her cell, thankful to be talking about what really mattered—the murder of her friend and not the stupid bump on her head.

"Pictures of the scene."

His eyebrows slowly lifted and she realized it was the first bit of emotion to crack the cool, calm, collected, *and demanding* demeanor.

"Of her body?" He asked.

"Her name is Hannah, and yes, the body and the room."

"What made you take pictures?"

"When I made the decision to remove her body... I knew it would be important for you guys to see what the scene looked like before."

His head tilted to the side with skepticism.

"Hey, I watch crime shows," she said defensively.

"What's Hannah's last name?"

"Winchester."

"How do you know her?"

"We work together."

Someone shouted his name from the distance.

"I'm going to need to get an official statement from you, but not until you're cleared by the doc. I need your cell phone."

"Of course. Whatever you need." Bobbi clicked open the pictures and like a beam of death shooting through the darkness, Hannah's once beautiful, delicate body was centered in the photo.

She closed her eyes and handed him the phone. "Also, someone was here when I walked in."

His hand froze. "Who?"

"I don't know. He sprinted out the back door—"

"Which door, exactly?"

"The kitchen."

The Lieutenant's gaze skittered to the team around the house. "And you didn't recognize him?"

"No. It was dark inside…" her voice trailed off trying to picture the scene in her head, which, shockingly, was a bit blurry. Maybe she did need to go to the hospital.

"Height, weight?"

"Um," she squinted deep in thought. "Normal height, I guess."

"Hair color?"

"Dark, I think. Dark ballcap, dark clothes."

"Was he carrying anything?"

"No, I don't… no, I don't think so, although I only saw him for a split-second."

"Any vehicles here when you pulled up?"

"No. And I didn't pass any, either."

"And you're sure you didn't recognize him?"

She chewed her lower lip wishing she had a photographic memory. "I just don't know…"

"*Jacob!*" He suddenly shouted impatiently.

She jumped.

Lieutenant Colson waved his hands in the air until an ambulance rolled to a stop next to them.

"An *ambulance?*" Her mouth gaped. "This is absolutely ridiculous."

The EMT jumped out, opened the back doors, and pulled down a stretcher.

"*No.* I am not—"

The Lieutenant's jaw set, nostrils flared. "Miss Cross, I will put you inside myself—"

Jacob Hill interrupted, breaking the mounting tension. "It's protocol ma'am. This is going to be your ride."

Just then—"Bobbi!"

The dark outline of a woman jogged down the driveway. The Lieutenant stepped forward, partially blocking Bobbi in a protective stance. Why the hell was he protecting *her*?

"I know her." Bobbi said as she stepped forward, not bothering to hide her irritation. "Payton—"

"Your *face.*" Payton's eyes popped to the size of golf balls. "My *God,* are you okay?" Wearing skinny jeans, designer black pumps and a couture blazer, Payton had obviously grabbed a shower after yoga and was headed back to work.

"I'm fine. But," her face fell as she looked at the house, black smoke swirling in the wind like a magic trick gone bad.

Panic froze Payton's face. *"Hannah?"*

Bobbi nodded, swallowing the knot in her throat, thankful when the Lieutenant broke the waterfall of emotion.

"Miss..."

Payton's shocked expression shifted to him. "Chase. Payton Chase."

"Miss Chase, this is a crime scene. I'm going to need to ask you to leave..."

Her eyes drifted back to Bobbi, clearly not registering what he'd just said. "Uh... She's dead?"

"Ma'am, please step aside."

"No... I...." Payton stuttered.

"How did you hear about the incident," the Lieutenant asked while trying to guide her away.

"Oh, I, uh, have a scanner in my car." She sucked in a breath and held her shoulders back. "I'm with NAR News."

Bobbi could practically feel him tense next to her. It was

no secret that the department's relationship with the media was a constant battle of love and hate.

"You need to step outside the crime scene, now."

Payton's eyes slitted with anger. "We're by the woods, for Christ's sake."

"The entire yard is a crime scene right now, and we don't need you or your team destroying potential evidence. The road, *now,* Miss Chase."

Not one to be intimidated, Payton stared at the six-foot hunk of muscle for a second, before finally looking at Bobbi.

"Where are you going?"

"They're making me check my head out."

Payton snorted. "So you'll be there awhile." Although Payton was never known to be a class clown, she had a quick wit.

Bobbi smiled and cut a glance at the Lieutenant who was shouting orders to put up more crime scene tape.

"I'll come by the hospital, okay?" Concern shown in Payton's deep blue eyes.

"You don't need to."

"Ma'am, let's get you checked out." The EMT said, impatient now.

"Fine." Bobbi ground her teeth, but realized she was being ridiculously difficult. She closed her eyes and took a quick breath. "Alright." She turned back to Payton. "I'll call you later, don't come by."

Payton solemnly nodded. "Talk soon."

Bobbi was lifted into the back of the ambulance, quickly followed by a slamming door. She looked out the window as the EMT slid behind the steering wheel. The scene was a circus. People running all over. Every single medic and law enforcement personnel had hightailed it to Hannah's, half were only there because they'd heard it over the scanner and wanted to take part in the action. Or, they wanted a good story to tell at Donny's Diner the next morning. That was the thing about small towns. Not much else going on otherwise.

A team of uniforms surrounded the Lieutenant while he yelled orders, and she realized just how tall he really was. His gaze flickered quickly to her, then cut away to the team as he said one last thing, and everyone split off.

4

QUINN STRODE ACROSS the lawn, his boots sinking in the fresh mud made from the fire hoses. With the headlights from the emergency response vehicles at his back, his silhouette stretched across the grass, which was covered in tracks and boot prints.

Fan-fucking-tastic.

All other vehicles had been ordered to park on the dirt road outside the driveway. Not that it mattered. Any evidence or tracks in the front yard had surely been trampled. The fire had been contained almost immediately which was good news, the bad news was the overkill amount of water that had been sprayed all over the damn place, no doubt washing away precious evidence at the scene. The house was still off-limits until the fire chief gave the okay, and although he was itching to get inside, he wanted to take another look at the body before Hannah was shipped off to the morgue.

He looked at his team, scrambling around the yard.

His team.

What a cluster fuck. He was used to big city departments, and the lack of divisions, structure, and organization in general had jarred him from his first day on the job at BSPD. But that was okay, he'd adjust. He'd adjust because the Lieutenant position wasn't the only thing that brought him to the suffocating small town they called Berry Springs.

The smoldering scent stung his nose as he stepped over to the black body bag next to the ambulance. Light from the opened back door of the vehicle spilled onto the body lying on top of the bag.

Two EMTs that he didn't know stood around watching the chaos and pretending to be busy. Not a lot for an EMT to do with a dead body.

Dr. Buckley looked up from his kneeled position next to Hannah's head.

"Poor, poor girl." The doctor muttered.

Quinn squatted down and looked the naked body over. Hannah Winchester was long and lean, with bright pink toenails and fingernails. A tattoo of a symbol—he was pretty sure it had something to do with yoga—colored the skin just below her navel, which sat in the middle of a six-pack stomach. Hannah was someone who took pride in her health. Long, blonde hair spilled around her head, highlighting the deep red stains of matted blood around a gnarly head wound. Blunt force trauma, no doubt about that. He cocked his head, getting a better angle. Whatever had busted her head open was small, but had to be thick and sturdy as hell. The butt of a gun, perhaps? The tip of a baseball bat? He took a slight inhale and allowed his gaze to go where everyone's had already been a hundred times. The red marks between her legs. He clenched his jaw, anger and disgust turning in his stomach. As a lifelong police officer, he'd seen a boatload of messed up shit, but sexual assault and rape were two things he never got used to. He did what he was trained *not* to do—he always imagined what it would be like if the woman was a family member.

That kind of fury did not sit well with him.

He leaned in closer and peered at Hannah's hands and fingernails. No scratches or scrapes, which indicated that she didn't fight her attacker. Interesting. Look at family and friends, first, he thought. His gaze slowly trailed up her torso, past her breasts, which appeared to be free of scrapes or bruising. No bite marks, which he'd seen a shocking amount of times on victim's breasts. He then looked at her neck, seemingly unmarked as well. She was raped, or it seemed pretty obvious that she was, but there were no other signs of sexual aggressiveness anywhere else. Had her attacker been in a hurry?

He looked at Hannah's face, a beautiful face in an almost serene, eerie expression.

"Do you know her," he asked Buckley.

"Hannah Winchester. Mid-twenties, although that's just a guess, really."

"She born and raised here?"

"Nope, but her granny was. Makes her one of our own." Thinly veiled anger colored the doctor's tone.

Pride. Although Quinn had only been an official Berry Springs resident for a few months, he realized very quickly everyone in this town was protective of each other, and didn't take kindly to strangers. Especially when an outsider was hired to serve and protect the place. He'd have to work for respect here, which, quite honestly, he didn't give a crap if he ever got. The small town cowboys could screw themselves. He had more important things to look after in Berry Springs.

Buckley continued, "She was one of my patients. Had strep throat recently. Nice gal. I knew her granny."

"What's her name?"

"Mavis Winchester. Died over a year ago."

So he couldn't question her. Dammit.

"Her folks live here?"

"Next town over. Live way out in the country. Never come into town much. I don't even know them, really. Live off the land. Major hippies, at least I think they are."

Well, he'd find out soon enough when he visited them to tell them their daughter was dead.

"What did Hannah do for a living?"

"Said she just graduated from the community college, I think. Teaches yoga occasionally at *Just Be Yoga,* a little building past the city park."

"Justin Yoga?"

"Just *Be* Yoga." He said with a bit of annoyance, as if Quinn should know every building in the town. Maybe he should.

Buckley continued. "They have daily yoga classes. My sister made me go a few months ago. Said I needed to work on my *Zen,* whatever the hell that means." He snorted. "Lasted five minutes in that suffocating sauna before sitting on my ass the rest of the class. Ain't for me. Hannah taught that class, is how I know. Anyway, Bobbi owns it. Girl you saved."

The girl he saved. Her face flashed in his head, the long dark hair, mesmerizing green eyes... the attitude. Bobbi Cross. He'd never forget the name, or the face.

He glanced at the house. "Hannah live alone?"

"That I don't know. That's her granny's old house. Heard Hannah inherited it."

Quinn glanced down at her lifeless, pale left hand. "Married?"

"Not that I'm aware."

"Boyfriend?"

Something flickered in the old man's eyes. "Don't know that either, but if so, I'd like to meet him in a dark alley."

Quinn watched him for a moment as the doctor avoided eye contact.

Heavy footsteps pounded the ground toward them, and Quinn looked up expecting to see a Clydesdale barreling toward them. What he got was a short, stocky, redhead with a look of steel in her eyes. In one hand she carried a bag half the size of her body, and in the other, a bright-red Slurpee from the gas station down the road.

"Got another one, huh?"

Another dead body, she meant. A pair of turquoise and brown cowgirl boots stopped at Hannah's head. Quinn and Buckley stood.

A smile instantly crossed Buckley's face. "Jessica."

She ignored both men as she looked down at the body, zeroing-in between the legs. *"Son of a bitch,"* she muttered. She set the bag down and yanked out two blue latex gloves as she eyed the bloody spot on Hannah's head. She popped on each glove, glanced up at the house, then back down at the body.

"Found here?" Jessica asked to no one in particular.

"No, she was pulled from the home," Quinn responded.

"Pulled from the house?"

"Yes, found deceased inside, and then carried outside."

"By who?"

"A witness."

She finally looked up, stared at him a minute. "You're the new Lieutenant, right?"

"Quinn Colson."

"Jessica Heathrow. Medical Examiner."

He'd heard the name, along with her spotless reputation and legendary ball-busting attitude.

"Well, welcome to Berry Springs, Lieutenant Colson. Why the hell was the body removed from the scene?"

"The house was catching fire. The witness, a friend of the victim, didn't want her to burn."

"Who found her?" Jessica asked again.

"Bobbi Cross." Buckley offered up, with no regard to privacy.

"No shit?" Jessica glanced up. "Damn."

"Can you tell how long she's been deceased?" Quinn cut to the point.

"Recent, for sure. She's not close to rigor. Although, I won't be able to tell you for sure until I finish my examination."

"You think within a handful of hours? Or under an hour?"

"As I said, I can't confirm that yet...but, the latter, possibly."

She chose her words carefully, not wanting to commit, which he understood and respected.

A minute passed as she aimed her flashlight and examined the head wound. "Pretty darn hard hit, right above the temple, too."

"Is it possible she fell?" Buckley asked.

"I can't tell you that at this moment, Buck."

Quinn was pretty sure he already knew the answer to that question. "I want her rape kit done immediately, first thing," he said.

Jessica looked up at him with raised eyebrows and an expression that told him the redhead didn't appreciate being told how to do her job. "Sexual assault victims are always treated with a sense of urgency. In my office, anyway. Who all has touched the body?" She asked.

"Bobbi and myself, and whoever did this. And the EMT's lifted her onto the bag."

"I'm sure they wore gloves," she said with a hint of attitude.

Quinn opened his mouth to explain that the reason he didn't put on a pair of gloves was because he needed to get both women away from the house as fast as possible, in case the place blew. In which case, her job would have been a hell of a lot harder. But he didn't care to explain himself to her, or anyone for that matter.

He glanced at the house, chomping at the bit to get in there. *Screw it,* he was going to push his way through. He looked back at Jessica. "I want to be at the autopsy." He slipped his card into her bag. "You'll hear from me shortly, Miss Heathrow."

"I have no doubt I will." She muttered as she looked back down.

He turned. "Willard."

Officer Travis Willard jogged over, late to the party. "Sir?" With the expression of a seasoned officer—complete with short, buzzed hair—but half the age of one, Officer Willard was a legacy officer, in his fourth year on the force. His father retired from a life-long career in law enforcement and had given his only son the bug. Willard was hardworking and focused. And just like Hayes—with perhaps less attitude—he was leery of the new Lieutenant, just like everyone else in town.

Join the club.

From the moment he'd met Hayes his first day on the job, Hayes made it clear that he wasn't a fan of an outsider coming in and telling him what to do. Hayes didn't trust him, and Quinn didn't give a shit, as long as Hayes showed up at work every day and put his heart into it. The moment his immature attitude began to hamper an investigation, Quinn would throw Hayes out on his ass. And enjoy every moment of it. Until then, he'd focus on keeping the less contentious relationship with Willard solid.

"I need you to check the back door. Our eye witness says she saw someone run out the back."

Willard's eyes rounded. "Bobbi did?"

Not only had word already spread who the witness was, but everyone seemed to know Bobbi. After seeing her up close and personal himself, he had a damn good guess why.

"Where is she?"

"On the way to the hospital."

"I thought she just passed out?"

"Gash on her head."

"You get a statement? Details?"

"Hardly." He decided against bringing up the pictures just yet. "Bottom line, no statement from her will hold up if she's concussed."

"Good point."

"Go to the back of the house. I don't want anyone messing with shit back there. Half our evidence has already been washed away. I'm going inside."

"I don't think they've cleared it yet."

He was done waiting. He stepped to the front door as Willard took off toward the back.

"How much longer?"

Fire Chief Dennis Carter pulled the towel away from his sweating face. He stared at Quinn for a moment with the same questioning eye he'd seen a dozen times over the last few months.

"We're making sure she's one-hundred percent contained, Lieutenant Colston."

"Colson." *Christ.*

"That's right. Colson. Sorry. Then, we'll need to conduct our investigation."

"You can do that while I do my own. What's your initial read on the cause of fire?"

"Ain't got that far yet, son."

Son.

"Did you tell your men to stay clear of the kitchen and the rest of the house?"

"Did our best."

There was attitude in the chief's voice and Quinn felt his patience wavering. He couldn't care less if no one liked him, what he did care about was finding the person who murdered Hannah Winchester, and to do that, they needed to work together and preserve as much evidence in the house as possible.

"I'm going to ask again, Chief, because I need to know. Did *your best* include staying out of the hallway and kitchen?" He reached into his pocket and began pulling on latex gloves.

The chief met his gaze and puffed his chest. He started to say something, but was interrupted.

"She's clear." Logan Black, a volunteer fireman, broke the tension as he raised his mask and stepped out the front door. Quinn didn't know much about the guy other than he was military and volunteered at the fire station when he wasn't deployed. Solid kid, alert, steely look in his eyes, and lacking the "stranger danger" attitude most Berry Springers had when they spoke to him.

Quinn nodded, took one last look at the chief and then stepped into the house. His foot splashed in a puddle.

Goddammit.

The charred scent hung heavy like a blanket in the air, but there was something else, too. A light, lemony scent. He frowned. The smell reminded him of sitting outside on his grandma's porch while she read stories to him when he was a little boy.

Weird.

He pulled the flashlight from his belt and looked around. The electricity had been turned off and they'd positioned a few lights at the entry which did little to illuminate.

Hannah's house was small, with a living room to the right, two bedrooms to the left and a kitchen in the back. He noticed Willard's shadow at the back door. Good.

Odd looking symbols and cloths hung from the walls—more yoga symbols, he guessed, and cheesy motivational quotes. The house was thoughtfully decorated, not cluttered, and clean. An end table lay haphazardly on the floor, with a smear of blood on the corner. He kneeled down and flashed the light, recalling Bobbi's story that she'd hit her head in the hall. That must've been the place. The tabletop was solid marble, with a dangerously sharp edge.

Damn.

Regardless, he'd run the blood to make sure. Beside the table lay a cracked picture of a young, beautiful Hannah sitting on a big, brown horse with who he assumed was her grandfather, who had a protective arm around her. Where were the pictures of her mom and dad? Maybe she wasn't close to them. He sure as hell understood that. They both beamed into the camera. What a wasted life.

He pushed to a stance.

"Looks like the fire was started in the bathroom." Logan stepped next to him. "Then caught the closet that backs up to it. But I want to show you something."

There was something in Logan's voice that made Quinn's eyebrows tip up. Logan led the way into Hannah's bedroom. Two lanterns placed at the doorway lit the small room. A haze of smoke still lingered in the air, and the lemon scent was stronger.

"What the hell is that lemon smell?"

"Noticed it, too. She's got oils and stuff around the house. Maybe some of that caught."

Made sense. He lifted his flashlight. Half the space was burned black, the other half still intact. His first thought was that the fire must've started mere seconds before Bobbi found the body... unless she started it.

Humph. His gut laughed at the thought, but good sense told him to look at everything. Every single thing.

He noted the blood on the pillow and the slight indentation on the bed where the body had laid. He wanted to pull out Bobbi's phone to check the pictures, but didn't want Logan to see, for now at least. He needed to know Logan's take on the fire and there were just too many variables at the moment to start exposing his investigation.

Logan led him to the bathroom, which was completely blackened. It was a typical small bathroom. Toilet, single sink over a cabinet, a one-person shower, and narrow doorway leading to the closet. He glanced out of the bathroom, into the bedroom. "Two doors lead to the closet."

Logan nodded. "A bedroom entry and bathroom."

Burned frames of disintegrated pictures hung haphazardly on the wall. Toothbrush holder, soap dispenser, and what remained of a tissue holder on the sink. He stepped further into the room and glanced at the small space between the toilet and sink. He kneeled down, peering at the six-inch cast iron candlestick holder lying on the floor. Long and skinny with a sharp point at the top to insert a candle, and a thick base at the bottom—perfect to bludgeon someone to death.

"Any wax or melted candle?"

"Yes, right around where you're standing. But that's not where the fire started." Logan motioned to the middle of the floor. "This is where the fire started." Then, he kicked open the crooked cabinet door under the sink. "And caught like crazy under here thanks to the hairspray and whatever else women put on their bodies. Walking fire hazards, they are."

Quinn pulled his phone from his pocket and took pictures of the holders.

Logan shined the light on the narrow door that led to the closet. "The fire spread, and then her clothes caught."

The closet was a complete loss. Not that it mattered.

Logan continued, "The number one cause of fire is candles, but, like I said, that's not where the fire started, so I'm ruling that out. No ashtrays or anything to indicate she was smoking." He illuminated the electrical sockets. "Fire didn't come from there, either."

Okay, that much was obvious. As if reading his thoughts, Logan continued, "What's striking me as odd is that the point of origin appears to be the middle of the floor." He illuminated the melted linoleum. "See the darker shades there? It appears a towel caught somehow, maybe this one, then this towel caught... then this one..."

The corner of a burned, blue paisley-print bath towel led to the closet.

"Our suspect used a trailer."

"Quite possibly, yes. Using the towels."

Arson seemed obvious from the get-go but a trailer was a dead giveaway.

Willard stepped into the bathroom. They nodded at each other.

Quinn stepped over to the shower. Only the rod of the curtain was left, but he noticed two loofahs and a washcloth inside. "The shower was wet when the fire started."

"Yes, which slowed the fire considerably. That and the humidity of the room."

Had Hannah been in the shower?

"Willard, set a marker here," Quinn pointed. "And two next to the candle holders on the floor by the toilet."

Willard pulled a yellow evidence tag and placed it next to the shower, then stepped past them.

Quinn turned, his mind reeling.

Assuming the killer was the one who started the fire, why the middle of the bathroom floor? Assuming Hannah was killed with the candle holder laying in the bathroom, why was her body found in bed? Nothing seemed obvious, and that was the first red flag. The second came when Logan motioned them into the bedroom.

"Here's where things get real interesting, Lieutenant." Logan illuminated the wall between the bathroom and bed.

"See that black *V*? That's one of the main ways we determine the origin of the fire."

Quinn focused on the spot, then glanced into the bathroom at the burned towels. "Wait. You're saying there were *two* separate fires?"

"Bingo."

Two separate fires. Brow knit in concentration, Quinn stepped closer to the *V* and squatted down.

"No outlet there, no frayed wiring, nothing obvious that would have set this exact spot on fire."

He looked at the blood-covered pillow on the bed, then back at the spot, about three feet away. He stood up.

"Wait." Willard glanced at the bed obviously thinking

the same thing. "Hannah was found dead, on the bed, right?" He placed another evidence marker next to the *V*.

"According to Miss Cross, yes."

"Okay, so if our suspect set the fire to destroy evidence, why the hell would he light it so far away from the body?"

"Assuming it's arson, yeah, that didn't make sense to me, either." Logan said.

"Right," Willard frowned. "What was he trying to cover up right here? I mean, why here? Maybe something's hiding in the wall?"

All valid points. But still, none that seemed to add up.

Logan nodded, "I agree. Something's off, for sure. If the fire was lit to cover tracks or destroy evidence, you'd figure the bed with the dead body would've been the number one priority."

"The fire had to ignite somehow." Quinn added as he paced the room, scanning every inch. He glanced at the bedroom window and shook his head—any fingerprints had surely been washed off by the hose. "We need to know how the fire started, first. Could be a simple lighter, candle, whatever, or he used an accelerant."

"If Hannah was in the shower, or if things had gotten wet, a simple cigarette lighter would have been difficult..."

"Exactly." Quinn said. "We need the surfaces tested for accelerant."

"Agreed, and it'll get done." The chief stepped into the room. "Along with examining the electrical system to rule that out."

"Hang on..." Willard paused, ignoring the chief. "If someone used an accelerant... wouldn't the point of origin be all over, or very large areas, at least? Meaning, not just in two secluded spots?"

Quinn shook his head as his brain started slowly putting

pieces of the puzzle together. The corners, at least—the corners of what his gut was telling him was going to be a very large puzzle with many, many pieces. "Not unless they had a limited amount of accelerant. They used it where they assumed would have the most impact. Towels that led to the closet, and then the carpet next to the bed."

"Again, why not light the *bed* on fire?"

Willard was right, that part made no sense. His hand was itching to pull out the pictures Bobbi had taken. "Willard, take pictures starting in the bathroom and work your way out. I want the entire house photographed. Hayes is swiping for prints." He turned to Logan and Chief Carter. "When will you have your official report written up?"

Logan glanced around the room. "I'll bag up the burned towel, remove a portion of the bathroom tile, and take carpet samples to send off for accelerant testing. That'll take a while."

"We don't have awhile."

"I'll put a rush on it, but no promises," the chief said.

"Once that's done, we'll write up the official report." Logan said and glanced at the chief. "But there's no question in my mind this isn't an accidental fire."

The chief nodded without hesitation. "We'll get out of your way, as soon as we get our samples."

"No samples until we get full photographs."

"Get at it, then."

As the firemen exited, Quinn turned to Willard.

"Did you know Hannah?" Willard was born and raised in Berry Springs, so it was a good bet.

"Met her a few times at Frank's."

Frank's Bar and Grill was the local watering hole. An old hunting cabin turned into a honky-tonk bar with a cowbell hanging over the front door and a constant flow of classic country out of an antique jukebox. Best BBQ he'd had in years. He loved the place. Felt like home.

"Were you two friendly?"

"A few casual conversations, in a group setting. Polite, but definitely not friends."

"Do you know if she was seeing anyone?"

A second ticked by, then Willard's eyebrows raised with an epiphany. "Actually, I saw her a few times recently with Chad Kudrow. Know him?"

Quinn shook his head.

"You will. Trust me, at some point in your career at BSPD, you'll meet him. Punk asshole if you ask me. Runs his own mechanic shop on the outskirts of town. Women seem to like him, no clue why."

"Why is he a punk asshole?"

"He's one of those drunks who spouts off and gets in fights. Check his record. He's spent a few nights in the cage for fighting."

Interesting. And from the little he knew about yoga-loving Hannah, they didn't seem like a fit. Again, something else that didn't appear to add up.

"Do you know if they were in a relationship, or just friends?"

"I don't think Chad has friends that are girls, if you catch my drift."

"When was the last time you saw them?"

"Ah, hell, I'm not sure. Maybe a week ago, I think. Don't quote me on that, though."

That was okay, he'd find out when he paid Chad a visit later. Quinn redirected the conversation.

"What's your take on the back door?"

"No obvious break-in—door or windows. Didn't see any obvious tracks, but didn't check the yard."

"Alright, that's where I'm headed. Get these pictures taken. Don't let anyone come in this room until you're done. Bag up the candlestick holders before Logan and Carter come back in to get samples. Come outside after."

"You got it."

5

LASHES OF LIGHT from Willard's camera bounced off the walls as Quinn stepped out of the bedroom. He glanced out the front door. Both ambulances were gone, along with the ME's truck, which meant Hannah had been zipped up and was on her way to the morgue. Logan Black was gathering tools to take samples, while the rest of the firemen were packing up. Hayes was focused on finding prints on the front door, and aside from Willard, he had the house to himself, for the moment, at least.

Quinn stepped into the living room and shined the flashlight. Quaint and cozy with a fireplace, love seat, paisley-printed armchair, and bookcase. The girl liked her paisley print. No TV, which he found interesting. Candles lined the fireplace mantel, along with several pictures—the focal point was a framed eight-by-ten of a smiling Hannah with her mother and father. He'd have to make that call soon. That was the worst part of his job, and it was something he never got used to. They'd ask how she died. For now, he'll say that it appears to have happened under suspicious circumstances, and leave the fact that she was raped and bludgeoned to death out of the description. Let the loss sink in before the father's worst nightmare hit.

He clenched his jaw with a rush of urgency to find the son of a bitch. Not only for the family, but for every woman in Berry Springs. Nothing was worse than a rapist, in his opinion, and no woman was safe until the guy was caught.

His gaze drifted to the next picture—college graduation.

He stopped cold on the next.

Four women and two men dripping in sweat, arms around each other, huddled in front of a small cottage with flowers along the sides. A sign above the door read *Just Be Yoga*. His gaze locked on Bobbi with a long, black braid of hair cascading down her shoulder. She was smiling, her cheeks a rosy red. She wore all black spandex, like a sexy ninja, and he found himself tracing the curves of her body. He was drawn to her eyes, a cat-like emerald green with depth that promised layers and layers of unpeeling until the true woman was revealed. She was smiling, yes, but there was something lacking in her eyes. Like a magnet, he leaned in further, searching the green irises. He saw many things in Bobbi Cross, including the edges of a thick brick wall she'd built around herself. He saw beauty, deception.

He saw strength.

He'd never forget seeing her step out of a burning house with a dead woman dangling from her arms. The blood trickling down her face, the sheer determination spilling from those green eyes.

Bobbi was petite, but muscular, and Hannah had a good four inches on her. The only way Bobbi would have been able to carry her outside—especially considering the smoke, haze, and hit to the head—was pure adrenaline. The kind that came from survivors.

In those eyes, he saw a survivor.

Quinn turned and walked into the second bedroom. A dozen cardboard boxes speckled the carpeted floor. Apparently, Hannah hadn't fully unpacked. He made a mental note to confirm that she'd been there a year, as Buckley had said. He checked the closet—empty—then the windows.

Next, the laundry room, then into the kitchen. He shined the light slowly around the small, cluttered space. Aged wallpaper with yellow flowers peeled from the ceiling. A few boxes sat in the corner next to a small dining table and mismatched chairs. Dirty dishes in the sink. A few pictures on the fridge, and he caught himself looking for Bobbi. No Bobbi. No boys.

A recycle can filled with aluminum cans, milk containers, three empty wine bottles, and an empty gallon of vodka sat next to a trashcan. Hannah liked to drink, but that certainly wasn't a crime. With a gloved hand he lifted the trashcan lid—banana peels, tissues, paper towels, wrappings. He closed the lid. He'd have someone go through that —not him. He made his way around the counter, then confirmed the window was securely locked. Next, he kneeled down by the back door. If Bobbi really did see the suspect run out the door, he surely touched the knob. He looked at the door frame—no nicks or cracks. Had the door been unlocked? Usually, he assumed people kept their doors locked, but one of the first things he'd learned when he'd moved to Berry Springs was people didn't bother to lock up. Tight-knit communities were way too trusting.

He straightened and looked out the small beveled window in the door, imagining the path he would take. Straight into the damn woods.

He turned and strode down the hall.

Click, click, click. Willard had moved to the living room, and Quinn could hear banging in the bedroom. Logan was removing samples for accelerant testing. *Good.* Now if Chief Carter could put a rush on the testing, maybe they'd have something.

He stepped outside, maneuvering past Hayes. It wasn't like the kid was going to acknowledge his presence anyway.

Quinn pulled his phone from his pocket.

"Jonas here."

"Jonas, Colson. I need you to look into something ASAP."

"Is there any other way?"

Jonas's official title at BSPD was Evidence Tech, but he was the station's go-to guy for research, admin work, or anything else that needed to be done. The thirty-something was smart as a whip, efficient, fast, and could hack into any system on the planet. A bit cocky, but he could back it up, and Quinn respected that. Jonas didn't give a shit that Quinn was an outsider, and they'd had a decent rapport right off the bat.

"You know a Chad Kudrow?"

"Yep. Traded punches with him at Frank's a few years ago."

Quinn's eyebrows tipped up. "You two got into it?"

"Yep."

"Over what?"

"Oh, some bullshit pool game."

"Who won?"

"I haven't lost a game of pool since the eighties."

"The fight, you idiot."

"Oh. Same, then. Haven't lost a fight since grade school. His punches were like having a peck on the cheek from your granny."

"My grandma doesn't peck."

"Fine. McCord's grandma, then."

"McCord's grandma has horns and breathes fire."

A boisterous laugh on the other end of the phone. "Anyway, yeah, I know the bastard."

Jonas was the second person to use "bastard" to describe the man.

"I need you to verify his whereabouts tonight. Find out where he is right now. Also, get me a write-up on him. Home life, job, what kind of car he drives, where he takes a shit."

"Well we all know he doesn't shit in the gym because—"

"I know, I know. He punches like a granny. Got it."

"Just making sure we're clear."

"Check his social media, too."

"Okay, I'll set aside the hundred other things you have me working on. You still at the Winchester residence?"

"Yeah."

"Is she as bad as I hear?"

How the hell did he hear about the condition of her body already? He'd never lived in a town where gossip was such a hot commodity. "It's not pretty. Get me a write-up on her, too. Check her social media accounts. I need to know every move this girl made in the last forty-eight hours. You know her?"

"Nope."

"Heard she hung out at Frank's some."

"Doesn't mean I know her."

"Alright. Get on Hannah's social media."

"Will do as soon as I locate twinkle toes."

Click.

Hayes walked up beside him looking at the front yard, now covered in tire tracks. "Looks like the party's died down. Pun unintended." He reached into his pocket and checked his phone. "Justin's asking if we need anything else."

"The EMT?"

"Yeah."

"No. How's Miss Cross?"

A barely visible smirk crossed Hayes's lips. "She's been admitted—

"What?"

"What, what?"

"What's with the smirk?"

"Oh." The smirk grew into a cocky grin. "She'd have a field day if she knew you were referring to her as *Miss Cross.*"

Quinn drew his eyebrows together.

"She's just not that kind of chick, ya know? I mean, she's one of the best target shooters in the state. Southern girl through and through. Not really a *Miss* kind of girl." Hayes shrugged, "Anyway, Doc's checking her over now."

Not a Miss kind of gal. "Okay. Keep checking for prints. Pay special attention to the back door."

Hayes nodded, keeping his eye on his cell.

"I'll be around back."

A cool breeze swept past Quinn as he rounded the corner of the house. He narrowed his eyes and scanned the dense woods that lined Hannah's yard. He made a mental note to check all trails and hunting roads that ran around her property. The suspect had to park somewhere, unless he lived close, which he'd also check.

A cloud drifted from the moon. Shadows stretched across the lawn, slowly swaying back and forth.

He paused at the back of the house and looked around. A small, ten-by-ten patio sat just outside the back door, with two lounge chairs, a grill, bag of charcoal, and four tiki torches at each corner.

He stepped onto the patio and kneeled down by a small, yellow jug tipped on its side next to the door.

Citronella Tiki Fuel.

Citronella—the lemony scent he'd smelled in the house wasn't hippie oils or incense, it was Citronella.

The guy used Citronella to light the damn fire.

He took a few pictures of the container, then carefully picked it up with the tips of his gloved hand.

Empty.

He placed the jug into an evidence bag, then stood and scanned the door, windows, and patio. Willard was right, nothing screamed break-in. He stepped into the back yard and shined his light. Berry Springs recently had six inches of rain—normal for springtime—and perfect for finding tracks.

Willard stepped out on the patio, avoiding touching the back door knob.

"Got pictures of the entire house." He joined Quinn on the grass.

"Anything stand out?"

"Not a thing."

"Logan still in there?"

"Yeah, think they should be done soon. Saw Hayes up front."

Quinn nodded toward the tiki fluid bagged on the patio.

Willard's eyes rounded as he walked over. "That's what that damn smell was."

"Yep. Odds are we found the accelerant."

Willard paused for a moment, frowning. "So, after he killed her, he searched for something to light the place on fire. Which makes me think this wasn't premeditated."

"Right... maybe the actual murder wasn't premeditated. Maybe things got messier than intended."

Willard nodded. "No sign of a break-in implies either she knew her attacker or possibly left her door unlocked, which doesn't sound like something a smart woman who lived alone would do, especially at night."

"People leave their doors unlocked all the time. Here, anyway."

"Or," Willard's eye widened. "The door was unlocked because she was expecting someone to stop by."

"Bobbi."

"Exactly. And the guy walked right in."

Quinn frowned, deep in thought. "Hannah gets home, gets in the shower, maybe had some time before Bobbi showed up. Bad guy walks in... surprised her in the shower."

"And if the candle holders are indeed the murder weapon, she was killed in the bathroom..." Willard chewed on his lower lip. "Killer freaks, searches for something to light the house on fire and the tiki fluid's the only thing he could find."

Quinn nodded. "Starts with the bathroom, then moves to the bedroom. Bobbi walks in and he hightails it out."

A moment slid by and Willard shook his head. "Bobbi's lucky."

Quinn had the same thought several times over the last hour. It was surprising that the suspect would risk keeping someone alive who saw him. Maybe he didn't have a gun? Didn't want to get up close and personal? Maybe all he was thinking at the time was to get the hell out? Which made Quinn wonder, maybe the suspect didn't recognize Bobbi either, therefore, didn't label her as a threat. No way she could ID him, if he didn't recognize her?

Just a few of the hundred questions rolling around in Quinn's head.

"What I don't get is the bed thing." Quinn glanced thoughtfully back at the house. "If the fire was started to cover his tracks, why the hell wouldn't he set the bed, or hell, even the body on fire?" It didn't make sense. Not a single bit. "The timeline also doesn't add up. The potential murder weapon is in the bathroom, where she was showering. But her body was found on the bed, positioned."

"Positioned?"

Quinn reached into his pocket and turned on Bobbi's phone. The morbid pictures of Hannah's raped, murdered body illuminated the darkness.

Willard stood silent as he flipped through each picture. "Holy shit." He finally said. "You're right. Someone crossed her legs and everything. They took the time to do this."

"She's also not in a sexually suggestive position." Like he'd seen before with rape victims. Positioning a victim after death wasn't uncommon—sick as fuck—but not uncommon. More often than not, the sexually assaulted woman was arranged in a degrading way, to further disintegrate any shred of decency in the victim's life. This wasn't the case with Hannah. In fact, it was the exact opposite.

Yet something else that didn't add up.

"Wait. So Hannah was showering, then raped, then killed in the bathroom, then placed on the bed?"

"Hannah showed no signs of struggle."

"It was consensual, then."

Quinn shook his head. "That doesn't add up with the red marks..." He waited to see if Willard was going to connect the dots that had been forming in his head the last thirty minutes.

"So then, she didn't fight, which means... Wait, *whoa.*" Willard stopped on a dime. "No *way.* She was raped *after* she was killed."

Quinn slowly nodded. "It's the only thing that makes sense. Killed in the bathroom—she had no time to fight—

then carried to the bed. Then, the guy had his way with her. He was rough with her."

"That's so *fucking sick.*"

It was so fucking sick, but potentially said a lot about the killer. Perhaps someone with a necrophilia fetish? Unfortunately, it wouldn't be the first case he'd seen involving it. The most common motivation for necrophilia was control— having sex with a non-resisting partner. In the three cases he'd worked in Texas, the necrophiliac was someone with low self-esteem and some sort of abuse in their past. A close second motivation was a sick sexual attraction to corpses, and the third was a need for one last rendezvous with a deceased loved one. No matter what the motivation, it made him want to heave up the lunch he hadn't eaten.

"We need to check to see if there are any local cases involving necrophilia... and I want the list of employees at the morgue."

Willard nodded. "I'm on it."

A moment of silence ticked by while they both tried to understand how someone could bang a corpse.

Willard shook his head. "I can't believe this. *Hannah.*"

"Was she into drugs, drinking, or hanging out with questionable people?"

"I don't get that vibe from her."

"What about her folks?"

"Not sure about them."

"I've got Jonas checking into her and Chad Kudrow. Apparently, he's not a fan of the guy either."

Willard grinned. "No, I wouldn't think so. They got into a fight a while back."

"I know all about it. According to Jonas, Kudrow fights like a girl."

Willard's brow cocked. "You must not know a lot of Berry Springs girls."

He thought of Bobbi... and had no doubt she could handle herself in a physical confrontation.

Willard continued, "Anyway, yeah Jonas won for sure but it wasn't a knockout. Kudrow gave him a run for his money."

"Any tickets given out?"

"The only thing that was given out was tequila shots by Frank afterward. Kudrow got what he was asking for and everyone was happy to see it. No one reported it."

They stepped into the woods, shining their lights on the ground.

Quinn considered the happy pictures in Hannah's house, the healthy lifestyle. "Kudrow just doesn't seem like the guy a girl like Hannah would date."

"Women like him for some reason. I think it's the whole bad boy persona or something."

"Women don't like assholes."

"Some do."

Willard nodded and started to say something but Quinn strong-armed him.

"*Stop.*"

Willard froze like a statue.

Quinn steadied his flashlight on a small patch of dirt three inches from Willard's boots. He kneeled down, Willard followed.

"Looks like we've got a fresh print."

"Well, son of a bitch."

"We need to get a cast of this immediately."

"Yes sir." Willard blew out a whistle as he gazed at the print. "First the candle holder—assuming it's the murder weapon—and now a footprint. Might be a slam dunk case."

Something in Quinn's gut told him this case was not going to be that easy. He narrowed his eyes.

"Shine that light closer."

Willard pointed his light, leaned in, then frowned. "Wait. Was he *barefoot?*"

Quinn stared at the blurry indentations of what appeared to be bare toes in the dirt.

No, not a single thing about this case seemed to add up, and it was at that moment that he was absolutely certain nothing about this was going to be a slam dunk.

6

*P*AYTON HELD HER breath and pressed her back against the tree as Lieutenant Colton—or was it Colson?—and Officer Willard walked by.

Her brand new Louboutin heels sank into the dirt, a thin beam of moonlight illuminating the shiny, black toe like a damn spotlight that said, *"Yes, I'm hiding right here, officers."*

She quickly slid her foot into the shadow that blanketed her.

If the Lieutenant would have walked four feet to the left, he'd have bumped right into her. But if there was anything Payton was good at, it was sneaking around undetected. A lifetime of walking on eggshells will do that to you.

She blew out a breath as they passed by.

Phew.

Having met the Lieutenant now, she had no doubt the man was no-bullshit, quick on his toes, and insusceptible to a pretty smile. He'd have her hands in cuffs before she could blink an eye, as he should—not that she'd mind that much, the guy was hot. Anyone lurking around the woods behind a murder scene was sure to be a suspect. But when it came to investigative journalism, danger was just part of the job. Well, for the good stories, anyway. The ones that made it onto the evening news and caught the attention of the networks. The ones that uncovered serial killers that had evaded police for decades. The ones that made careers. And that's exactly what Payton had her eye on—replacing Lanie Peabody as lead anchor on the local news. Conquer small-town politics first, then all the way up to the *Today Show.* She just needed a few breaks, and thanks to the tenacious genes her father had given her, determination and relentlessness came as easily as breathing. She got the same vibe from the Lieutenant, which wasn't going to make things easy for her—even if he was easy on the eyes. Funnily enough, though, those piercing, almost-black eyes hadn't done a thing for her. It had been so long since she'd been in a relationship, she doubted her hormones even worked.

Payton took another deep breath, and once their heavy footsteps faded, she leaned around the tree, peering through the prickly pine branches.

She felt like a peeping tom, but she wasn't. Someone else was, and that peeping tom had taken Hannah Winchester's life.

And Payton knew exactly where to start looking.

She waited until the Lieutenant and Willard were deep in the woods before slinking back into the shadows.

She silently made her way through the woods as she devised a plan.

Unfortunately, that plan didn't include noticing the pair of eyes watching her from behind a bush.

QUINN PULLED INTO a parking spot next to a chipped wooden sign that read *Berry Springs Hospital.*

He blew out a breath and checked the time—12:43 a.m.

His stomach clenched, but not from hunger, although he should be starving. He hadn't eaten a thing since noon, and even then, it was a bag of chips from the vending machine with a questionable sell-by date. It had been a hell of a night, and so far, the forty-three minutes of the next day weren't looking so hot, either.

After Logan had taken the tile and carpet samples he'd needed, and Willard and Hayes had bagged up the evidence from the house, Quinn had sent them to the station to log everything into the system and get ready to send to the crime lab at the ass crack of dawn. Then, Quinn did the worst part of his job—he'd driven to Mr. and Mrs. Winchester's house to tell them that their dear Hannah had passed away.

It went as expected. Over the years, he'd learned there were three responses to learning your child had been murdered. The most common response was hysteria. Shrill screams, sometimes followed by a faint. A close second was denial. And finally, total and utter shock, which was sometimes accompanied with a calmness that always unnerved him. This was the preferred response. At the Winchester house, he'd gotten the first two. Hannah's mom was absolutely hysterical, inconsolable. So much so, he'd hadn't been able to get a lick of useful information from her to help find who could have done this to her daughter. The father sat solidly in reaction number two—denial. Nope, we had the wrong girl and needed to rush the autopsy because then we'd see that the dead body was not his daughter. No, there was no way his daughter was dead. He'd just talked to her earlier in the day, so it was impossible that she'd been murdered hours later.

The visit had been a ping pong game between the two that had completely drained him.

And his night wasn't even close to over.

Quinn grabbed his cell and pushed out of the car. Nothing but the sound of a gentle breeze against his ear as he made a quick mental note of the cars in the lot. A haze settled under the fluorescent light posts. The evening had dipped into the fifties, and based on the humidity in the air, he guessed a few spring storms weren't too far off.

He walked up the short sidewalk to the main entrance, lined with freshly planted flowers. Average wait time in the ER was over an hour, but someone sure had the time to garden. He stepped through the sliding glass doors of the Emergency Room.

"Well, Lieutenant *Colson.*" A sweet, southern voice called out from behind the front desk. Maryanne Simpson worked part-time at Donny's Diner, and the other half working the overnight shift at the hospital. With fire-red nails, blonde hair teased high above her overly made-up face, and a questionable-sized chest for her small frame, Maryanne was a fifty-seven year old widow who'd invited him over for "coffee" three times since he'd moved to town. He'd stumbled his way out of the first invite by asking about her husband, who she'd stumbled on remembering his name. Definitely no love lost there. He'd made up random excuses the next two times. Policemen were busy, after all.

"Evenin' Ms. Simpson."

Her eyes scanned his uniformed body like a cat sizing up its prey—a feral cat.

"What brings you in tonight, honey? Everything okay, dear?"

"I'm here to visit Miss Bobbi Cross."

"Ah." Maryanne chuckled. "Good luck with that. Girl came in hotter than a two-headed rattlesnake, cussin' every other word. Kept on it all the way to her room."

Well, at least that meant Bobbi was stable.

Maryanne began clicking keys on her computer. "Good thing she didn't have one of those guns she sells on her."

He chewed on that for a moment. Everyone seemed to have something to say about Bobbi Cross, and he wasn't sure if Maryanne liked the girl, or not.

As the heavily-perfumed receptionist typed away, Quinn looked around the waiting room.

Huddled in the corner was a teen he instantly recognized from a drug bust a few weeks ago. Passed out. From the looks of his quivering friend next to him, he'd probably been on a bender and his buddies finally decided he needed medical treatment. Quinn stared at the friend, who was doggedly avoiding eye contact. If the kid had enough good sense to bring in his buddy, the kid might make it. He just needed someone to pull him out of the crowd that had sucked him into the dark side. God knows Quinn knew plenty about that.

A comfortable space away from the "druggies," a young, panic-stricken man rubbed his pregnant wife's back as she practiced her breathing. The pained look in her eyes made Quinn shift his weight. By the size of her stomach, the woman might be holding a pair of twins before the night was over. He watched the man, laser-focused on his wife, completely consumed by the moment, with a mix of sheer terror and excitement in his eyes. He was significantly younger than Quinn, and Quinn had a very surprising split-second moment of jealousy. What would his life be like today if he'd had babies at that age? Would he be happier, more content? More fulfilled? He was probably a decade older than the father-to-be, with no kids on the horizon. Not even close. Not that he minded much, or, at least he didn't think he minded. Quinn was focused on his new job, and besides, he had another relationship he was hellbent on ironing out.

The doors slid open behind him and a wide-eyed father and sobbing, young boy shuffled into the lobby.

"Well, little Paulie Kimble," Maryanne pushed to her feet and looked at little Paulie's daddy. "What's wrong?"

Paulie's dad didn't even notice Quinn as he breezed past him, solely focused on getting help for his five-year-old son.

"Think he mighta broken his arm. Fell out of his bunk bed."

Little Paulie wailed and rubbed his arm.

"Oh, poor baby, let me get you checked in."

"Thank you, Maryanne."

Paulie turned to Quinn, his watery eyes focusing on the badge on Quinn's hip.

Quinn kneeled down. "Oh, man, buddy." He looked over

Paulie's arm. Bruising was already starting to show around the elbow, but no swelling. If Quinn had to guess, the arm wasn't broken, possibly fractured, but no doubt hurt like hell. "I'd ask which bunk you were on, but by the looks of that arm, I'd say you were on the top bunk, huh?"

Paulie sniffled and nodded, his eyes clearing and showing a gleam of excitement now that he was talking to a "policeman." It was a look he'd seen many times when he visited elementary schools or local events. It always surprised him how many little boys idolized cops. When Quinn was little, he wanted to be a race car driver.

But life had different plans for him.

"My brother sleeps on the bottom bunk. I get the top." Paulie said proudly.

"What's your brother's name?"

"Rocky."

Quinn's lip curled up as he glanced at the father who shrugged innocently. *Paulie and Rocky.* Rocky was a good movie, sure, but probably not worthy of naming your kids after. But what did he know about that, anyway? He'd have gone with Smith and Wesson if it were him. He turned back to Paulie. "Well, did you get him?"

"Get who," the boy asked skeptically.

"The monster in your room."

Paulie's eyes widened, then he nodded enthusiastically.

"So you saved your brother, then, huh?"

The boy's quivering lip started to settle as he tipped his chin up proudly and nodded.

"Wow." Quinn shook his head. "It's a good thing you were around, then. You took care of a monster and saved your brother and all you got out of it was a hurt arm? Man, you are one strong kid."

Paulie smiled from ear-to-ear.

Quinn smiled. "The doc is going to examine your arm, and it's no big deal. You be strong in there, okay?"

"Okay."

He put his hand on the now composed child. "You always take care of your brother, okay? No matter what. Older brothers have to be strong all the time."

"Yes, sir." He said like a soldier taking orders.

Good kid.

Quinn stood and Paulie's dad gave him an appreciative nod.

"Okay," Maryanne said, finally. "I've got little Paulie all checked in, y'all go take a seat. And, Lieutenant, Miss Cross is in room eight." She buzzed open the double doors. "Go on back."

"Thanks, Ms. Simpson."

The receptionist winked. "See you around, Lieutenant."

And he had no doubt she would.

Quinn walked down the blinding-white hallway, nodding at the giggling nurses as he passed. He came to door eight and paused. A thin folder with *Cross, Bobbi Sue* typed neatly across it sat in a holder attached to the door.

Bobbi *Sue.* He grinned, something told him the southern firecracker would be less than thrilled if her middle name was common knowledge.

The door was ajar and the flicker of a television danced across the dimly lit beige walls.

He lightly knocked, waited a minute, then knocked again.

He glanced at the clock on the wall reminding him that it was almost one in the morning. He contemplated, then slowly pushed open the door. He wanted to talk to her while everything was still fresh, assuming she wasn't concussed.

A thin curtain divided the small room, leaving only her feet and legs visible, covered with a blue and white blanket.

"Miss Cross?" He quietly announced himself as he walked into the room, surprised she was alone. No family, friends. No husband or boyfriend?

Common sense was telling him he should leave, but his legs carried him forward. He peered around the curtain.

Bobbi Cross lay asleep in the hospital bed, sitting up as if she'd done everything she could to fight sleep. If he had to guess, she'd argued to be released up until the exhaustion finally took over. Shiny, dark hair wove over the white pillow, encircling a smooth, feminine, porcelain face, with a bandage on her forehead. Relaxed, dark eyebrows rested calmly above closed eyes. He remembered the color behind them—a green as sparkling as spring's budding meadows. His gaze trailed to her lips, pouty, pink with a slight indentation running down the middle of the full, bottom lip. Something awoke in his stomach, a slight tickle that took him by surprise.

Bobbi Cross was absolutely beautiful.

"She just fell asleep."

Quinn jumped and tore his hypnotic gaze away from the sleeping beauty. *Christ,* he'd been *staring* at her like some creeper. He cleared his throat, squared his shoulders and turned to Dr. Buckley, apparently the only doctor in all of Berry Springs that was working tonight.

"Heard she was a lot to handle."

"She doesn't like being handled," Buckley replied in a low whisper, as if not wanting to wake a sleeping bear.

"How is she?" He flinched, afraid the question came off as too personal considering Buckley had just caught him watching the woman sleep, so he quickly followed it up with, "because I'd like to formally interview her."

Buckley nodded. "No concussion, but she had to have four stitches above her eye. She'll have a scar. Not that she cares."

Quinn nodded. Bobbi didn't seem the type to fuss over her appearance, like most women did.

"Her oxygen level's perfect, no coughing. I think she got out of there before inhaling too much smoke. Regardless, I did a full blood panel. Everything looks good, including her carboxyhemoglobin and methemoglobin levels—no carbon monoxide poisoning. Didn't want to put her through a chest X-ray. She's in good shape. Will have a headache, but she's fine."

"How long are you keeping her?"

He glanced at the clock. "She can go home when the sun comes up. I just wanted to keep an eye on her for a bit."

Quinn looked back at Bobbi, focusing on the bandage above her eye, and something else awoke in him—anger. The innocent woman had been hurt. And he didn't like it.

"She's been through a lot, Lieutenant. She's a strong girl, from good stock. But she just saw her friend murdered. Brutally."

He nodded. He'd seen plenty of death himself. He knew the personal ramifications all too well.

"Has no one come by to see her?"

"Her dad's house hunting in the Keys, and her brother's in DC for work."

So, she wasn't married. He wanted to ask about friends or boyfriends, but considering he'd already been caught drooling at her, he didn't push it. Shouldn't be anything thirty minutes in Donny's Diner wouldn't tell him, anyway.

"I hope she'll help in your investigation. But..." The doctor paused, sadness filled his eyes. "Why don't you just wait until morning. Give her some time—"

"I don't need time, Buckley."

Both men snapped their heads to the hospital bed, where Bobbi's green eyes were now open, alert—and loaded.

Her gaze flickered to him, lingered a moment, then shifted back to the doctor.

"Why don't you release me so you can get back to planning your date with Alice?" She winked.

Buckley grinned. "Well her humor sure is intact, along with her imagination." Buckley looked at Quinn. "She's been trying to set me up with a woman in her yoga class."

"That's right—the one you couldn't stop staring at the *one* time you came."

"Human beings are not meant to do physical fitness in one-hundred degree rooms, Bobbi."

Quinn watched the back and forth with amusement.

"It cleanses you, releases toxins. Didn't they teach you that in medical school?"

It was interesting, watching her. He knew she'd been through hell, and probably felt like hell, but she was doing everything in her power to act like she was okay. His gaze drifted to the bandage again, blood seeping through the middle of the gauze. She wore it with a certain aloofness as if the gash was nothing more than a paper cut.

Buckley shook his head and rolled his eyes. "Anyway," he crossed the room to her bed. "How's the head?"

"Fine."

"Sure it is. I sent in some pain pills to Robby. He'll have them ready for you when they open in a few hours."

"Thanks, but I don't need them."

"Oh, that's right. I guess another thing I didn't learn in medical school was that pain meds were to help with pain.

I'll get your release paperwork ready and Sandy will bring it in shortly."

"Thanks, Buckley."

Buckley stroked the top of Bobbi's head. "Let me know if you need anything, okay?" He glanced at Quinn, his face hardening. "I have no doubt you'll catch the son of a bitch."

Their eyes locked as the door closed behind the doctor.

She cut right to the chase. "Did you find him yet?"

"We will."

She nodded, that steely look of determination in her eyes.

"Every bit of information, big or small, will help, which is why I'm here."

Bobbi glanced at the clock and her eyes rounded. "Wow, I didn't realize... *geez,* I've been asleep for over an hour."

"Superhuman adrenaline will do that to you. You crashed." He took a step forward, stopping at the edge of her bed. She sat up straighter, the blanket falling around her waist. Lean, muscular—yet feminine—arms stretched out of the blue checkered gown that draped over two very erect nipples, and based on those two perfect little bumps in the gown, he guessed the nipples sat in the middle of some very nice breasts. She either didn't notice that her nipples were on full display, or didn't care. He assumed the former.

"Adrenaline crash," she repeated as if letting the information sink into a fuzzy brain.

"Miss Winchester's got you by probably twenty pounds and you carried her through the front door like she was a blowup doll. Your adrenaline was working overtime."

"I didn't even..." she paused. "Maybe you're right." She shook her head. "I'm sorry I took her out. There was no way I was going to let her burn to ashes in there." She laughed a humorless laugh. "Doesn't matter, really, does it? But, I guess, to me it did. At that moment, it mattered."

"To you, and her family. It does matter. They have a body to bury now. And the ME has evidence to search for now. It does matter."

She looked down for a moment and a heavy silence filled the room, then, her eyes widened and darted from the counter to the bed stand. "You still have my phone?"

He reached into his pocket and handed it to her. "I sent the pictures to my cell phone. I hope that's okay." He'd also refrained from searching through all her texts, reminding himself that her relationship status didn't have anything to do with the investigation. She'd received a few texts from her friend, Payton, while he'd had it. Other than that, no calls or any other communication.

"Of course that's okay." Bobbi took the phone, checked it for a moment, then clicked it off. "No one knows about it yet, I guess. Besides Payton." She met his gaze and narrowed her eyes. "They will, though. The entire town will know about it, and it'll cause an uproar."

"The sooner we get this guy, the better, which is why I want you to take me through your entire evening again. If you're up for it."

"Yes, I'm up for it." Determination pulled at her pretty face again. She dove into her story, the words tumbling out with an eagerness to help the investigation.

"I'd just gotten out of class—yoga. I have a yoga studio. Hannah is, well, was, one of the instructors. Anyway, she'd gotten a few things we need for a retreat I have coming up and I went by to pick everything up. I'd freaking *just* talked to her. She was expecting me."

"Where had she been?"

She chewed on her sexy bottom lip, and he felt his attention wavering.

"She didn't say."

"Do you know what she did during the day?"

Bobbi's gaze fluttered to her hands, clasped in her lap. Quinn noticed. "No, I don't."

"Do you know if she was seeing anyone?"

Another hesitation. "I know she'd been hanging out with someone." She looked up, a hard look in her eyes. "Chad Kudrow. Don't care much for the guy, and I told her that, too."

Nobody seemed to care for the guy, and that was a red flag. He'd find out why soon.

"Were they in a relationship?"

"I don't think so. Maybe just a casual thing. But, I'm telling you, that guy's no good." She stared at him for a moment as if wanting the words to sink in. He got it. Chad was an asshole.

"Anyone else? She have a best girlfriend?"

"No, I don't think there was another guy in her life. Friends? Let's see…. I know she has some childhood friends she still hangs out with, but, I'm sorry, I don't know who, or their names. She and I were friends, but it mostly centered around work."

"Did she mention any arguments or anything lately?"

"No. I've thought about it a hundred times. No, she didn't. She was a really nice girl."

That seemed to be the general consensus.

"Did you tell her folks?"

He nodded.

"How are they?"

"About as you'd expect."

Bobbi gritted her teeth, leaned forward. "I should do something for them... get them food... something..." She started to rip the covers off, but then paused, remembering she was partially naked. He hadn't forgotten. She also seemed to become aware that she didn't have a bra on, and she quickly puffed out the gown so it didn't cling to her front.

Dammit. That view had been officially the best part of his day so far.

"We've got to find this guy, Lieutenant." Apparently, the display of her nipples didn't throw her off.

"We will, and I need you to focus, ma'am. Finish taking me through your night."

The slightest bit of amusement flashed in her eyes. Calling her ma'am seemed to momentarily disarm her. Note to self.

"Okay." She said, resigning and sitting back. "So, I get to the house, and saw smoke. Just barely... I mean, I wasn't even sure it was smoke, but it was enough to alarm me so I ran in—"

"The door was unlocked?"

"Yes. Like I said, she was expecting me."

"How long had passed from the moment you two hung up to the moment you got to her house?"

"Oh, well, I'd stopped by the range—

"Range?"

"Shooting range. B's Bullseye. I own it."

No way. "Nice place. I was just there earlier, actually."

Something flickered in her eyes. She scanned him from head to toe and every sexual sensor in his body came to life.

"What time were you there?"

"Before my shift started. Probably thirty minutes before I got the call about Hannah."

The corner of her mouth curved, and with a twinkle in her eye, she said, "You're a hell of a shot."

He stared at her for a moment, then it hit him like a ton of bricks. "You're lane one?"

She grinned.

No freakin' way. He'd been target shooting not twenty feet from her thirty minutes before saving her life. *Lord help me,* stunning beauty *and* a hell of a shot.

"You're not too bad yourself."

She cocked a brow. "For a girl, you mean?"

"For anyone."

She nodded in appreciation. "Thanks. You had me, though. I hadn't seen a bullseye like that in a while."

They stared at each for a moment, until she tore her eyes away and continued, "Anyway, I was there, at the range, for a while... maybe forty-five minutes to an hour."

How had he missed her? Regardless, "forty-five minutes to an hour" was a lifetime in a homicide investigation.

"So after I ran inside her house, I yelled her name, and that's when I saw him."

"You're sure a him?"

She paused. "Well, good question I guess, but yeah, I'm sure." She nodded. "Yes, definitely a man... especially with everything that happened..."

With the sexual assault, she meant.

She continued, "He darted out of her bedroom, down the hall and through the back door. I didn't chase him."

"Why?"

"Because I knew something was wrong. I knew in my gut Hannah was dead, or hurt, at least."

"How tall was the guy?"

"Normal height. I'd say six foot or so, dressed in black.

And that's all I remember. The house was dark, so I couldn't get a good look."

"Did you get a look at the face? The side? Even the ears?"

She nodded. "The side, technically, but I'm telling you, he sprinted out that door like a flash."

"Hat?"

"Yes. A baseball cap. Dark."

"Think about the clothes. Picture them in your head. Do you see anything? Logos, kind of clothes, things like that?"

She closed her eyes and was silent a moment. "He had a jacket on... and I think there were reflective lines on it."

Quinn smiled. "Good job. An athletic jacket possibly."

"Yes."

"Anything else?"

She shook her head. "Then I went into her bedroom—that's where the smoke was coming from—and you know the rest."

"I've already asked you this, but I want to make sure. You didn't see or pass any cars on the way to her house?"

"No. He had to have parked in the woods or something." She looked down, hiding the sadness in her eyes. "I just can't believe this. She didn't deserve this. She was a sweet girl. It should have never happened..."

There was a hint of guilt in her voice, and it was that moment that Quinn realized Bobbi Cross was not going to leave this to the authorities. She felt partially responsible for not showing up at Hannah's earlier. Maybe if she had, she could have stopped the tragedy that had happened. It was a ridiculous thought, but unfortunately, he knew that kind of irrational thinking all too well. Quinn knew guilt like the back of his hand.

"Miss Cross—"

"Bobbi." Her voice was soft as she looked up.

"Bobbi, do you know anyone who would do this to Hannah?"

"No." Her eyes glazed over. "Not in a million years."

The door opened and a surprisingly perky nurse walked in—for one in the morning, at least. She cast him a look before walking to the bed.

"Well, Bobbi," she said with way too much energy. "Your wish is granted. You're released." The nurse's gaze shifted back to him.

"Thank you." Bobbi flashed him a grin. "Sandy, this is Lieutenant Colson. New to these parts. Been here a few months."

How did she know that, he wondered. Probably heard it at the diner.

"Well it's very nice to meet you, Lieutenant," the nurse said with a wink.

He glanced at Bobbi, who was grinning ear-to-ear.

"Anyway," Sandy finally looked away from him and focused on the patient at hand. "Here's additional information on concussions. Doc doesn't think you have one, but just in case you start feeling dizzy again, come back in. And here's how to keep your sutures clean, and lastly here's instructions on the pain meds that I know you won't take."

"Thanks."

"Now, do you have a ride to your car?"

Bobbi's face dropped. "*Shit.* No, my car is..."

She looked at Quinn.

"Still at Hannah's. I'll take you."

8

QUINN PACED THE cracked sidewalk outside of the Emergency Room. The haze had turned into a light fog, slowly snaking across the parking lot.

It was almost two in the morning, with no sleep in sight.

He took a deep breath, inhaling the late night air. He hated the smell of hospitals. Hated everything about them. Hospitals reminded him of how fragile life was—a concept that he knew all too well.

The *whoosh* of the sliding doors behind him had him turning and his heart giving a kick.

Wearing curve-hugging black yoga leggings and a fitted *Just Be* yoga tank, Bobbi strode through the doors. Her long, black hair cascaded around her shoulders, sweeping just below the breasts he'd fantasized about earlier.

She walked in strong, confident strides. If it weren't for the bandage on her forehead, he'd have no idea she'd carried her friend's murdered body from a burning house hours earlier, almost dying in the process.

Quinn cleared his throat, quickly reminding himself he

was on the job. He needed to focus on the investigation, not those curves that made him want to stand to attention.

"How're you doing?" He took the plastic hospital bag from her hands.

"Good."

He cocked his head.

"Alright, fine. My head hurts."

He nodded, pleased with her admission. He'd just won a small battle with her and, if he had to guess, those victories were few and far between with this woman.

"You should take those pain meds."

"Nothing that a glass of whiskey can't fix."

"Whiskey, huh? Off the bat, I wouldn't have pegged you as a whiskey gal, but having spent some time with you now..."

"I drink it when the occasion fits."

"I'd say tonight's a damn good night for whiskey, then."

A cool breeze swept past them. She shivered.

"Didn't you have a flannel?" He started to open the hospital bag.

"No. Don't." She put her hand on his arm and he remembered that her shirt was covered in Hannah's blood. He quickly closed the bag and stepped closer to her in an attempt to block the wind.

"I had yoga tonight. Hence, the outfit." She glanced at him. "I don't usually run around town wearing painted-on clothes."

Damn shame.

Quinn opened the passenger side door of his truck. "I'll crank the heater."

He grabbed a camo coat from the back and handed it to her. She hesitated, then took it from his hands. "I didn't take you for a hunter, but having spent time with you now..." She smirked.

Touché. "It's warm. Put it on."

Quinn slid behind the steering wheel and pulled onto Main Street. Like most small towns, Berry Springs shut down at eight p.m.. There wasn't a single car, truck, or tractor on the road. They drove in silence a moment.

"I don't believe this."

He glanced over at her, the streetlights flashing across her face. She was wired, not tired or emotionally drained like he'd expect from someone who just pulled a body from a burning building, or hell, anyone at two in the morning. Her wheels were turning.

"Hannah was a sweet, calm person. She didn't deserve this," she said as she placed the coat on her lap.

"If I had a nickel for every time I saw a victim that didn't deserve what they got. You can't think like that, though. You have to get them justice. That's all you can do."

"I *saw* the damn guy, Quinn."

Quinn. He liked the way his name rolled off her tongue. He also liked the fire that came out of her when she cursed.

"What are the odds of that? I mean, I should be able to help more for Christ's sake." She let out a frustrated growl, that oddly enough, kind of turned him on. "It was dark and he bolted out of there, but I still feel like I should be able to at least describe the side of his face."

"Like you said, it was dark and you were in panic mode. It's understandable."

"Not an excuse."

"Keep trying to remember, something might spark. And if it does, you call me or come to the station immediately."

She nodded, then said, "What did you find at the scene? Anything?"

He paused a moment. He didn't want to tell her about the candle holders, footprint, or the empty tiki fluid container. Not only because it was an open investigation, but because every instinct in his body told him that Bobbi was going to stick to the case like glue until they found the suspect. She was going to do her own investigating. And he didn't want that for two reasons: One, it was his investigation. Two, he didn't want her sticking her nose anywhere near a raping, necrophiliac, murderous bastard.

At his silence, she said, "I get that you can't tell me, but I'll find out anyway."

His brow cocked. "I've learned incessant snooping comes hand in hand with small towns, but you need to understand..." His voice was sharp. "That is exactly the type of stuff that makes our job harder. People meddling where they shouldn't and, in some cases, spreading enough gossip to spook the suspect and send him past the border. And then we'll never find him."

Quinn didn't look at her, but felt the cab chill as his statement lingered. He flicked on his turn signal and turned onto the dirt road that led to Hannah's house.

A string of yellow *do-not-cross* tape flapped from an oak tree. He scanned the inky-black woods that lined the road, looking for any side roads or trails. He'd canvass the area at first light.

He rolled to a stop at the end of the driveway and was pleasantly surprised the tape he'd used to block the entrance was still intact. He cut the engine and they both got out. The silence of early morning settled around them, along with the faint smell of smoke, and the subtle eeriness that came with a murder hanging in the air.

The house was barely visible through the dark night— no electricity, no lights, no life.

He met her at the tape. Her eyes were glued to the house, memories undoubtedly flashing through her head. She'd have nightmares for weeks. Months, maybe.

A gust of wind swept past, although this time, she didn't seem to notice. He took his coat from her hands, opened it and stepped behind her.

"Put it on."

Still transfixed on the house, she mindlessly slid her arms inside and he wrapped it around her shoulders.

Quinn pulled the flashlight from his belt, clicked it on and lifted the yellow tape. She dipped under and he followed. Her Jeep was still parked at the side of the house. Thankfully, they'd been able to leave it there without inter-ruption.

They walked silently through the front yard while Quinn scanned the woods. A sixth sense had him hyper aware of every sound, every movement, every leaf that blew in the trees. His fingers itched to grab his gun. He glanced over his shoulder. There was a very real possibility that whoever killed Hannah could still be lurking around the area, and the thought made him want to get Bobbi home as soon as possible.

He picked up his pace.

They were almost to her Jeep, when she suddenly stopped at the front door, just feet away from where she'd passed out.

"I want to see inside again... I want to see if I remember anything." She stepped up to the front door.

"You need to get home, rest, Bobbi. Doctor's orders."

"It might jog my memory. I just want one look."

Quinn inwardly groaned. Damn the woman.

"One look, Bobbi, that's it. Quickly. I lead. Do not step anywhere I don't, do you understand?"

She nodded.

They'd already bagged up the evidence, but he didn't want to risk anything. Things tended to turn up in the light, although that was a long shot thanks to the water from the hoses and everyone who'd trampled the scene before he could process it. But he'd be damned if they added to the damage that was already done.

White powder coated the knob and door frame. Hayes hadn't found a single print on the front or back knob, which was suspicious in itself. Someone covered their tracks.

Quinn stepped over the threshold. The burned-tar smell had settled but was still stinging. Bobbi moved beside him. He shined the thin beam of light around the house, pausing on the table, toppled-over next to the door.

"That's where you hit your head."

"Geez." She kneeled down and ran her finger along the sharp edge. "No wonder why I needed stitches."

"And that's why you should be in bed right now."

She pushed to a stance, ignoring him. He had a feeling she was good at ignoring comments she didn't agree with. Her gaze froze on the doorway to Hannah's room.

"That's where he came out." She said in a breathy whisper. "He ran out of the room when I called her name."

"Remembering anything else?" He followed her as she walked to the room.

Bobbi shook her head, then glanced back at him. "I don't have any blank spots. I remember everything that happened, just wish I could remember more *detail*."

"It might come." He stepped forward and illuminated the scorched master bedroom.

"*Geez*," she whispered behind him. A moment passed. "Only half the room burned. That's good, right? What's that smell?"

He raised a brow, surprised she'd noticed. "What do you think it is?"

"Smells like Citronella."

"Nice work, detective. You're right. We think he used tiki fluid from the back porch."

The flashlight swept over the bed and he felt her tense next to him. The bedding had been removed and bagged up, but speckles of blood from Hannah's head had seeped onto the white mattress.

"The fire was in the bathroom when I walked in." She carefully walked to the bathroom, his light guiding the way.

Quinn watched as she squatted down in front of the cabinet under the sink and sifted through the remaining contents. Then, she looked through the drawers.

She was looking for something.

He narrowed his eyes and watched her as she sat back on her heels. Bobbi might not remember the suspect's face, but she was definitely keeping something from him.

She turned and looked around the floor. He shined the light to follow her gaze.

"Stop," she said. "Shine the light there."

He panned over. "Where?"

Bobbi snatched the light from his hand and squatted down where the corner of the shower met the floor. She shined the light into the tiny crevasse of the corner.

"There."

He kneeled next to her, squinted, and leaned forward.

"It's blood, isn't it?"

About an inch above the floor, a small speck of red splattered the paint. The fire hoses washed the other spots away, but this one was perfectly nestled in the corner of the wall and shower. He glanced back at the floor around the toilet where the candle holders had laid. The positioning made sense. Assuming the blood was Hannah's, this confirmed that she was definitely attacked coming out of the shower, with the candle holders, and the suspect tossed them across the room after she'd crumbled to the ground. It was an important confirmation. One that he'd missed.

"How the *hell* did you see that?"

"It is, isn't it? It's blood." Hope pitched Bobbi's voice.

"Looks like it to me." His mind started to race. "I need to take pictures and get a sample." He stood.

Bobbi followed him into the bedroom and he paused to take one more look around. He scanned the floor from the bathroom to the bed for the hundredth time that evening. The light lingered on the bloody mattress and he suddenly felt Bobbi step closer behind him. He froze. He could practically feel the heat of her body against his. Her breath was fast against the silence, the tension like weights in the air. He stood still, not sure what she was needing. But then, when he felt her fingers lightly grab the back of his shirt, he knew—the thick wall Bobbi had built around herself was crumbling and she was on the verge of a panic attack. She'd had enough. Her mind, body, emotions—the woman had had enough.

He moved his head, looking over his shoulder. Her skin had paled, her eyes were panic-stricken—wide-eyed as a deer. She stared at the bed with an expression that told him she wasn't in the present moment. Bobbi was reliving seeing Hannah for the first time, naked, bludgeoned to death.

"Hey," he said softly as he turned. Her finger clenched his shirt tighter. "You okay?"

She ripped her eyes away from the bed and stared at him, inches from his face. Darkness shaded her, but there was no mistaking the red rims around the wide, green eyes.

A light breeze from the opened door blew a strand of hair across her face.

He inhaled. A chill flew up his spine.

Quinn grabbed Bobbi's shoulders, his gaze shifting to the dark hall. He sniffed again.

Gas.

"We need to get out of here."

His tone snapped her back to the present. He started pushing her out the door.

"What? What's going on?"

"Gas."

"*Gas?* But wasn't everything turned off?"

"Someone turned it back on." He pulled his gun and scanned the hallway before nodding her toward the front door. "Go. Outside, *now.*"

Bobbi nodded, her fear palpable. Quinn waited until she was off the porch, then quickly searched the house. Room to room, his instinct telling him someone had not only just been in the house, but were very likely still close by. Quinn looked out the front door at Bobbi's silhouette, before turning back to the kitchen. A small candle flickered on the stove across the room.

"*Bobbi, run!*"

He turned on his heel and sprinted down the hallway.

"*Run!*" He yelled again and jumped off the porch.

As Quinn hurled himself over Bobbi's body, the house exploded in a million pieces behind them.

9

*B*OBBI CLOSED THE front door and tossed her purse on the floor, followed by the hospital bag.

She heaved out a breath, then squeezed her face at the pain in her ribcage from when Quinn had shielded her from the explosion.

And saved her life.

For the second time—*in one night.*

She looked around her dark house, not believing the night she'd just had. She closed her eyes, inhaling deeply. The fresh scent of lavender oil hit her nose, a subtle reminder to relax.

Relax. *Yeah right.*

Bobbi checked the deadbolt—a habit her special ops brother had instilled in her—then glanced out the front window and watched Quinn's taillights disappear into the night. Or morning, really.

After the explosion, Hannah's house turned into a circus —*again*—and by the time they'd given their statements and Quinn had done his job, he'd insisted on following her home to make sure she arrived safely.

One thing was for certain, Hannah's killer had been watching them and wanted to destroy whatever evidence hadn't been taken care of in the initial fire. The fire that Bobbi had thwarted with her visit.

The house was nothing but rubble. It was a miracle they were still alive.

She was a walking zombie by the time she'd pulled into her driveway with Quinn on her bumper. He didn't get out of his truck, just waited behind the steering wheel with a steely look in his eyes until she closed the door.

Her hand drifted to her forehead and she winced at the touch. The numbness from the lidocaine had worn off and was replaced with a stabbing pain in her skull.

Bobbi padded down the hall, a mixture of exhaustion and edginess wafting over her. The house was dead silent, dark as the inky blackness outside.

So this is what three in the morning looks like.

She flicked on the kitchen light, then quickly turned it off—way too bright for the headache she had. Instead, she turned on a dim light above the stove, barely illuminating the large stone and marble kitchen.

Bobbi pulled down a glass from the cabinet, filled it with water and chugged. The coolness felt good against the cotton in her mouth. She could hear the water splashing in her empty stomach. It had been almost a full day since she'd eaten, but food was the last thing on her mind. She glanced at the clock—so was sleep.

"I'd say tonight's a damn good night for whiskey."

With Quinn's voice in her head, she grabbed the whiskey bottle from the counter and walked into the living room. Her gaze skimmed the sweeping windows that looked out to the mountains in the distance. Usually, the view gave her a feeling of peace, a window to the outdoors that she loved so much. Not tonight. She couldn't even make out the massive peaks in the pitch-blackness. No peace tonight.

Tonight, she felt vulnerable—an unfamiliar feeling for her.

She set the whiskey on the coffee table and stacked a few logs in the fireplace. There was something about a fire that soothed her, and maybe watching the flames would send her into a hypnotic daze of sleep.

The fire caught and she grabbed the whiskey and sank into her oversized brown leather chair.

What a night.

Bobbi tipped up the bottle and sipped, the burn watering her eyes. Whiskey wasn't typically something she drank straight up, but tonight was a different story.

She took another sip and stared into the fire.

Hannah was dead.

Not just dead. Murdered.

Unbelievable.

Her mind started racing, wishing Quinn had told her more about the investigation. She felt like she was a big part of it, and wanted to help. Somehow.

She thought of Hannah's parents, whom she'd never met, and her stomach sank. Quinn had been the one to tell them and she hoped he'd done it with grace. Although the man had a hard exterior, she'd seen a softness in him when he'd turned to her during her almost-panic attack.

Quinn didn't remember her, but she definitely remembered him. From the moment he kneeled next to her in Hannah's front yard, she remembered those eyes. That ruggedly handsome face that would make any woman do a double-take. There was a roughness, an edge, a strength to him that wasn't just from his height. She remembered how her heart had skittered when she'd seen him in the woods months earlier. An instant physical reaction. She'd cautiously asked around, and while people weren't sure of his name, they'd told her he'd just moved to town to join BSPD. It was hot gossip at the time, because people didn't like someone they didn't know coming in and overseeing the rest of the officers. *What does he know about Berry Springs, anyway,* they'd said.

Based on what she saw tonight, she was guessing he didn't give a shit what other people thought.

She didn't know anything else about him, other than he was an unwanted outsider.

Bobbi took another sip, leaned her head against the leather. A familiar scent caught her nose.

Him.

Her eyes widened and she looked down. She was still wearing his coat! She'd been so flustered with everything that had gone on, she hadn't even thought to give it back, and he hadn't asked.

She ran her fingers along the front, imagining him inside it. While the coat engulfed her, Quinn probably stretched the hems with those broad shoulders. A small smile crossed her lips. She slipped her hands into the pockets and fingered a pair of leather gloves. Everything about the coat was warm and comforting. Like Quinn. She wrapped it tighter around herself and sniffed the collar. *That smell.* It was the same scent she'd noticed when he'd been at the range. The same smell of his chest when he cradled her in his arms.

She took a deep breath.

How long had it been since she'd been close enough to smell a man's skin? How long had it been since she'd been with a man? A *real* man. A man that was strong enough to handle her. A man that made her feel feminine and taken care of.

That was the thing about tough women. Men often thought they didn't need, or want, to be taken care of, but in reality, every woman wanted to feel like their man would do anything for them.

Every woman wanted to be saved.

Bobbi had dated on and off over the years, but nothing serious. In a small town like Berry Springs, finding a decent crop of men to date was tough. And when she'd opened her shooting range, she became so consumed with running both her businesses that she stopped having time to date— that's what she told herself anyway. Bobbi taught yoga in the mornings and evenings, and worked the range during the day. Most days she felt like she didn't have enough hours to get everything done. She felt like she was in a constant state of exhaustion. But her hard work was worth it. Bobbi had paid off every penny of her debt, and recently remodeled her house, which had proven to be an entirely different workload on top of her regular workload that she hadn't expected.

But it was all worth it.

The small, run-down rock house she'd purchased years earlier now had a state-of-the-art kitchen, new master bedroom and bath, and new hardwood floors throughout. Everything about the remodel was focused around bringing the outdoors inside, highlighted by the earthly color palette she'd chosen. The house was filled with indoor plants, waterfalls in each room, and scented oil lamps. It was her own little Zen Palace to unwind.

But *Zen* was anything but the way she was feeling.

The fire crackled and hissed in front of her, taking her

back to the moment she pulled Hannah's limp body from the bed.

Her stomach rolled.

Unable to sit, Bobbi pushed out of the chair and walked to the windows. She placed her hand on the cool glass and watched the haze of heat blur around each finger.

She wrapped her arms around Quinn's jacket and gazed into the blackness where the mountains rested in the distance, always beautiful, tall, solid, strong, never moving.

An anchor.

A knot caught her throat.

To everyone around town, Bobbi was that—solid, strong, never showing emotions, never wavering. An anchor. But the truth was, she was a total mess inside. An emotional basket case that kept it all together on the outside, but was craving so much more on the inside. She'd battled discontentment for years, and although she'd created a comfortable rhythm for herself, she felt like she was missing something.

Her brother said it was because their mother walked out on them when they were children. Another man, so she'd heard. Since that day, Bobbi had never seen or heard from her mother again. The woman had made a new life for herself, a new family on the west coast, that's all Bobbi knew. It was true abandonment. Sure to cause some psychological issues. She knew that, but she didn't have to accept it. Although it was hard to ignore the fact that's what she did to every guy she dated—she abandoned them. Just like her mom did to her. *Fear of getting too close and then being walked out on?* Her brother had asked once.

All Bobbi knew was that dating, or men, for that matter, had never filled the deep hole she felt in her life. And lately she began to wonder if it was her. If something was wrong with *her*. Her impending thirtieth birthday made her think about the future in ways she'd never had before. She had her businesses and dream home, but that was it.

No man. No family.

She was restless, edgy, always moving, never content. Perhaps worst of all, tonight, she felt scared.

No, she wasn't an anchor. Anything but.

And it was at that moment, for the first time, she wished she had an anchor in her life—someone to hold her close until she fell asleep.

The mountain ahead of him turned a bright shade of coral as he rounded a hairpin corner. Quinn glanced in the rearview mirror at the cascade of colors shooting up from the mountains behind him. Pinks, oranges, and yellows pushing their way into a deep indigo sky where the stars were beginning to dim.

It was going to be a beautiful sunrise, and he reminded himself to enjoy the moment while it lasted, because his gut told him it was going to be one hell of a day. Not just because he was on two hours of sleep, but because day one of a homicide investigation was always a shitshow. After he'd followed Bobbi home the night before, he'd gone back to Hannah's one last time just to make sure the fucker who tried to blow them up wasn't still hanging around. After that, he'd gone home and put together some notes for the eight-thirty meeting Chief McCord had already scheduled.

It was barely sunrise and Quinn already had a list of things to do as long as the Mississippi.

But that could wait. He had something else to do, first.

He glanced at the clock—6:24 a.m.—then at the temperature on the touchscreen in his truck. It was a refreshing sixty-one degrees, a bit warmer than usual for a Berry Springs spring morning.

Quinn turned down a long, narrow driveway that wound through a thicket of pine trees littered with branches. He made a mental note that the underbrush needed to be trimmed, too. He passed a massive woodpile which had doubled in size since his last visit.

Good.

The small, two-bedroom house with gray siding and the beginnings of a wraparound porch was dark, he noticed, as he parked behind a beat-up red Chevy. He yanked the keys from the ignition and pushed out the door.

As he walked down the stone pathway he'd built with his own two hands, he noticed a few bags of soil next to a stack of lumber.

Good.

Quinn inserted the key and walked inside. The scent of a microwave dinner lingered in the air suggesting his brother hadn't been asleep very long. Well that was too bad.

He quickly scanned the house, as his eye had been trained to do ever since his brother had been released from prison seven months earlier. No beer cans, liquor bottles, cigarettes. No sign of visitors. No one crashing on the couch.

Good.

His gaze landed on a half-assembled wooden chair in the living room, surrounded by tools and wood clippings. He smiled. His brother was a very talented carpenter. Better than he ever was.

He turned and walked into the master bedroom, where blackout curtains covered the windows. He flicked the lights.

"Morning, sunshine." His voice boomed against the silence.

His little brother sprang to attention, kicking the covers and sitting up, his hair standing on its ends, eyes squinty and red.

"Geez, Quinn."

"Six-thirty and sixty-degrees outside, bro." He ripped off the covers. "Time for our run."

His brother groaned and ran his fingers through his sandy blonde hair that, in Quinn's opinion, had gotten too long.

"It's a good damn thing I don't own a gun."

"They don't *let* you own a gun."

"Thanks for the reminder." Landon swung his legs over the side of the bed and blew out a breath. "Give me five minutes, you dick."

Quinn nodded with a smirk, then walked into the kitchen to get the coffee ready for when they returned. Landon might have been off the hard stuff, but he couldn't go a morning without coffee. Technically, he was supposed to avoid any stimulant, but Quinn figured he gave his little brother so much crap about everything else, he'd let the coffee slide. He reached into the cabinet and raised his eyebrows at the selection—two fancy, nine-dollar bags of coffee. A moment of panic shot through him. He shook his head, forcing the thought out.

Stop, Quinn. No, Landon wasn't dealing again.

He set two mugs next to the pot as his brother walked in. He couldn't help himself, so he said, "Getting a little ritzy with the coffee, huh?"

His brother eyed him before bending over and lacing his running shoes. Landon was used to Quinn prying, watching, spying—constantly worrying—about every single thing in his life. But that was Quinn's job... and he'd fucked it up once, and he'd be damned if it ever happened again.

"Just trying to keep up with you, big shot *Lieutenant*." Landon flashed a smirk. "Let's go."

Quinn followed him out the front door. They didn't bother to lock it. Only one other person lived down the dirt road besides his brother—him.

They took a minute to stretch, then, in their ever competitive nature, took off sprinting through the yard, starting too fast for their four mile jog through the woods. They burst through the tree line, into the woods where they'd hacked out a small trail that led to the main hiking trails on Summit Mountain.

The fresh, mountain air cleared Quinn's lungs and the grogginess in his head. Fresh oxygen pumped through his veins, giving him a much needed jolt of energy. Sunlight cut through the canopy of trees like spears of light. A pair of squirrels chased each other around a thick maple tree ahead of him.

"How's the new job, anyway?"

Quinn surprised himself by hesitating. "Good. Off to a good start." He partially lied. Good was definitely an over-statement for the ice-cold welcome he'd received from the locals. But he knew that Landon knew the truth, which was, the only reason Quinn moved to Berry Springs was to watch after his little brother. To make sure Landon stayed on the right track—*this time.*

Quinn and Landon grew up as thick as thieves in a small town outside of Dallas, Texas. Hellions, they were, according to almost everyone they crossed paths with. Both boys excelled in sports. Due to his size, Quinn chose football, and Landon chose basketball, due to his speed and agility. Landon was being scouted for a free ride to college on a basketball scholarship, until he blew out his knee. That one moment changed the kid's entire life.

Quinn had gone on to play college football and was wrapped up in his own life of the game, girls, and doing everything he could to keep his grades up. He didn't realize Landon had become addicted to the pain pills he'd been prescribed after his knee surgery.

By age twenty-two, Landon was addicted to heroin and had become one of the biggest drug dealers in Texas. By the time Quinn realized what was happening, it was too late. He'd lost his little brother to drugs and not even a four-day stint in ICU from an overdose stopped the kid. Landon's father—their mother had walked out on them at the beginning of Landon's addiction—had completely given up on his youngest son. A move that Quinn would never forgive. It was up to Quinn to take care of his younger brother, which was a lot for a twenty-seven year old to take on. Landon made it out of ICU and went on to get busted several times after. He became a regular in the county jail as the years dragged on, until the inevitable happened—he was caught with over seventy grams of heroin. Possession with intent to sell. Combining that with his long list of previous arrests, the judge threw the book at him and gave him ten years in prison. Quinn visited him every day and watched his brother fade from a strung out, wild-eyed druggie, to a dead-behind-the-eyes ball of emotionless depression. Landon served two and a half years of his sentence.

The day Landon was released from prison, he moved to the mountains to get "away from everything and everyone." That day, Quinn put in his notice at Dallas PD. He was all his little brother had in the entire world. Luck was on his side that Berry Springs was looking for a Lieutenant to join the force. Moving to the small town had been a huge change, but he didn't care. What he cared about was helping his brother stay on track. And although Landon knew Quinn moved to Berry Springs because of him, he had no idea that his fall from grace was the entire reason Quinn got into law enforcement in the first place.

On day two of Landon's freedom, Quinn drew up a fitness routine for him. They'd both always been fit and muscular, but the drugs had destroyed Landon's body. Quinn figured one way he could help his brother stay on track was to retrain his brain to take care of his body, instead of destroying it. He and his brother had also loved to build things and had a small carpentry business in high school. Landon had abandoned the business but Quinn had picked it back up after college. The week Landon was out, Quinn bought him a garage-full of new tools and lumber, which Landon turned into a profitable little side business. Landon had a few dollars in the bank now, and had put on fifteen pounds of muscle since he'd gotten out, thanks to the weight bench Quinn had gotten him and the challenging trail runs up the mountain every morning.

"Tree." Quinn said over his shoulder as he jumped over a fallen branch. He listened to his brother's steps to make sure he didn't fall.

"The porch looks good."

"Thanks. A wraparound's a lot more work than I realized." Landon's breath was still strong, not labored yet. His lungs were getting stronger.

"It'll be worth it, though. Maybe put in a porch swing, too. Harold approve of all this?"

Harold was the owner of the house. A good ol' boy that Quinn liked immediately. Harold was renting the house to Landon, allowing him to fix it up with the intent that he would buy it someday.

"Yeah, he's always wanted the house to have a porch, I guess."

"Noticed the soil." Quinn slapped a branch away from his face. "Branch."

Landon swiped it away. "Need to get a few more bags. I'm thinking about planting some vegetables out back."

A swell of pride rushed through Quinn. His brother was staying busy.

"Plant me some jalapeños."

"There's not enough in the world to feed that need."

Quinn chuckled.

"I still don't know how you eat those things raw, sick bastard."

"Real men eat them raw."

"Real men plant their own shit. Pick up your pace, Sally. What the hell's wrong with you this morning?"

Quinn hadn't realized he'd been jogging slower than usual. Maybe it had something to do with the zero sleep he'd gotten.

They veered onto the manicured hiking trail and began the torturous ascent up the mountain, side-by-side. Quinn sucked in the cool, clean air perfumed with budding flowers. His lungs were already burning. He glanced at his brother who was barely flushed. Landon was doing so good and it took everything in Quinn's power not to grovel at his feet every day and beg him to stay that way. He'd never felt so desperate about anything in his life.

They passed a young female jogger, in low-cut spandex. Instead of imagining what the woman looked like naked, Quinn found himself immediately thinking of Bobbi and wondering what she was doing. He cleared his throat. The last thing he needed at that moment was to get a crush on a local. He needed his focus on the investigation, not Bobbi's mesmerizing green eyes. Or her breasts, for that matter.

"Need any help loading up furniture for the farmer's market this weekend?" Quinn asked.

"Naw. Only got two chairs and a few other things to sell this week."

"The chair in the living room?"

Landon glanced down for a moment, and Quinn noticed.

"No, I'm actually making that for someone."

Quinn stumbled on a rock. "What?"

Landon didn't respond.

"Did you say you were making the chair for *someone?*"

Landon set his jaw, obviously not wanting to talk about it. Quinn couldn't tear his eyes away from his brother.

"A *girl?* Landon... have you met someone?"

His brother rolled his eyes and shook his head. "Just lay off, alright? I don't want to talk about it. It's not a big deal."

It *was* a big deal. A big fucking deal. And Quinn wanted to know the name of this mystery girl immediately so he could run her through the system and then chase her out of town, if need be.

They ran in silence for a moment.

"You'll tell me when you're ready, okay?"

Landon nodded, then cut him a glance. "Like you're anyone to talk to about relationships, eh?"

"What the hell's that supposed to mean?"

"Dude. Seriously. Did you even date when I was inside?"

No, he didn't. He was too riddled with guilt, worrying about his brother to put his emotions anywhere else. Truth was, it had been over four years since Quinn had a real girlfriend, and that had crashed and burned. He'd dated here and there—a man had needs, after all. But nothing that stuck. He didn't want to think how long it had been since he'd had sex, but he knew one thing for sure, it was before he moved to Berry Springs.

"Probably dated less than you did in prison." Quinn quipped, switching the subject.

"Ha. Ha."

Quinn laughed, and as they pressed up the steepest part of the mountain, his thoughts raced with who the hell Landon had met in Berry Springs.

*L*OADED WITH COFFEE and a rush of endorphins from a four mile run, Quinn checked his GPS one more time.

Yep, he was on the right track. He glanced at the clock—8:07 a.m.. Maybe not a respectable hour to drop by someone's workplace and ask them if they had anything to do with a homicide, but he didn't give a shit.

He squinted at the sign ahead.

Kudrow's Car Repair

Quinn turned into a small gravel parking lot in front of a garage encircled with a dozen rundown, rusted vehicles in the grass. The place looked sketchy at best.

He parked next to a dumpster, got out of his truck and was welcomed by screaming rock music. The kind that made his skin crawl.

He was already on edge when he walked into the garage's office. Cluttered, messy, dirty, stinky. The scent of motor oil clung to the air along with a hint of pot. A calendar with half-naked women hung proudly behind an old computer with oiled fingerprints all over it. A ratty couch sat next to a tiny, dirty bathroom. A large window overlooked the garage, with a car in each bay.

He peered over the desk at the computer which was off —dammit.

Feeling like his brain was being pelted with shards of glass, Quinn glanced up at the surprisingly expensive-looking speaker and considered ripping it off the wall, but movement caught his eye.

He let himself into the garage.

"Chad Kudrow?" He yelled over the blaring music.

The mechanic rolled out from under a sedan. The moment he saw Quinn's uniform, his beady eyes narrowed. Not intimidated by law enforcement, apparently.

"Mind if we turn that down?" Quinn yelled, a little louder than he probably needed to.

Kudrow hesitated, then pushed off the floor and took his time putting a tool away. Then, he washed his hands, taking care to make sure they were as clean as a damn Saint. He was making Quinn wait—a subtle *your-in-my-territory* move. The guy had some balls. Finally, the mechanic walked over to the stereo and clicked it down. The ear-pricing music faded to a respectable level.

"You're Chad Kudrow, correct?"

Kudrow wiped his hands on a towel, eyeing Quinn. Dressed in a plaid shirt—unbuttoned enough to showcase a torso full of tattoos—dirty jeans, and combat boots, Quinn wondered how the kid had earned a reputation as a ladies' man. His dark hair was buzzed short, a contrast to the thick beard he sported. He looked to be pushing thirty, although possibly aged more by hard living.

"That's me." His voice was deep, gruff.

"Nice shop."

"Thanks."

"You own it?"

Kudrow shifted his weight. "Few years."

"Just you?"

"Yeah. You need a car looked at, or something?"

Quinn wondered what *or something* was. "No, actually, I wanted to talk to you about Hannah Winchester."

Something flickered in the kid's bloodshot eyes and a little warning bell went off.

"Know her?"

"Yeah, I guess."

"How so?"

"She brought her car in a few weeks ago."

"What kind of car trouble was she having?"

"Oil leak."

Interesting that Kudrow remembered immediately. He didn't seem the type to have a stellar memory.

"You fix it?"

He nodded.

"And that was it?"

"It, what?"

"Is that the last time you saw her?"

"Uh, I ran into her at Frank's a few times."

"Did you two have a relationship?"

"No, man." He said a little too quickly, and a little too defensively.

Quinn kept waiting for Kudrow to ask what this had to do with him, but he didn't. Did he already know about Hannah's death? Through town gossip, or because she died by his tattooed hand?

"What did you do last night, Chad?"

The mechanic's dark brow cocked, obviously knowing where this was going. Familiar territory, apparently. "I was here. Working. A bit backed up."

"What time?"

"I worked the day shift, then went home for dinner, then came back."

"What times, Chad?"

"I got to work around eight." He looked at the clock. "Left about six in the evening, came back about eight."

"Lunch?"

"Ate here."

"Were there other employees here?"

"Guy named Randy worked with me during the day."

"What about when you came back at eight?"

"No. Just me here."

"So you weren't here from six to eight?"

"I was at home."

"What time did you pack up and leave for the night?"

"'Round midnight."

The kid didn't strike him as a workaholic.

"Anyone with you at home?"

"Not sure if that's any of your business."

Kudrow was either starting to clam up or smarten up, so Quinn quickly asked another question.

"When was the last time you spoke with Miss Winchester?"

He shoved his hands in his pockets. "Few days ago."

"What was the nature of that conversation?"

"Just asking how her car was running."

"Follow-up customer service is very important, huh?"

A car pulled into the parking lot.

"That's my eight-thirty." Kudrow said quickly.

Quinn glanced at the two twenty-something kids, dressed head-to-toe in black, as they stepped out of a lowered sedan with spokes coming out of the wheels.

Quinn cocked a brow and look back at Kudrow. "I'm

assuming the appointment is to take off the window tint that's darker than legal?"

Kudrow narrowed his eyes. The guy was done talking.

"Alright then, Chad." Quinn handed him his card, and watched him closely as he said his next words. "Hannah Winchester was murdered last night. I'd like you to call me if you think of anything that can help me find who did it."

Kudrow's eyes never left the card as Quinn turned and strode outside.

Quinn nodded at the punk kids who warily stepped aside to let him pass. Good to know someone there was intimidated by law enforcement.

Following his instincts, he took a moment to look around. He scanned the vacant cars scattered around the garage, the stacks of old tires, the rusted bikes. A large wood pile stacked neatly against a tree. He passed the dumpster, then paused and turned around.

Quinn kicked over a stump from the wood pile, stepped up, and peered inside the dumpster.

A zing of excitement shot through him.

Barely visible underneath a black trash bag was the corner of a blue, paisley-print bath towel.

Fifteen minutes later, Quinn pushed through the front doors of the station.

"Morning, sunshine." Carrying a steaming cup of coffee, Jonas breezed by the front doors looking as alert and impeccably dressed as always. "Cuttin' it close... although, if I was almost blown to pieces last night, I'd probably be late, too."

Quinn looked at the clock on the wall—8:28 a.m.. "I've got two minutes to spare, Jonas."

They passed by the bullpen abuzz with ringing phones,

chatter, and the ding of a video game somewhere in the background.

"I seem to remember someone telling us that if we're not five minutes early, we're late," Jonas said as he nodded at the newest dispatcher who had a rack the size of Summit Mountain.

Quinn, who considered being on-time a show of respect, cocked an eyebrow. "I hope that attention to detail carried over in the reports you have for me... right now."

Jonas lifted the folder in his hand. "Hannah Winchester and Chad Kudrow, all tied up in a little bow for you, Lieutenant."

"Good. Now, go make me look smart."

Quinn stepped into the conference room behind Jonas. It was a full house. Chief of Police David McCord sat at the head of the table—naturally—Hayes and Willard beside him, and Detective Dean Walker stood in the corner on his cell phone, looking tanned and rested, fresh from his honeymoon. Jonas motioned to the only chair left, and Quinn shook his head. He'd rather stand.

McCord leaned his elbows on the table.

"Okay, boys, let's get going. Dean, welcome back. Colson's already landed his first homicide. I know you're buried getting caught up, but work with him if he needs it. I'm keeping Quinn as point on this."

Dean nodded, eyeing "the new guy."

McCord looked at him. "As suspected, word about Miss Winchester's death is already out. The explosion woke the entire damn town up. Whataya got so far?"

McCord notoriously lacked people skills, but Quinn didn't care. No bullshit, no small talk. Two of Quinn's favorite qualities in a person.

Quinn walked to the front of the room, slipped a thumb

drive into the computer and flicked on the projector. As he clicked through files, he began his update, "I just got off the phone with Jessica. Miss Winchester's autopsy is slated to begin at one-thirty this afternoon. She'll get her in earlier if she can, but she's already pushing her to the front of the line. I'll be there."

"Did she confirm TOD?"

"More or less. Looks like Miss Cross found her not long after she was killed. Jessica implied Hannah could've been deceased less than an hour by the time she got to the morgue."

"Blunt force trauma?"

"Likely cause at the moment."

"And sexually assaulted, right?" McCord, always straight to the point.

Quinn nodded. "Yes, red marks between her legs indicate that. Also, she was found naked on her bed." He glanced at Jonas. "Hit the lights." Jonas flicked the switch and the room was illuminated with Hannah Winchester's naked, dead body.

"Let's back up for a sec. As you know, Bobbi Cross spoke with Hannah on the phone at 7:47 last night. I confirmed this by checking her phone. Miss Cross says they had a short conversation and that it was agreed that she would swing by Hannah's house to pick up something for her yoga class, after she stopped by her shooting range. At approximately 9:15 Bobbi pulled up to Hannah's house and noticed smoke. She ran inside where she saw someone running out the back door, then she found Hannah's body in her bedroom." All eyes shifted to the image on the wall. "She called 911, and before she removed the body from the house, she took these pictures for us, to document the scene. I was the first one on location."

"Have you gotten Hannah's phone records, yet?" McCord asked.

Quinn looked at Jonas, who said, "Not yet. I'll get them today."

Quinn nodded to the image on the wall. "You can see Hannah's body is strategically placed, and it's important to note that the placement is not derogatory, as with most rape cases where the vic is positioned post mortem. If anything, her legs and arms being crossed are shielding her. Covering her up."

"That's interesting," McCord said.

"Yeah, it is. Makes me think there were emotions involved, possibly."

"Meaning?"

Detective Dean Walker cut in. "Regret, maybe. Remorse for what he'd done."

Quinn nodded. "Exactly. Maybe there was some sort of love or respect there. Or, the placement could be a symbol." He clicked to another picture dated years earlier. "I did a quick search of related crimes in the area where the vic had been positioned in a symbolic way. This is Ginny Thomas, murdered by her former boyfriend for cheating on him. You can see he positioned her hands in a sexually derogatory way... with some interesting toys I've never seen before. The boyfriend's still in jail, so we know this isn't connected." He clicked to another picture. "And I understand everyone is very familiar with this case. Three years ago a group of anti-government bastards went on a killing spree, branding each of their vics with their group symbol. Dr. Katie Somers was the only survivor. The bad guys are still in jail, for life. Those are the only two similar local cases I could find, and I don't see an immediate connection here." He clicked back to the photo of Hannah on her bed. "As I noted, there doesn't appear to be any sign of struggle, which possibly means one of two things—she knew the suspect, or was raped after she was killed."

The room fell silent. Quinn looked at the rounded eyes around the table.

"You're saying we have a fucking murdering *necrophiliac* running around Berry Springs?" Hayes asked.

"If she was killed first, yes. Jessica will confirm that."

"What about local cases involving necrophilia? Any?" McCord asked.

"None, but Jonas, I'd like you to extend that search nationwide. Look for the same type of woman, too. Fit, health nut, hippie-type. Young. Hell, even look into the yoga connection."

"Will do."

"Good thinking... what about the people that went to her yoga class?" McCord asked.

"Bobbi keeps a sign-in sheet at her front door but unfortunately, not all signatures are legible, and there are a lot of them. We're filtering through them."

Willard shook his head. "I don't see a necrophiliac being into yoga."

"There's a lot of sick fucks out there, Willard." Dean added, with a look that said he'd seen his fair share.

"Fucking a dead body is beyond sick... hell, is that even considered rape?"

"Great question. So necrophilia is interesting, for lack of a better word." Quinn continued. "Believe it or not, most states, including ours, have no laws prohibiting it. It's a very difficult thing to prosecute because technically the corpse isn't considered a person under law, so you can't charge for sexual assault or rape. It'd be like banging a loaf of bread, in the court's eyes. So a corpse cannot be considered the victim of a sex crime. I read a few cases where they were able to charge the perp with theft, because technically the corpse was owned by the family, but that's about it."

"What about desecration of a corpse?"

"Not sure if having sex with a dead body applies there."

"Dead body or not, they'll find the sick bastard's DNA in her."

"Hopefully. Or, a fingerprint, or hair... it's a good bet Jessica will turn up something." He switched to the photos Willard had taken from the scene. "Now let's talk about evidence. This picture is of two, cast iron candle holders in the bathroom. Possible murder weapon. Jonas, you send these off to the lab already?"

"Yes, sir, along with the bedding, container—"

"Container?" McCord asked.

"Yes, found on the back porch. We think the suspect used tiki fluid to light the fire."

"Which is why he didn't bother to take the murder weapon. Thought the house would go down in flames," Willard added.

"Also," Quinn said, "shows he wasn't prepared."

"So Bobbi showed up and wrecked his plans, but he sure as hell was prepared when you guys went back later. You two are damn lucky." McCord said.

Quinn's jaw twitched. It made his stomach sink to think how close Bobbi had come to losing her life a second time that night.

"Do you think he knew you two were going to come back?"

"It's a possibility. Or, we just showed up at the wrong place, wrong time. He'd turned on the gas and was very likely in the house when we got there. It also tells me he'd quite possibly been watching, waiting, from woods the entire time."

"That's ballsy."

Quinn shrugged—or just morbid curiosity. "Before the explosion, the fire department took samples to determine the exact accelerant used in the initial fire. Logan Black will let me know as soon as he hears back. It's also important to note that the suspect set two separate fires initially, presumably to destroy evidence, but oddly enough not the bed where the dead body was."

He glanced at the looks of confusion around the room. It confused him, too, but the more he thought about it, and the more he considered the positioning of Hannah's legs and hands, he felt confident that the suspect possibly knew her, and there were emotions involved. It wasn't just a random murder. Maybe he didn't want to set her body on fire. Couldn't do it, or couldn't watch it light, at least. Regardless, Quinn had nothing to go on but his gut with that theory so he kept it to himself and moved the meeting forward.

He clicked pictures. "Lastly, we've got a footprint outside. Interestingly enough, it looks to be a bare footprint."

"*Bear* footprint?" McCord asked.

"Bare. As in, no shoes. We took a cast and collected soil samples." He looked at Jonas. "Anything back on that yet?"

Jonas looked at his watch. "No, remember boss, it's only eight-forty-five."

Quinn cocked a brow and stared at him.

Jonas straightened. "Alrighty then, I'll follow up immediately and light a fire under their asses."

"Good. Okay, so, they'll scan for fingerprints on the candle holders and container, and for DNA on the sheets." He clicked to the picture of the blood drop Bobbi had found in the bathroom. "We've also got this... or, had it, anyway.

Before the house blew, Bobbi noticed this spot in the bathroom. I was never able to get a sample—because the shit blew—but it confirms our theory that Hannah was killed in the bathroom, assuming the blood was hers."

McCord looked at Hayes. "Any prints in the house?"

"Only Bobbi's on the front door knob, interestingly enough. None on the back door knob."

"He wiped them clean, and maybe had gloves or used a dish towel to go through the back door on the way out."

"I think so, yes," Quinn nodded. "My guess is he was possibly cleaning up after himself when Bobbi showed up."

"So the dude is stupid enough to leave behind the murder weapon, but smart enough to wipe down the door handles?" Hayes asked.

"Again, I think it's safe to assume he thought the house would burn down initially. But, to your point, I sincerely do not think we are looking for a seasoned criminal. There are way too many things that don't add up for someone who knows what they're doing."

"Agreed," McCord nodded. "And that makes our job that much more difficult."

"And Bobbi didn't get a good look at the guy? Not at all?" Dean asked.

"Unfortunately the lights were off and the guy sprinted out. She couldn't tell a thing about him other than he was, quote, normal height, and that she felt strongly that it was a male. Remember, she was in shock, probably. Last thing she expected. It was an impromptu visit to pick up something for some yoga thing they're doing together."

"Yoga thing?"

"A yoga retreat, focusing on mindfulness and meditation," Willard said.

All eyes cut to Willard.

Jonas cocked a brow. "You into yoga, Willard?"

"I've gone before."

"Didn't know men did yoga."

"Sometimes. Nothing wrong with being centered."

"I'm sure your center gets very stimulated being around sweating women in leotards with their legs up in the air." Jonas smirked.

"What the hell's a leotard?" Hayes asked Jonas.

"It's what your mom left at my house last night." Willard quipped.

Dean rolled his eyes in the corner.

"Stay on task, boys." McCord nodded toward the screen.

"So, how is our beauty, Bobbi?" Jonas asked, followed by a twinge of jealously shooting through Quinn. Every man in town knew Bobbi.

"Stitches, but fine," he said, keeping it short and sweet.

"And she doesn't have any idea who could have done this?"

"No."

"What about Hannah's folks? They have anything useful to say?"

"No, but I plan to follow up today."

McCord leaned back and blew out a breath. "So to recap. Bobbi Cross found Miss Hannah Winchester dead, naked, on her bed, with a hit to the head. Possible scenario is that Hannah's showering, some pervert comes in, kills her in the bathroom, then drags her to the bed and has his way with her. Then, sets the shit on fire and gets the hell out when he hears Bobbi come in. Later, you take Bobbi back to Hannah's, to get her Jeep, and the house blows up."

Quinn nodded. "In a nutshell."

"Okay. Who are your suspects?"

"If you would've asked me an hour ago, I'd say none yet.

But, I'd gotten wind that Hannah was possibly involved with Chad Kudrow over the last few weeks. So, I paid our boy a little visit this morning. Kudrow didn't come clean about the relationship and was vague at best, but he doesn't have an alibi for last night. Says he was working in his shop, alone."

"Hardly makes him a suspect."

"I'm not finished." He clicked to a picture of Hannah's bathroom that showed a bath towel, still intact. He pulled his cell phone from his pocket. "As I was leaving his shop, I glanced in the dumpster and saw this." He turned the phone around. "A blue, paisley-print bath towel."

Everyone looked at the projector, then back at his phone. The towels were an exact match.

Quinn nodded. "It's not enough to consider him an official suspect, but I want a search warrant issued immediately to confiscate it and search Kudrow's business and house, and get his phone records."

"Why not bring him in for formal questioning?" Willard asked.

"Kid's not gonna talk, that much is obvious. Us showing up on his doorstep with a warrant will."

McCord sat stone-faced for a moment, then finally nodded. "I'll see what I can do."

"Do it fast."

Quinn's demand was met with raised eyebrows around the room. He didn't give a damn. He turned to Jonas. "Jonas, what did you dig up on Chad and Hannah?"

Jonas passed a few pictures around the table. "Since our boy is the current conversation, I'll go into him first." The table flipped through pictures printed from Chad's social media account. "Kudrow is a mom's worst nightmare. High school dropout turned local drug dealer. Spent a few nights in jail for multiple DWIs, paraphernalia, and possession—"

"Possession of what?"

"Heroin."

Quinn stiffened.

Jonas continued, "Eventually opened a mechanic shop on the outskirts of town. As you all know, rumor has it he runs drugs out of there, but we've never been able to pin it."

Or, never cared to try, Quinn thought.

"He's twenty-nine, never been married, but appears to have tons of girlfriends. Hangs out at Frank's often, lives alone. Folks have a trailer on the west side of Summit Mountain. Dear daddy's the same story, a pair of DWIs and now draws disability from the government, which I think is bullshit, but that's just my opinion. Mom doesn't work. There's no pictures or messages or any sign of Hannah on his social media account, or hers, for that matter. So my impression is that if they were in some sort of a relationship, it certainly wasn't serious."

"The fact that Kudrow has an extensive record will make it easier to get the warrant." Hayes added.

Jonas nodded, and continued, "And Hannah," he passed out a few more pictures. "Age twenty-six, went to college and studied horticulture, but never actually graduated. Her grandmother passed away, leaving her the house and a chunk of change. Works at *Just Be Yoga* part-time and that's it. No house payment. Lots of social media posts about motivational mantras, finding yourself, etcetera. Seems like a bit of a drifter, if you ask me. A hell of a nice looking one."

"Show some respect, Jonas." Hayes rolled his eyes.

"No disrespect to acknowledge a woman's beauty, dead or alive."

"Did you say horticulture?" Willard asked.

Jonas nodded. "Normal hippie major these days."

Quinn frowned. "I'll be anxious to see if there's any

drugs in her system." He looked at Jonas. "Does *rumor have it* that Kudrow deals pot, too?"

"Think he does a little of everything."

Hayes leaned in and looked at the pictures. "She seems like the kind of earthy chick to use pot for relaxation or whatever."

"Way to label someone, Hayes."

"I'm just saying maybe that's how she knows him. She buys drugs from him."

"It's a good assumption." Quinn looked at Jonas. "And labeling, guessing, and assuming is what we've got right now. No room to be politically correct as long as I'm around."

"Hear, hear," Dean said.

Quinn glanced at the clock, feeling the weight of things to get done immediately. "Chief, you push the warrant. Jonas, get that evidence pushed through and I don't care if you have to sell your soul to the devil to get it done. Hayes, I want you to get a list of Hannah's most active friends on social media from Jonas and go visit each of them. See what they know, or think. I'm going to check the roads around Hannah's house. The suspect watched us the whole damn time, parked somewhere, and I'm going to find it. See if I can get some tracks or something. Then, I'll head to the autopsy. If anyone is contacted by the media, direct them to me. Don't say a damn word." He looked at McCord. "Anything else?"

The corner of the chief's lip curled up in the closest thing to a smile Quinn had ever seen. "Nice work, Colson. Get on it, guys."

11

*B*OBBI PARKED UNDERNEATH a pine tree and climbed out of her Jeep. The moment her shoes hit the rocky ground, she took a deep breath.

The woods. Her happy place, usually. Not that day.

Thick clouds greedily absorbed most of the early morning light. A bleak dimness colored the woods, doing nothing to help her mood.

Bobbi closed her eyes and focused on the babbling creek in the distance. She forced herself to quiet her mind, the racing thoughts, the gruesome images of murder in her head.

She took a shaky breath.

Spring was in the air.

Unfortunately, so was death.

Bobbi had awoken with a splitting headache and a knot the size of a baseball on her head. The right side of her forehead was so swollen she was concerned the stitches would pop, but that was the least of her worries.

After a night of pacing and a handful of whiskey shots, Bobbi had finally forced herself into bed at four in the morning, only to wake up three and a half hours later drenched in sweat from a horrific nightmare that one of her friends had been raped and murdered. When she realized it wasn't a dream, sleep had escaped her. She'd forced herself out of bed, made a pot of coffee, checked emails, and was pulled back to reality with her hefty to-do list. It's funny how, even when tragedy hits, the world still spins. Life goes on, and things need to get done. She'd fought it, though, and sat on the deck watching the sun rise, but eventually kicked herself in the ass, reminding herself that nothing positive comes from wallowing. Hannah was dead, nothing was going to change that. All of her thoughts needed to be focused toward finding the bastard who did it.

In the meantime, life went on. Aside from yoga. Bobbi decided to cancel classes for a week out of respect for Hannah. It was the right thing to do.

After a quick shower, she'd pulled on a pair of faded blue jeans, a vintage T-shirt that said "hang in there, baby," and slid into her favorite pair of flip-flops. Dan the Weatherman warned rain was on the way, but before that, temps were expected to reach seventy-five. Normally, that would have Bobbi doing cartwheels.

After two ibuprofen, a grainy protein smoothie, and short ride into the mountains, Bobbi was tackling the first item on the day's to-do list—working on the impending yoga retreat.

She slung a bag over her shoulder, grabbed a box from the back of her Jeep and stepped onto the manicured pebbled trail that led to the luxury resort nestled deep in the woods. Shadow Creek Resort had seventeen cabins, a main lodge, an event center, and an overlook on top of the highest mountain in Berry Springs. Each cabin was thoughtfully secluded on either side of Shadow Creek, hidden between soaring trees and complete with wrap-around decks and state of the art appliances. Several Victorian-style wooden bridges crossed over the water. Lighted trails wove their way around the mountain encouraging hiking, picnicking and *being one* with nature. The main lodge was a log cabin with a five-star restaurant and spa. The resort had been featured in several magazines and even a few TV shows. The property looked like something you'd see in a Disney movie with fairies and little gnomes, a magical place in the woods, especially in the Springtime. It was sold-out year round and Bobbi had shelled out two months earnings just to reserve the place for her weekend yoga retreat. The owner, a former soldier named Rocco, had given her the "BS" discount—only available to those born and raised in Berry Springs. Although she was pretty sure she was the first person to receive this discount. Hell, she'd take it where she could get it.

As long as everything panned out, Bobbi was on track to not only make her money back, but a nice profit as well. If that happened, she planned to make her retreat a twice-yearly thing, which was her goal.

Getting the retreat going had been an unbelievable amount of work. Double—triple—what she'd anticipated. And triple the stress, too. Regardless, she needed to pull it together because people from all over the south were traveling to little Berry Springs just to attend, and her name was on the line.

Bobbi's footsteps crunched on the rock pathway as she walked deeper into the woods. Due to the remote location of the cabins, the walking trail was the only way to access them. Usually, golf carts or four-wheelers were waiting to take guests, but not that morning. It was quiet. Eerily so. No tourists, no joggers, no one.

The thick canopy of trees closed in around her, darkening the already dim light.

She glanced over her shoulder.

Where *was* everyone?

Just then, distance footfalls behind her.

Bobbi glanced over her shoulder again, but saw no one.

She told herself she was probably just hearing things, but just in case, she picked up her pace. Hell, after the night she'd had, she was very likely delusional.

The sound of the creek grew louder and after taking a curve in the trail, the woods opened up to a rocky beach with soaring mountains on either side of the sparkling water.

"Hey, Bobbi."

She jumped like a stray cat, juggling the box in her hands.

"Whoa, sorry, didn't mean to..." Wearing khaki overalls and hiking boots, Rocco stepped out of the woods and froze mid-stride. "Holy *crap,* you okay?"

After swallowing the knot in her throat, she inwardly groaned. So the bandage and swelling on her forehead truly looked as horrible as she thought it did—*fan-freaking-tastic.*

Bobbi glanced down. "Yeah... I just... fell."

She met his gaze, gauging his reaction. Did he know about Hannah? Had he heard the gossip? She sure as hell didn't want to be the one to spread the gossip and based on the bags under the guy's eyes, he didn't look like he was in any mood to talk about death, either.

"Hell of a bump." Rocco frowned. "Stitches?"

As he took the box from her hands she noticed a voluptuous pin-up girl tattooed on his forearm. The suggestive image seemed out of place for the notoriously introverted former Green Beret. Although he was barely six-foot, the former solider was all muscle. At thirty-five, Rocco had served six tours in Afghanistan and retired after his parents had died tragically in a car accident on an icy night in the mountains. Rocco purchased the resort with the boatload of money he'd inherited and lived in a small cabin just off the premises. Rumor was he rarely left the property. Bobbi had only seen him a handful of times in town, once at the post office and once at the grocery store. People seemed to keep their distance from him.

Rocco had hired a bubbly, extroverted businesswoman named Pauline to manage and be "the face" of the resort, while he took care of everything behind the scenes. Bobbi had done ninety-percent of her correspondence through Pauline and was surprised at seeing Rocco at all.

She avoided the stitches question. "Where is everyone?"

"I've closed the place down for the few days leading up to your retreat. Needed to get a few things done to the cabins. Spring cleaning, things like that. You headed to the shed?"

"The shed" was a spare cabin used as storage.

She nodded. "I've got more boxes in my Jeep."

"I'll send Jimmy in the four wheeler to help you out."

"Thanks."

Just then—

"Hey, Bobbi!" Shuffling down the path with a box each, Alice and Kinsley stepped out of the woods. Alice's gray hair hung to the side in a tight braid, like the expression on her face. A messy bun bobbed on top of Kinsley's head, her face flushed with emotion.

Bobbi forced a smile. "Well, hey, there."

From the flurry of texts she'd gotten over the course of the morning—and hadn't respond to—everyone knew about Hannah, apparently. Not just about the murder, but that Bobbi had found her. Nothing was a secret in Berry Springs. Well, almost nothing.

"I'll get this in the shed for you and keep it unlocked," Rocco said, and before she could thank him, he disappeared into the woods.

"I didn't expect to see you guys here," Bobbi said as Alice and Kinsley walked up, trying to keep it light.

"Oh *my...*" Kinsley's mouth gaped when she saw the bandage. She dropped the box. "Oh my *God*, Bobbi, are you *okay?*"

Dammit. "Yeah, I'm fine. Of course I'm fine." It wasn't about her, and she was sick of people pitying her.

Frowning, Alice nodded to the bandage. "Seriously. How'd you get that?"

"Fell on my way out of the burning house."

Alice shook her head, grief squeezing her face.

Kinsley's eyes filled with tears. "I can't believe it, Bobbi. Do they know who did it?"

"I don't think so... not yet, at least."

"Oh, God, this is just so... you must be a wreck! What the heck are you doing out of bed? What can I do? This is so, *so* awful. How are you?" Kinsley spouted questions like a wind-up doll about to explode.

Knowing Bobbi better than anyone else from class, Alice turned to Kinsley, and in her ever-motherly tone, said, "Bobbi'll be just fine. Our girl's a tough one." She turned back to Bobbi. "Now. What can we help you with, dear? We figured you'd be here, so here we are. With bells on." She winked.

Bobbi flashed Alice a *thank-you* smile. If she had to answer one more question about how *she* was, she was going to spontaneously combust.

"Thanks for coming, then. I'm taking stuff to the shed."

They fell into step together, walking along the rocky

beach. Kinsley was still sniffling. Bobbi chose to power through and keep the subject off death.

"We need to start decorating the cabins and setting stuff out. Rocco's sending someone to my Jeep to help with the boxes."

"Bobbi, I'm sorry," Kinsley shook her head. "But I can't stand here and pretend nothing happened. You saw the guy? That's what I heard. Is that right?"

Bobbi sucked air into lungs that felt like they were about to cave in. She'd rather give a detailed account of her last pap-smear than talk about what happened in Hannah's house. ... And draw a picture. But she knew the questions wouldn't stop until she addressed them.

"Technically, yes, I saw whoever did it running out of the house. But it was dark. I couldn't make out the face."

"How *scary*. Bobbi, you're so lucky."

Her jaw clenched. Thinking of herself as lucky made her feel guiltier than she ever had in her life. Survivor's guilt. She knew she was lucky. It was a shock to everyone that the killer hadn't gone after her. Part of what had kept her up all night was wondering... was there a chance he still would?

Kinsley continued. "And the police really don't have any leads?"

Bobbi thought of Quinn and the resolute look in his eyes. If anyone could find the guy, it was him.

"I really don't know," she said. "I wasn't allowed to stick around. They forced me to go to the ER to get my head checked out. After that, I was taken home." She decided to leave out the part about the house blowing up, mainly because it appeared Kinsley didn't know about that. "It was pushing three in the morning by the time I got home."

"Who's they? Who forced you to go to the ER?"

"Lieutenant Colson."

Kinsley's eyebrows raised. "That *new* cop?"

Bobbi nodded.

"He is *sooo hot.*" Kinsley's watery eyes twinkled.

Alice grinned. "Handsome, *and single,* so I hear."

Bobbi rolled her eyes and shook her head. Alice, along with Bobbi's brother, had been pushing Bobbi to settle into a solid relationship. Give someone a chance. Anyone, they'd both said.

"Don't even start, Alice."

Kinsley had gone from quivering baby to excited puppy in two seconds. "I saw him jogging the other day, and sweet baby Jesus, that guy is built like a *tank,* B."

Bobbi wasn't about to admit that her imagination had drawn up the same image. Although in her fantasy, his shirt was off... Fine, he was naked.

"Heard he's never been married, either, and no kids. Nice package."

Bobbi's brow lifted. A mind of its own.

Alice rolled her eyes. "I mean, all *that* is a nice package. Not his *package,* package. Pervert."

"Well I don't doubt he has a nice package as well." A wicked grin crossed Kinsley's face as they stepped up to the shed.

"Well you two are welcome to find out." Along with every other woman in Berry Springs who was probably throwing themselves at him. The thought reminded Bobbi to keep her thoughts and fantasies under control. She wasn't about to step in line for that guy. Or any guy for that matter.

"Hey, ladies!"

Bobbi looked over her shoulder to see Wells barreling down the shoreline in a four-wheeler. Wearing his green park ranger uniform, he stopped next to the shed, skidding on the loose rocks. Like everyone else, he immediately zeroed in on Bobbi's bandaged forehead. He scrunched his face. "Geez, B, how many stitches?"

Three thousand. "Just a few. It's fine."

"I'm sorry to hear about everything."

"Tell that to Hannah's parents." Her gaze drifted to the scratches on his arms and she frowned. "Get into a fight with a piranha?"

He glanced at his hands, then rolled his eyes. "Fell into a damned barbed wire fence this morning hauling your damn fairy lights all over the place. Hurts like a bitch."

"Want some of my bandage?" She reached up and touched her face. "There's plenty of it, trust me."

"Only if it comes with a shot of whiskey."

"That I can guarantee."

He laughed.

Returning to the gruesome subject, Kinsley asked, "When's the funeral?"

"I think it will be a while before they release her body."

"Why?"

Bobbi paused. Did they know Hannah had been sexually assaulted?

A moment of silence settled around them, giving her the answer.

"Well," Wells said, in a lighter tone, changing the subject. "I'm starting on the tree lights today." He glanced at one of the bridges that arched over the creek. "Want me to light those up, too?"

"That might be nice. Ask Pauline first to make sure it's okay."

"She's already given me the green light to do whatever I want. They want this place looking as nice as possible, too."

"Perfect. And just make sure the trails are trimmed. We're really going to push nature walks."

He nodded. "... Good for healing."

Another moment of silence.

"You got more boxes in the Jeep?"

"Yeah."

"Well, load up, ladies, I'll take you there."

Alice slid in next to him on the four-wheeler and Kinsley jumped onto the back.

"Go ahead, guys, I'll walk. I'm going to check out a few things, first."

"You sure?" Alice frowned.

"Yep. Go ahead. See you in a sec."

"Alright, then."

Bobbi watched "her team" take off into the woods. The sound of the growling motor faded, leaving the peaceful song of nature around her. She hadn't anticipated how difficult it was going to be to talk about Hannah and everything that had happened. It made it more real. Not something she could just compartmentalize while going on with her life. And if she knew anything about Berry Springs, Hannah's murder was going to be the talk of the town until the bastard got caught, so she'd better get used to it.

Bobbi walked to the creek. The water level was still up from storms earlier in the week. Probably to her chest in the deepest spots.

The water moved swiftly, cresting over boulders and branches, bubbling over rocks.

She slipped out of her flip-flops. The sun sparkled like diamonds as she stepped into the water. It was ice-cold and felt invigorating against her warm skin. She focused on the silky feeling weaving through her toes, washing away the sickness she felt inside. She closed her eyes and took a deep breath.

And another.

An image of Quinn flashed through her mind and her eyes opened.

It surprised her how the mere mention of his name sent both Kinsley and Alice into a schoolgirl frenzy. Perhaps his body was the only thing to pull them out of thoughts of murder.

There was no denying Quinn Colson was hot. A hottie who had saved her life.

A hero by all counts.

And she owed him a thank you.

12

QUINN HOVERED OVER the geographical map spread across his desk, marking all the potential roads Hannah's killer could have used to hide his vehicle. If Quinn could find the spot the guy parked, maybe he could find more prints, or tire tracks, or, if he got *really lucky*, maybe a local hunter caught a full image of the guy on a deer cam.

His phone rang,. He ignored it. He had two voicemails from Lanie Peabody from NAR News wanting an exclusive.

Yeah, right.

He figured he had at least a half-day until he'd have to give a statement to the press, just to get them off his back.

God, he hated the press.

When Quinn's brother had gone to prison, they'd painted a picture of a soulless, violent, ruthless drug lord. The scum of the earth. But the truth was, Landon had stumbled into the wrong crowd after his basketball career went up in flames. His new friends had pulled him into the world of addiction and emptied his bank account in the process.

To Quinn, true scum was kicking someone when they were down.

Fuck that.

Quinn's stomach growled and he glanced at the clock— 10:11 a.m. He frowned. When was the last time he'd eaten? He grabbed the cup of coffee he'd mindlessly poured earlier, lifted it to his lips and snarled. It smelled like burned rubber. Damn station coffee. He'd be lucky if he made it through his career without getting a hole in his gut. He thought of his brother's high dollar coffee and wondered what he was doing. Hanging out with the *mystery woman,* perhaps?

A knock sounded at the door.

Quinn looked up and sloshed the coffee on the map.

"Oh, shoot! Here…" The one and only Bobbi Cross breezed into his office, grabbed a handful of napkins from the trashcan and tossed them on the map.

He cleared his throat. *What the fuck?* The mere sight of the woman had his body jerking in all the wrong places. Or, right places. He wasn't sure which.

"Sorry," she said. "Didn't mean to—"

Scare him? No. Quinn Colson didn't get scared, and he sure as hell didn't want a woman thinking he did. He quickly cut her off before the word stripped him of his masculinity.

"No, don't worry about it. Been a long morning."

Quinn dabbed up the coffee, surprised that it hadn't disintegrated the map. He straightened and looked her over, shocked to see her standing in front of him. She didn't fit in the surroundings. The cold, bleak, gray walls that had seen more crime than the back alley of an inner city seemed to blur around her. Her long, dark hair was windblown, falling over her shoulders—a kind of bedhead sexy that made his gaze notice the way her T-shirt and faded jeans hugged the kind of curves that only came from hours in the gym, which made them even sexier. But even that perfectly-formed ass couldn't distract from the knot on her forehead, which pulled him out of his lustful haze and into murder. And also into a fresh rush of anger.

He pushed the emotions away and nodded to the bandage. "How's it feeling today?"

"Oh, this?" She said as if it were a paper cut. "It's fine." She grabbed the coffee-soaked napkins and tossed them back into the trashcan. Helpful.

"What brings you in today, Miss Cross?"

A tiny smile crossed her succulent, pink lips. "Bobbi."

"Bobbi, then."

She held up the camo coat he hadn't even noticed in her hands. Apparently her ass could distract from that.

"I wanted to return your coat... and, to say thank you."

Bobbi glanced down as if the words were as difficult to say as "it's time for your prostate exam." Because she was an unappreciative woman? No. Because she was the type that was embarrassed that she needed help in the first place.

"It's my job." He took the coat from her hands.

The unemotional response seemed to ease her. She looked up, those big, green eyes finding a way to sparkle under the oppressive fluorescent lights. She gave a quick nod, then quickly changed the subject.

"Any developments?"

"A few." He wanted to give her enough to know that the investigation wasn't stagnant, but not so much to drag her deeper into it than she already was.

She cocked her head with the same attitude he'd seen

the night before when he demanded she go to the ER. That little attitude was kind of growing on him.

"Anything you care to share, Lieutenant?"

"Quinn."

"Quinn, then."

His lip curled up, then he said, "You mentioned Hannah had been spending time with Chad Kudrow?"

Her sculpted brows lifted. "Yeah?"

"Can you remember anything specific about what she said? A time, place, anything?"

"Ah..." She lifted her gaze to the ceiling. "The first time she said something about him was a few weeks ago... two, maybe? We were cleaning up after class and she asked if I knew him. I didn't; just heard of him, and I asked why. She said she'd taken her car to him. Come to think of it, I bet that's when they first met."

It made much more sense than running in the same circle, which Hannah didn't seem to fit. What also didn't seem to fit was the way Bobbi's gaze left his every time he asked about the Kudrow connection.

"And you don't know if they went out on a date, or hung out at all?"

"I know she saw him a few times at Frank's Bar. That's it."

"If she was asking you about him, there must have been more to it than getting a tune up."

Bobbi swallowed, shrugged.

He stared at her for a moment, letting the silence stretch out. What wasn't she telling him? He figured she'd cave to the uncomfortable silence and begin talking again—like most people did—but she didn't. Bobbi was completely comfortable standing her own in awkward silences.

"Do you know if they were intimate?"

"I really don't know. And that's not something I'm willing to guess at." She shifted her weight. "Is there anything else I can help with? With the investigation, I mean."

"Anything you remember would be helpful. Anything at all. We're reaching out to her social media friends, school colleagues, and her parents again." He glanced down at the map covered in curvy lines, reminding him of the curves he'd seen in Bobbi's hospital gown. "And I'm going to try to figure out which road this guy took to get to her house, and where he parked. Where the hell he was watching us from last night."

"Kudrow smokes, you know."

"A few things, I hear." And Bobbi was smart. The moment he'd noticed an ashtray in Kudrow's shop, he was itching to get to the woods. If he had a nickel for every crime that had been solved by the suspect tossing a cigarette butt covered in DNA, he'd have quite a few nickels. "But yes, to your point, a cigarette will be one of the few things I'll search for."

Hayes breezed in without knocking, or even looking up from the phone in his hand.

"Lieutenant, I..." He looked up. "Oh. Well, hey Bobbi." He scrunched his face in disgust. "*Geeeez,* how's the gash?"

Bobbi shook her head and muttered, "I'm taking this stupid bandage off."

Hayes leaned forward, his nose wrinkled like a Shar-Pei. "Wouldn't matter. Based on the purple around it, you'd look like you went one-on-one with Mike Tyson anyway... and *my God,* that thing is *really* swelled up."

She crossed her arms over her chest. "Thanks, Hayes."

"How many stitches?"

"Four." She said impatiently.

"That's not bad. Shouldn't scar too much. Nothing compared to the battle wound on your arm, anyway."

She stiffened. Quinn frowned. *Battle wound?*

Hayes continued, "That was what? More than ten stitches, right?"

Bobbi cut Quinn a glance.

"What're you guys talking about?"

Hayes looked back and forth between he and Bobbi. "You know... the bike wreck?"

Quinn's frown deepened. What the hell were they talking about? He looked at Bobbi who was staring at him intently now. He felt completely left out of an inside joke.

Hayes's phone beeped and he glanced down at it.

Quinn cocked his head at Bobbi. "What am I missing here?"

"Hey, I gotta take this call." Hayes lifted the phone, then breezed out as quickly as he came in.

"You don't remember me, do you?" She asked once they were alone, a shy smile on her lips.

His eyes widened. *Remember her?* If he'd seen that face before, he'd never have forgotten it.

"We've met before? Aside from last night?"

"Well, we didn't technically meet, but it was a few months ago."

A few months ago. "I'd just moved here."

"Sounds about right. You were with Hayes. I think you'd just started at the station."

A line of concentration ran between his brows, pulling at his memory strings. Then it hit him. "The biking trails."

She glanced away, but nodded.

The memories came flooding back. He'd never actually

seen her. Only her backside. But, he remembered. He remembered that hair, the strong lines of her body. He'd noticed her and he hadn't even seen her face.

"I remember. That was my first week on the job. My second day, I think. I was riding with the team to learn the roads. Hayes interviewed you while I interviewed the other guy and spoke with the medics."

"Grady." There was something in her voice that suggested it was a hard topic for her to talk about.

"Yeah, that's right. Grady... Grady Messick."

Her lips pressed in a thin line. He stared at her for a moment, surprised at the emotion in her face.

"I didn't realize you'd gotten hurt."

"It was nothing. Nothing compared to Grady."

He paused. "It was an accident, Bobbi. A very obvious accident."

She shook her head. "I could've killed him."

He narrowed his eyes, confused by her reaction. There was no question to anyone that what had happened that afternoon in the woods was one-hundred percent unintentional. It hadn't even made town gossip.

"Well, technically anyone could've killed him, then." Quinn said. "Kid was barreling down the trail on his dirt bike. It was bad timing is all. You were jogging, and you crossed paths. He hit a tree, and, you?" He nodded to her arm.

"Just a rock. Anyway, I wasn't paying attention. Just running damn full speed like I always am, trying to get a workout in before heading to work for the day." She shook her head. "He swerved to miss me. Buckley said his disc was a millimeter away from slicing his spinal cord."

"But it didn't." Quinn searched her face, her rigid body

language, and realized it wasn't anger in her eyes. It was guilt.

"It's my understanding his surgery was just for a slipped disc. It could've been a lot worse."

She nodded.

"Do you know how many near-deaths I've seen in my career? Hell, Bobbi, they happen every day, to everyday people. But that's the thing, the worst never happened. I also heard through the grapevine that someone paid for every penny of his medical bills. I'm guessing that was you."

She looked away—an obvious yes—then she changed the subject. "Anyway, so yes, we've met." She smiled, although a bit forced.

His gaze lingered on her for a moment, intrigued more than ever. Bobbi Cross was one sexy, southern Annie Oakley, but behind that tough cowgirl exterior was a sensitive woman. One that took the blame when she didn't have to. One that now was going to carry the weight of her murdered friend on her shoulders.

With his impeccable timing again, Hayes walked back in.

"That was T-Bone at the lab."

"*T-Bone?*" Bobbi raised her eyebrows. "Professional name."

"Travis... something. I don't know, everyone just calls him T-Bone. Anyway, he can be called anything he wants if he keeps bringing us information like this."

"What information?" Quinn asked.

"The footprint we found outside of Hannah's house. Or, the *bear* footprint as McCord would say." He grinned. "The soil sample showed traces of blood in the print."

Quinn's heart skipped a beat. "Who's blood?"

"Not the suspect's. Hannah's."

Dammit. But, at least now they knew the print definitely belonged to Hannah's murderer.

Hayes continued. "And our barefoot bandit wasn't barefoot at all. The print had traces of rubber, and shows a weaving print on the sole. He was wearing shoes. The tread can help narrow down the type, maybe even the brand."

"Shoes with toes has to be a small segment to search."

Hayes's nodded. "That's right. That'll narrow it down significantly."

Bobbi frowned. "Toes?"

"The footprint we found outlined each toe, which is why we thought he was barefoot."

Her eyes rounded. *"Toe shoes.* Yes. They call them five finger shoes. A lot of people wear them in the water. They're like rubber socks, kind of."

"Five finger shoes," Quinn repeated and picked up the phone.

"Jonas here."

"Jonas, I need the list of every shoe store in the area that sells those ugly-ass toe water shoes. Five finger shoes, I guess they're called."

"Five finger shoes?"

"You know, the kind that fit around your toes, like rubber socks."

"Oh. Yeah, those are ugly, aren't they?" Quinn heard a shuffle of papers as Jonas wrote it down. "Will get on it right now."

"I'm going to have Hayes send you an image of the print, maybe you can narrow down the brand based on that."

"I'll give it a shot."

Quinn looked at Hayes. "What size was the print?"

"Ten."

Quinn turned back to the phone. "You hear that? Size ten five finger shoe."

"Yep, got it."

"Text me the list as soon as you've got it compiled."

"You got it."

He hung up. "Hayes, I need you to look at anyone on Hannah's social media account that posts about outdoor sports. Canoeing, kayaking, fishing, paddle boarding, swimming, camping, anything."

Bobbi nodded. "Those shoes are definitely worn by outdoorsy types. Athletic."

Hayes read from his phone. "Based on the shoe size, T-Bone estimates the print belongs to someone anywhere from five-eleven to six-foot."

Quinn glanced at Bobbi. "That aligns with what you saw, right?"

"Yes, and remember, I noticed reflective fabric on his jacket."

Quinn nodded. "So we've definitely got someone into health, sports, an active lifestyle."

Hayes nodded in agreement. "Once I get my list from Hannah's social media, I'll have Jonas pull each person's height and weight from the DMV."

"Perfect. Also compare Bobbi's list of attendees at her studio. But check Kudrow, first. And follow up on that warrant. Check with McCord." He began folding up the map. "I want that damn thing by the end of the day."

Hayes turned on his heel and walked out, without a *"sure, boss"* or *"you got it."* At least he didn't roll his eyes this time.

"That's not all of the roads around her house, you know," Bobbi said, peering at the map.

"No?"

"No. There's a few roads hunters use that aren't even roads, really. Wouldn't be on the map. Only the locals would know about them."

He stared at her for a moment.

Two eyes were always better than one. Especially a pair that looked like that.

"Let's go, then."

13

"*H*ANG ON, LET me grab some boots from my Jeep."

Quinn watched Bobbi jog to her vehicle, counting the ever-growing list of things that took him by surprise. Bobbi Cross, sharpshooter, yoga enthusiast, business owner, whiskey drinker, and a tough-as-nails beauty that carried a pair of shitkickers in the back of her Jeep.

Dear God.

A flame of desire warmed his skin as he watched Bobbi bend over and slip on the boots. Quinn cleared his throat and looked away.

He needed to be careful with her.

Very careful.

She jogged over—boobs bouncing like a goddamn Baywatch episode—and jumped into his truck.

"Take a left onto the highway."

Yes, ma'am.

They drove down Main Street. The morning was growing darker, drearier, with each passing hour. The electricity of impending rain hung heavily in the air. Spring's inconsistent weather was on full display, complete with a gusty seventy degrees.

Quinn flicked on the turn signal.

"Where're you going?"

"Food," he said.

Bobbi raised her eyebrows, then nodded in an approval of this impromptu stop.

He pulled up to the tiny black speaker box. "Two sausage egg and cheese biscuits, hash browns, coffee with creamer and sugar—the real stuff—and a water." He caught her gaping expression and winked, "Watching my figure."

"Oh yes, the non-recyclable water bottle erases all two-thousand of those calories."

He grinned. "What'll you have, ma'am? A steamed carrot with green tea?"

Bobbi rolled her eyes and leaned over him, her breasts sweeping against his arms. A tingle shot through his groin. He bit the inside of his cheek.

"I'll take the exact same, minus one biscuit."

"Well, well, *well.* Those in glass houses..."

"I know, I know." She sat back, to his dismay. "I haven't eaten since lunchtime yesterday... I probably could eat two biscuits, to be honest."

Quinn turned back to the speaker. "Make that two biscuits, please."

"No. I won't eat it."

"Then we'll feed it to the birds. Everyone wins."

He drove around to the window.

"Well, howdy there, Quinn."

"Hey there, Missy. How's basketball going?"

The blonde high schooler handed over the water bottles and coffees, almost spilling them in the process. She giggled. "Whoops, sorry, Lieutenant. Ah, it's going. Made point."

"Very important position. Practice every day and keep those grades up."

"Yes, sir." Missy handed over the food, blushing now. "See you guys later."

Bobbi took the bag, grinning.

"What?" He asked.

"Missy has a little crush on you, *Lieutenant.*"

"Yeah?" He'd be blind not to notice, but it still felt awkward, especially considering he was two decades older than the girl, which made him wonder how much older he was than Bobbi.

As Quinn pulled onto the highway he fought a smirk as Bobbi ripped into her bag like a bear coming out of hibernation. No prim and proper here, nope, this was one hungry woman.

She took a shockingly large bite of her biscuit and looked at his coffee on the console. "Want me to stir in the sugar and creamer?" She asked between chewing.

He had a weird moment of fantasizing of being that sausage rolling around in her mouth. *Christ,* he needed to get it together.

"Sure, thanks."

While she worked his coffee, Quinn maneuvered the road with one hand and bit into his biscuit. *Heaven.*

After securing the coffee lid, Bobbi unwrapped his hash browns, placed them on the console, then squirted ketchup on a napkin next to it.

"Maybe I don't want ketchup on my hash browns."

"This is the south. Everyone eats ketchup on their hash browns." She dipped her biscuit in it. "And their eggs, for that matter."

He couldn't hide his grin any longer. Bobbi was funny. In a less obvious way. He didn't bother telling her that he was born and raised in the sticks and used ketchup almost as much as hot sauce. *Almost.* Instead, he took another bite and they rode a few minutes in silence. He had to refrain himself from watching her eat with such gusto. Damn unexpected turn on it was.

"Turn here."

He hit the brakes. "What? Where?"

"This road, here. Right *here.*"

"You mean that *hiking trail?*" Quinn yanked the wheel.

Bobbi raised the coffee as they bounced over the ditch. "This is exactly what I was talking about that you wouldn't see on the map. Only locals know it and use it."

She was right. He wouldn't have noticed the "road."

A branch swept the side of his Chevy and he cringed. At least he wasn't in that new Silverado he'd been eyeing the last few weeks.

Bobbi swigged her coffee. "So this road hugs the base of the mountain and smaller roads shoot off from it. Lots of places to get lost, or do illegal things, or have sex, for that matter." Another massive bite of biscuit.

He cocked a brow. "Sex, huh?"

She smirked and rolled her eyes, a mouthful of food in her cheek.

He smirked back and forced himself not to say one of the hundred perverted things jumping around in his head.

"I think I busted some kids a few weeks ago for smoking marijuana around here."

She grinned.

"What?"

"Oh, nothing. You're just so formal, Lieutenant."

"What? You mean using the term *marijuana?*"

Bobbi shrugged, still smiling. Her breakfast was bringing color back to her cheeks.

"Sorry, I'm not as cool and hip as you young bucks. Would you rather me call it *weed?* Or pot?"

"Young bucks?"

"That's right."

Bobbi crossed her arms over her chest and narrowed her eyes. "How old do you think I am?"

"Oh," he laughed boisterously. "*Hell* no. I am not falling for that trap, Miss Cross."

"Come on. I won't get mad."

He shook his head. "No, ma'am."

"Alright, I'll do you first."

He almost choked on his hash brown. "Okay..."

She rubbed her palms together. "You're thirty... eight. And based on your tightass vernacular and choice of occupation, I'm guessing you've never smoked *pot,* and have always been pretty straight-laced. And based on how many times you've called me *ma'am* and *Miss Cross,* I'm assuming you were raised by a strong woman who you respected very much."

"Alright, fine." He looked at her with a glint in his eye. "You're twenty... five. Based on your humor about my tightass vernacular, I'm guessing you've taken a few puffs off the cheeba—"

She tipped her head back and laughed loudly at this.

Quinn continued, "And based on the twinkle in your green eyes every time I've called you ma'am and Miss Cross, I think you like it. Lastly, I don't think you think you're as badass as you come off, Miss Cross."

Her laugh and grin quickly dried up, so he quit while he was ahead.

"Turn here." Bobbi pointed to another trail, then said,

"Okay... my *thirtieth* birthday is tomorrow night, so thanks for that compliment."

So she wasn't too much younger than him, after all. Or, not in the *creepy-old-man* zone, at least.

"And everything else?" He asked.

"No cheeba for me. My former special ops Marine brother would have my hide."

"Former special ops, huh?"

"Yes, very mean, former special ops Marine."

Note to self. "And the rest?" He asked as he glanced at her.

"I'll tell you the rest when you tell me more about you."

"Okay. Fine." His truck hit a hole and bottomed out. He cringed, then said, "You hit the nail on the head. I'm exactly thirty-eight. Good to know the wrinkles have set in. And being a cop makes you straight-laced, well, most people, anyway. Lastly, you're right. I had a strong, solid woman who had my utmost respect."

"Not your mom," she said intuitively.

"My grandma." His tone had shifted. He didn't want to talk about how his mom walked out on them, disowning them when his brother started getting in trouble.

"You're not close to your mom."

Quinn shook his head. "Uh-uh, not till you open up to me first, Miss Cross."

Bobbi pointed ahead. "Park here."

"Yes, ma'am." He winked and edged between two budding oak trees.

Bobbi pushed out of the truck and they met at the hood. They were out in the middle of nowhere—nothing but miles and miles of dense forests. Miles and miles to search. Quinn focused on the sounds around him, the wind howling through the trees, the birds calling above them, the calming stillness that accompanied nature. The clouds had grown dark and brooding, blocking most of the light. The breeze swifter. Rain was definitely coming in.

They needed to get a move on.

"Hannah's house is about a mile west of here," Bobbi pointed. "Like I said, this road wraps around the mountain, with a few exits. And remember how we pulled onto it from the highway?"

Quinn nodded.

"Would be super easy for the killer to have pulled out and blended in with everyone else."

"You think he parked here?"

"It's possible," she said. "I don't think there's another clearing like this for a while. And considering Hannah's house is a straight line... worth checking for sure."

He surveyed the dirt. No viable tracks, no cigarettes, no beer cans or anything worth noting. He did a one-eighty noticing various small paths through the woods.

"How many people come out here?"

"A lot. Teenagers, hunters, and hikers in general. These paths lead to the main hiking trails."

A lot like his brother's place.

They really were looking for a needle in a haystack. Quinn glanced at the ominous cloud above. "Well, let's do what we can before the rain hits."

Bobbi nodded and they fell into step together, making their way through the darkening woods, taking the clearest path that led to Hannah's house.

The winds had picked up.

"Hannah didn't deserve this, Quinn." Bobbi's face was tight, jaw clenched.

"Of course she didn't. No woman does." Unfortunately,

he'd seen enough sexual assault crimes to last a lifetime. And, no, not a single woman deserved it.

A hawk swooped between the trees, seeking out its prey. A fitting move under the circumstances.

"Even if she was hanging out with someone like Kudrow." She paused. "I just don't want her name dragged through the mud. Those guys, Kudrow's whole crew, are a bunch of assholes. Wastes of society."

He wanted to check his cell to see what progress had been made on the warrant, but would rather keep her talking. More often than not, the small details that people didn't think mattered were the turning points in investigations.

"She was a good girl." Her voice wavered. "A *good* girl."

"We'll get him, Bobbi."

Quinn felt her staring at him as a moment dragged out.

"I believe that," she said.

"Until then, you—every woman—should be vigilant. More cautious than usual."

Bobbi nodded, then asked, "What made you become a cop?"

His shoulders tensed. Talking about his brother was not something he liked to do. He walked a few steps before answering.

"I saw how bad people can completely turn someone's life upside down. They prey on the weak. I didn't like it, and I didn't feel like anyone was doing much about it, so I stepped up." And, that was the truth. More or less.

He could feel by her gaze that she knew there was more to the story.

"How long have you been in law enforcement?"

How long ago was the day he found out his brother was addicted to heroin? "About ten years."

"Dallas, right?"

Quinn nodded. "Started out working the beat, then became a detective, then accepted the Lieutenant position there."

"I can definitely see the detective in you."

It's what made him a good cop. He knew that.

"You from Dallas?" It was more of a statement than a question.

"No, a town just outside... but somehow I think you already knew that."

She smiled. "A new guy in a small town is big news. To all the single women, anyway."

"Good to know. How long until this 'shiny new toy' phase wears off?"

"Until someone snags you up."

He laughed. "In that case, maybe I should get my sport coat dry cleaned."

"You own a sport coat?" Bobbi winked.

"First dates only... which is why it needs to be dry cleaned."

She laughed. "Normally I'd call bullshit, but you don't strike me as a ladies' man."

"Ouch."

"Because of the *sport coat*. No one wears a *sport coat* on a first date around here. Or since the fifties."

"Nothing wrong with a little wining and dining."

"That's true." She glanced at him, a glimmer in her eye. "For the first date, only?"

"That's right. Then it's microwave dinners, faded flannel, ripped boxers and mismatched socks."

"Thanks for the visual."

"Anytime. How about you?"

"When was my last first date? Well, lets see... there was

snow on the ground... and uh... let's see... what year was that?"

He laughed. "I meant, what made you become a business owner, but let's go with this. No dating for you? I'm definitely calling bullshit here."

"I might be a lot of things Quinn, but a bullshitter I am not."

"A nun, then?"

She did another one of her *tip-her-head-back-and-laugh* laughs. Warmth spread over him listening to it.

"They'da kicked me to the curb long ago."

"Lesbian, then?"

Her eyebrows shot up and she laughed. "Hate to disappoint, but no."

"Damn."

She rolled her eyes.

"Well, just in the short amount of time I've been in Berry Springs, it's obvious every man in town wouldn't mind taking you out on a date. I'd say you've still got the shiny new toy thing going for you. Since birth, probably."

"Gross." She deflected the veiled compliment.

"I didn't mean it like that, you sicko."

Bobbi looked down, clearly uncomfortable with compliments, then said, "Anyway, to answer your *intended* question, I started my yoga studio five years ago."

"No offense, but the whole yoga thing throws me with you."

"What? You picture me in a tobacco spitting contest instead?"

"Are you wearing a bikini?"

Another eye roll.

He laughed. "I'd kinda like to see that."

"With or without the bikini?"

"Oh, without. Definitely."

"I didn't mean..." Bobbi laughed. "I meant..." Her voice trailed off. Was she getting flustered? Was he able to throw Bobbi Cross off her game? *"Anyway,* I've always been drawn to yoga, especially in a nature setting. I stumbled onto it, actually. Started meditating during my hikes without really realizing I was meditating. I'd find a nice tree, sit down and listen to the nature around me. Close my eyes, focus on the sounds, the feeling of the wind against my skin. I'd breathe deeply. There's nothing to ease the mind like being in the middle of the woods."

"Amen." He wholeheartedly agreed.

"So, I started reading books about meditation and mindfulness—you know, being in the moment—and it just opened up a part of me that I felt like had been busting to get out." She laughed. "My dad and brother thought I was crazy. Military guys. And it's funny, if anyone needs more Zen in their lives, it's those guys." She glanced at him. "And law enforcement folks, too. I'm actually thinking about offering free yoga to you guys. Even thought about coming to the station to do it. It can change lives, you know."

The thought of Bobbi stretching and bending in skintight clothes in front of his colleagues sent a shockwave of possessiveness through him. Knocked him off balance a bit. Where the hell had that come from?

"Would you be interested?" She asked.

"I'm, uh, not very bendy."

"I'll bet given the right situation you are."

The unintended sexual innuendo dropped like a lead weight between them.

She cleared her throat. "Anyway, in an ironic twist, I also love to shoot. Dad taught me when I was young—I was shooting Folgers cans in the backyard with a BB gun by age five. After a few years running the studio, I guess I got the entrepreneurial itch. So, I filled a need in town and opened an indoor-outdoor shooting range."

"Fantastic facility. I hear it's doing really well."

"Glad that's the gossip, and yeah, it's keeping me busy. Especially with the yoga retreat I've got coming up. There's not enough hours in the day."

"For personal time."

Bobbi nodded, smiled. "Yeah, loop that into your dating question."

"I get it. Hard to find the time sometimes."

A few seconds passed.

"Yoga and guns." He looked at her. "I can honestly say that I have never met a woman like you in my life, Bobbi."

"Not sure if that's a good thing, or a bad thing."

Quinn stared at her, wanting to tell her that he thought it was a very good thing. Wanting to show her what a good thing he thought it was. She locked eyes with him, and an understanding of attraction flickered between them. And dammit if his stomach didn't do a little dance.

She tore her eyes away.

A few minutes passed in silence as they trudged through the woods, but he couldn't resist getting to know her more.

"You said your dad and brother thought you were nuts for getting into yoga. What about your mom?"

Her toe caught a branch and she stumbled. He grabbed her arm, steadied her. *Note to self, avoid all future mom questions.*

Bobbi shook it off and pushed forward. "She left when my brother and I were babies."

Sounded familiar. And the layers continue to peel off her.

"I get it."

Her head whipped to him. "You do?"

"Mom left my dad. But we were older. Teenagers. Being a baby must've been tough."

"Why'd she leave?"

"Wasn't the kind of woman to stick around when things got tough. Yours?"

"Another man. Or, that was the rumor anyway."

They walked a while without speaking, a silent understanding of the pain of abandonment.

A low rumble of thunder sounded in the distance.

"There's her house." Bobbi's voice perked up. "Hannah's. Right between those trees. See it?"

Quinn stopped and began scanning the area.

"We know he ran out the back door and then disappeared, right? And we're coming up on the side of the house, so maybe we need to walk south."

He nodded and they veered. "We also know he went back into the house before we came back to get your Jeep, so he probably walked all over. Look for fresh tracks."

Bobbi nodded. "Let's split off, then. You take south, I'll take north."

Quinn glanced up at the menacing clouds that were close to cutting loose. They didn't have much time.

"Holler if you see anything." Bobbi started to turn and he grabbed her arm. "Hey. Keep your eyes peeled. Head on a swivel, okay?"

They broke off.

He hadn't made it thirty feet when he heard, "Hey! *Quinn!*"

Quinn spun on his heel and jogged in the direction of her shout. Bobbi was squatted down behind a thick oak tree, staring at something on the ground.

"What'd you find?"

"Look, here."

Careful to stay out of her line of sight, he stepped around and squatted.

Bobbi pointed to multiple tiny holes in the ground. He squinted and leaned closer.

"What the hell is that?"

"Looks like little stab marks in the ground, right? And look here." She pointed. "Each stab is side by side. There's a little shuffle here, but for the most part, they're side by side."

"Yeah, I see..."

She looked at him wide-eyed. "These are high heels."

"High heels?"

"High-heeled shoes or boots. The stems punched into the damp ground. Someone wearing high heels was hanging out behind this tree."

Quinn frowned and looked at the holes again. He was no high-heel expert—not that there was anything wrong with that—but the holes did look like impressions from those tiny spike heels he'd seen at the club a few times.

"It doesn't appear to be recent, or today at least," he said.

"Last night?"

"Possibly. What was a woman doing hanging out in the woods?" He stood and looked around. "There's another... and another." Following his gut, he searched a wide circle around the little stab marks in the dirt. He stopped behind a bush, about seven feet behind the oak, narrowed his eyes and kneeled down. "I'll be a son of a bitch."

Bobbi stepped over and he pointed to the ground.

"Looks like another print from a five finger shoe, doesn't it? Faded, but, look, you can see the heel indent, and..." He leaned in even further. "Toe imprints."

"I see it." Bobbi's eyes widened. "Can you get a cast of this one?"

Quinn glanced up and smirked. "Well, *Detective* Cross—"

She cocked a brow. "I like that."

"Noted," he said as his thoughts wandered to dirty detective uniforms. He stood. "No, we couldn't get a cast from this one. Too faded. And I don't see any more."

"Me, either. So, wait... the killer was watching whoever was wearing the heels?"

It certainly appeared that way.

"Let's see where the heels go, then."

They followed the tracks through the woods until they faded into the driveway and disappeared into everything else that had treaded through Hannah's front yard.

Quinn stopped, tilted his head to the side. "What was your friend's name?"

"What friend?"

"The one that came here last night. Works at NAR News, I think."

Bobbi's eyes rounded. "Payton Chase... No *way*. Why the hell..." Her voice trailed off as the clouds opened up and a deluge dropped down on them.

14

*H*UNCHED OVER HER computer, Payton glanced over her shoulder one more time before clicking into the folder. She'd be fired in two seconds if her boss found out she'd hacked into someone's personal medical records.

Two. Seconds. Flat.

She glanced at the clock glowing above her boss's office —8:11 p.m. It had been raining cats and dogs since lunchtime and nothing sounded better than her flannel PJs and a glass of wine. Payton shifted her gaze to the dark windows. She'd better get going before the storms started back up, but rain or no rain, she had something important to do and time was of the essence.

She'd tried to get the files the honest way, slipping Maryanne Simpson at the hospital a fifty for a quick peek at the records. After promising a bottle of strawberry wine on top of that, Maryanne finally obliged and just as Payton had slipped around the desk, old man Clemens burst through the front door complaining of chest pains. Payton had been shooed away, with no one else to bribe.

But that wasn't going to stop her. Not much did.

Her pulse started to pick up and she glanced over her shoulder one more time before diving in.

The office was quiet, dark, with only a few lights on. Everyone was either home, eating dinner with their families, at Frank's drinking and laughing, or perhaps on a romantic date at Evening Shade Inn at the top of Summit Mountain.

Not her. No sir, not Payton Chase. Payton was working, as she always was, chasing her dream of becoming the lead evening news anchor. Her small circle of friends had faded away years ago—tends to happen when you never go out—around the time they started telling her she needed to work less. But the truth was, Payton loved to work. She'd grown up with a silver spoon in her mouth and with the isolation that came with that. She watched her gold-digging stepmother and stepmother's snotty friends focus their lives around material things, gossip, and rich men, and decided she never wanted to be like that. She was going to have her own career and never be dependent on money, or anyone for that matter, to make her happy.

Payton had inherited a few things from her father— money and her relentless drive and work ethic. What else had she inherited from him? She had no clue because she didn't even really know her father. He was never home during her childhood. His job took him all over the world, twelve months a year. Not that she cared. According to her stepmother, he had the emotional capacity of a rock. And as the lonely years went on, Payton worried she'd inherited that little personality trait from her dad, too—and it had manifested in an emotionless workaholic.

But, Payton didn't care. She loved the satisfaction that

working hard gave her. Loved the feeling of independence it gave her.

Yep, everyone else in Berry Springs was out celebrating the end of the day, but not her.

She heard shuffling from the hallway and froze. The red glow of the Exit light washed over the doorway that led into a darkened hall. Payton tried to shrink behind her cubicle, with no luck. The top of her head stuck out like a beacon. She had zero privacy, and zero opportunity to be snooping around in places she shouldn't.

The janitor stepped out of the shadows, pushing a cart full of supplies.

"Miss Chase..." His low, gravelly voice called out. "Go home."

Payton quickly minimized the screen and stood, not that she needed to, she could see him from over the top of her shoebox.

"Evening, Gerald. I'll go home as soon as you do." She winked. She learned long ago that a little wink and smile could get her far in this business.

He shook his head and waved a frail, thin arm. "But I wasn't here at five-thirty this morning, Miss Chase."

Well, he had her there. Payton got to work at five-thirty every day, after a full workout and healthy breakfast.

God, she was pathetic.

Gerald pushed his cart into an office while calling out, "I've got about twenty minutes left here, then I'm kicking you out with me."

"You got it."

She waited until he was completely out of sight and took another look around, before sinking back into her crooked, uncomfortable office chair, speckled with some very suspicious stains.

A line of concentration ran across Payton's forehead as she violated about a hundred privacy laws and clicked into the files of the man she thought possibly had something to do with Hannah's death.

She pictured his face in her head as she clicked through each attachment, and her stomach did a little dip. There was always something *off* about him. From the moment she'd met him, she'd gotten a weird vibe. A creepy vibe. Nothing she could put her finger on exactly, just a feeling, deep in her gut. She'd never forget watching the way he stared at Hannah from across the bar one night at Frank's, one of the few nights she'd gone out. The guy gave her the chills. The moment she'd heard the call about Hannah over the scanner, his name popped into her head. Why? Call it a woman's intuition.

Payton skimmed each file—nothing, nothing, nothing. Boring, boring.

Come on, there has to be something here.

Then, she hit the mother load. Payton lifted her finger off the mouse—a mental evaluation?

Holy shit.

She opened a restricted file and gaped at the reports from a mandated psychologist. She clicked on one.

Holy...

"Don't you have a life?"

She jumped out of her seat, her finger clicking the mouse rapid fire. Finally, the screen went blank. Payton turned and swallowed the basketball-sized lump her in her throat.

"*Geez*, Jax," a nervous giggle sounding like a tickle-me-Elmo-doll squeaked out of her. "You scared me."

Jax Timbow, NAR News sports anchor, crossed his arms over his chest with a suspicious look in his eyes.

Had he seen what she was doing?

"Don't you have anything else better to do?" Jax asked.

Better than breaking the law? Nope. She forced her shoulders to relax. "Not all of us are social pillars of society, Jax. And by social pillar, I mean regulars at Frank's. Don't they have a seat named after you or something?"

The twenty-six year old former baseball-star grinned. "You know, there's a whole world out there that you don't know about."

"I'm familiar with honky-tonk bars."

"I mean *fun*."

"*Hmm.*" Payton thoughtfully scratched her chin. "I'm not familiar with that word."

He laughed, a twinkle in his eyes. Jax was attractive, and close to her age, but for some reason she'd never looked at him as anything other than a cocky ladies' man.

"Besides," she continued with a hint of defensiveness in her voice. "I go to yoga."

"Oh, wow, you're so social that you go to a place where you don't say a word ninety-percent of the time. *Wow.*"

"We hang out after, sometimes." After the words came out, Payton realized it wasn't true. Bobbi, who she genuinely liked, had asked her to meet them for a drink several times, but she'd always said she needed to work.

"Come on." Jax said with his trademark cocky smirk. "Turn off that computer and I'll buy you a drink. Maybe I'll even show you some *fun*."

She cocked an eyebrow. "For some reason, I think you'll find some *fun* with or without me."

"You're probably right. But it would be good for you. People talk, you know."

"What do you mean, *people talk?*"

"You know," he cocked his hip onto her desk, sending

her water bottle teetering on its side. He didn't even notice. "There's more to being a journalist than sitting behind a computer."

"I know." Payton had done more stakeouts than she cared to admit.

"No, I don't mean hard-hitting crime investigation like you pretend to do." He laughed. She didn't. "I mean, *being a part of the community.* Don't you think people might actually open up to you more if they liked you? Knew you, even? When you go door to door with your investigative notebook—"

"Pretty sure it's just a notebook."

"Whatever. When you ask them questions to help solve whatever crime you've drummed up in your head, maybe they'd give you more than 'no comment' if they actually knew you."

"People do know me."

"Your family, but not you. Hell, you've spent half your life in private schools on the other side of the country."

Payton fought a cringe thinking of her family sending her away for an 'ivy league education' when she was so young. And, as much as she hated to admit it, Pretty Boy Jax had a point. She needed to intertwine with the locals again.

Feeling a bit disheveled now, Payton turned back to her computer. She'd let Jax get under her skin. Not cool.

"Well," she said, dismissing him. "I'm going to pass on all the fun tonight. Be careful out there."

Jax lingered behind her a moment in a way that had her watching his reflection on her monitor.

"Suit yourself, Chase."

Payton watched his silhouette disappear down the hall. Her shoulders sagged. What did he know anyway?

"Come on, Miss Chase. Time to get on home now."

"Alright, alright, Gerald."

Payton dragged the files to her thumb drive and watched the wheel turn on her screen as the files copied at snail speed. Gerald started slowly making his way to her postage stamp, eyeing her computer.

"Come on, come on," she whispered as she tapped her fingernail on the desk.

"What're you working so hard on anyway, dear?"

"Uh…" She felt her forehead begin to heat.

Download complete.

Phew! She ripped out the thumb drive. "Just catching up on some stuff."

"Shut 'er down. Let's go."

Payton shoved the drive into her purse and fell into step next to Gerald as they slowly made their way down the hall and out the front door.

Water dripped from the awnings, streetlights reflected in the puddles scattered across the parking lot. The smell of rain was heavy in the air.

"Night, Gerald."

"See you tomorrow."

"Hopefully," she said with a wink.

Payton walked across the lot to her BMW SUV, maneuvering between the puddles. The engine purred to life and she glanced at the clock. A drink sounded good. An ice-cold beer maybe, and *maybe* a lighthearted conversation with the locals who'd forgotten she'd even existed.

She bit her lip and tapped the steering wheel.

What the hell?

Payton reversed out of the lot, hung a right and as she headed into town, her thoughts drifted to the files sitting innocently in her thumb drive. More than a few things stood out to her. Definite red flags. Her gut had been correct.

But was it possible he'd really killed Hannah?

Maybe if she just did a little drive-by his house. Just to scope it out—for the third time since last night.

With thoughts of a social life long gone, Payton did a U-turn in the middle of the road and headed across town.

Maybe she was being ridiculous. Maybe she was way off. But bottom-line, an innocent woman had been murdered and she owed it to Hannah to follow her instinct. She just hoped she wouldn't become the laughing stock of town if she was wrong.

After a few turns through the woods, Payton slowed and craned her neck as she drove by the small, rundown house with molded siding.

A light was on.

What was he doing?

Probably normal stuff, Pay. Making dinner, watching television, reading. Or... her eyes narrowed...*murdering another young woman, perhaps?*

She rolled her eyes at herself. Maybe she should've been a detective. But really, a journalist wasn't too different from a detective. She just wished journalist got the same amount of respect.

She wondered which light was on—his bedroom, perhaps?

Hmmm.

Payton slowly rounded the corner, the house slipping just out of view, and her car just seemed to pull itself to the side of the road. The moonless night blanketed the woods in an inky black. Perfect for a little investigating. She glanced up at the sky, still holding off on its next deluge. Fate perhaps? An open door that she should just walk right through?

Yep.

She turned off the engine and after grabbing her binoculars and slipping her keys in her pocket, Payton quietly shut the door and slipped into the shallow line of trees that skirted the road. She hunkered down and jumped from tree to tree, wet earth and the sweet scent of budding flowers perfuming the air. Her high-heels sank into the mud with each step like a suction cup. Each leap was like removing her foot from quicksand and by the time she got to the back of the house, her quads burned. Maybe she'd just invented the next workout craze.

After glancing up and down the dirt road, Payton darted across the gravel into a field that skirted the house. *Geez*, if someone saw her, she'd have a free ride home courtesy of a black and white... if she wasn't shot with a twenty-two first.

Her heart raced as she jumped behind a tree, and took a moment to grab her breath. A gust of wind whipped her hair around her face.

Payton blinked, realizing she couldn't see more than a few feet in front of her.

Her stomach suddenly tickled with nerves. Maybe she shouldn't have gotten out of the car. The night was too dark for anyone to be lurking around in. She shuddered against the sudden drop in temperature.

A little warning bell went off in her head.

She shouldn't be out here.

Payton looked over her shoulder, knowing that there were miles of woods behind her, but she couldn't see a thing. It was like being dropped in the middle of the ocean at night.

Payton turned back to the house. Maybe just one quick look, then she'd head home. And then maybe drop this whole thing all together. She inhaled, straining to listen for any cars coming down the road that might see her car.

She was about twenty feet from the back door of his house. She'd be able to see into the windows if she could just get close enough.

Just then, a raindrop bounced off her nose. *Great.* Payton swiped her face and glanced over her shoulder again. When she turned back, the house had gone totally dark. The single light that was on had been turned off.

She frowned and pressed the binoculars to her eyes. Maybe he'd gone to bed...

Her heart stopped. Her entire body froze with instinct.

She felt the subtle movement of air right behind her.

He was here.

Her eyes rounded in terror a second before a blinding pain exploded in her skull.

15

SPRINKLES OF RAIN reflected like diamonds in Quinn's headlights as he drove up his driveway. Another round was about to hit. The cherry on top of an afternoon he'd spent in a constant state of damp. He glanced at the clock—8:54 p.m.

He needed a fucking shower. He needed food, sleep, and after spending a few hours with Bobbi Cross, he needed to get laid.

He immediately ticked the last need off the list, convincing himself that he just didn't have the energy tonight... nothing to do with the fact that he had zero prospects.

After he and Bobbi had gotten caught in the rainstorm while they were canvassing Hannah's yard earlier, Quinn had driven to NAR News headquarters off Main Street, to understand why Payton Chase had been lurking in the woods around Hannah's house—if it had been her, anyway. Unwilling to admit Payton might have been up to something sinister, Bobbi had come up with a few conclusions to their high-heeled peeping tom, including the interesting thought that perhaps Hannah's killer had been a woman. Far-fetched, but an angle to consider. In which case, Payton was a long shot at best. Or, maybe Hannah had been murdered by *two* people—the stilettoed mystery woman and the man Bobbi had seen running out. They'd also considered that the tracks could have been made by Hannah herself, although Bobbi couldn't remember a single time she'd seen Hannah wearing high heels. Regardless, they were both confident the tracks were made with a pair of heels.

Once inside NAR News, Quinn was told by some jacked-up dude named Jax that Payton was out working a story, and Jax promised he'd let her know Quinn had stopped by. Based on the protective and suspicious look on the kid's face, Quinn would bet his life savings that Payton would never get that message.

After that fruitless trip, he'd arrived late for Hannah's autopsy and was met with an annoyed glance from the prickly medical examiner who hadn't bothered to wait seven minutes until he showed. Did he expect Jessica to? No. He didn't tolerate people being late, and certainly didn't expect any special treatment. But, did he have no doubt that she would've waited for anyone else on the BSPD team? Absolutely. Berry Springs was a tight-knit community where red tape and boundaries were constantly crossed to help each other out, including in police investigations. He appreciated that, though, because red tape, bullshit policies, and political correctness were three of his least favorite things. And more often than not, they hampered investigations. But the well-meaning citizens sure as hell weren't about to help *him* out. He wondered how long it would take before the locals quit considering him an evil outsider.

After the jaw dropping autopsy, he'd gone to a few of the most popular clothing and shoe stores in the area asking if anyone had purchased a size ten five finger shoe within the last few years. Apparently, there'd been more than a few because this request was met with "you'll have to give me some time to pull that," to which he responded, "you have twenty-four hours." This made him less likable than he already was. He'd lucked out on his last stop and was printed out a list of buyers, which he immediately forwarded to Jonas.

Then, after giving an impromptu, but very necessary, statement to the press in front of Donny's Diner, it was back to the station to catch up on all the other crap he had to do. Unfortunately, Hannah Winchester wasn't the only homicide in Berry Springs.

He was officially beat.

Quinn rolled to a stop as his cell rang. Someone at the station was calling. The rain had picked up, sliding down his windshield in sheets. He groaned and glanced at his house wanting nothing more than an ice-cold beer in his hand instead of a ringing cell phone.

"Colson here."

"Colson, it's McCord."

Fantastic. He'd left the chief a voicemail about the autopsy and had expected a call. He'd expected the man to call an immediate meeting.

"What the hell do you mean Hannah's body was wiped clean?" McCord demanded. To the point.

"Hannah's body was wiped down with bleach, post mortem."

"Like, *laundry* bleach?"

"Exactly. With a washcloth, according to Jessica. If I had to guess, the same washcloth he used to open the back door as he was hightailing it out."

"Every inch of her?"

"Yep. Her hair was even soaked with it."

"Did you get the bottle?"

"It was destroyed with the rest of the house."

"Dammit. Okay, give me the Cliffs Notes of everything else."

Quinn took a quick breath and dove in. "Jessica determined the cause of death was blunt force trauma to the head, as we suspected. She estimates the object used was small, possibly a two-inch shaft or base."

"The candle holders."

"It's a good bet at this point. I already called the lab, they're working on it as we speak."

"Good."

"The penetration also happened post mortem."

"Sick son of a bitch."

"My thoughts exactly. And he wore a condom."

"What about the red marks between her legs?"

"Post mortem." He swore he heard the chief gag. "Guy was probably on a crazy adrenaline rush. Jessica said it looked like fingernails pierced Hannah's thighs from where he gripped her. I had both Hayes and Willard go through the outside trash for the second time looking for the condom. No luck finding that, or the washcloth used to wipe down the body."

"Two easy things to slip in a pocket. Or, he probably never even took off the condom until he got home."

"Agreed."

"So no DNA at all?"

"Nowhere on her body, inside her body, not under her nails, nowhere."

"What about the bedsheets? If he did remove the condom..."

Quinn glanced at the clock again. He should already

have those results. "I've got two voicemails in. Will keep following up." He closed his eyes feeling a twinge of a headache between his temples.

"Lots of DNA on sheets, Colson... hell, a piece of pube hair is a safe bet. What about her tox?"

"She had a significant amount of hydrocodone in her system, taken within the few hours before her death."

"Interesting."

"Yep. I spoke with Buckley already, he never wrote her a script and he checked with the other doctors, too—nothing. Jonas is going to check with the pharmacy."

"She could've bought them illegally."

"Right. Which is another tie-in with Kudrow here."

"Did you find any pills at the scene? In her purse? Car?"

"No." And that was odd. Legal, or illegal, they should have found the pills somewhere in her house.

"Okay, let me know where that rabbit hole takes you. We need to get this necrophiliac off the streets. Sick bastard. I want to throw the book at this guy."

"Where's the warrant to search Kudrow's place?"

"Just spoke with the judge. You'll have it first thing tomorrow morning."

He nodded in relief. McCord came through... a few hours later than Quinn would've liked but he came through, nonetheless.

"I'll be in late tomorrow morning then."

"Fine. Anything else?"

"Got a list of names from a few local shops that carry those five finger shoes. We're comparing that list with Hannah's social media and people who fit the height and weight estimates based on the size of the print." He cut off, not wanting to get into the high-heel prints they'd found in the woods, or that they could belong to Payton Chase. Not until he talked to her first.

"Saw your statement to the press. Damn vultures. They won't stop until we've got someone in cuffs. I want an update after you get to Kudrow's. And I want to sit in while you interview him."

"You got it."

"I want to find this fucker and close the book on it, Colson."

"No more than I do."

"See you tomorrow. Get some sleep."

"Will do."

Quinn blew out a breath. Sleep. Yeah right.

He yanked his keys from the ignition and jogged to the front door. He shook the rain out of his hair as he stepped inside. He'd never been so excited for a set of dry clothes in his life. He took a deep breath, inhaling the earthy scent of sawdust.

Home.

Quinn flicked a light and maneuvered through the stacks of lumber lying next to the entryway. The day he'd accepted a position with BSPD, he'd purchased the small rock cabin nestled deep in the woods, five country-road miles from his brother's house. He'd started the remodel the day he moved in, with plans to completely gut the place. It was two-bedroom, one-bathroom, with a small living room and even smaller kitchen. His favorite place was the large back porch that invited everything from deer to black bears to his doorstep. The property was surrounded by hiking trails and backed up to Shadow Creek—a fantastic spot to go fly-fishing, he learned.

That was his first big purchase in Berry Springs, his second came a week after he'd arrived. During an afternoon of hiking, he'd stumbled onto an even smaller log cabin for sale at the peak of the Summit Mountain, with a view of the surrounding mountains that he couldn't resist. He also couldn't resist the price tag, so he'd purchased it, with plans to fix it up and sell it, or perhaps move into it after. Or, give it to his brother if Landon's current landlord backed out of their deal. Owning two houses probably wasn't the best financial decision, but it wasn't like Quinn had a family to support. It also gave him plenty to do on weekends when everyone else was spending time with loved ones.

Quinn walked into the kitchen and yanked the fridge open. His stomach soured at the selection. He made a mental note to go grocery shopping, then shut the door and leaned against the counter. He eyed the whiskey bottle and thought of Bobbi.

What was she doing?

It was the same thought that had crept up a million times over the afternoon. A thought he'd pushed away, tried to ignore, but was as relentless as the look of determination in those bright green eyes.

God, she was beautiful.

After their journey through the woods, he'd realized he wasn't just attracted to her physically. There was more. Bobbi intrigued him, awoke something in him that had been hibernating for decades... or perhaps, something he'd never even felt before. No matter how much he tried to focus on finding Hannah's killer, he couldn't get Bobbi off his mind. Those eyes, those curves, those lips. The juxtaposition that was Bobbi Cross. Yoga, guns, and now, a seductive sorceress that had captivated his thoughts.

A sorceress he'd let seduce him any day of the week.

He felt a wave of heat over his skin, and growled with frustration. He pushed off the counter. He needed to release some energy, the pent-up anger, and the sexual frustration he'd been feeling over the last few hours.

After a quick change of clothes, Quinn made his way into the garage, a makeshift gym and tool shop. A space every man needed.

He set the classic rock to blaring and took to the weight bench. With every grunt, every bead of sweat, his mind began to clear. Quinn was on his last set when he heard the crunch of gravel outside. He sat up, wiped the sweat from his face and looked at the clock—9:17 p.m.

He turned off the music, walked into the house, and looked out the front window. A black and white. His heart sank as his thoughts immediately went to Landon.

In nothing but a pair of mesh shorts and Nikes, Quinn strode outside.

Hayes stepped out of the car with a forced smile. Of all the people—*Hayes.*

"Hey." He glanced at Quinn's chest. "I'd ask if I was interrupting something, but considering your chronic lack of female companionship—"

"What's going on?" Quinn cut in.

Hayes stepped onto the porch. "Just left my folks' house. They live at the base of the mountain and thought I'd swing by."

"At nine o'clock at night?" Quinn pushed open the front door, motioning Hayes inside. There was definitely something off about the kid's demeanor. Hayes wasn't his usual aloof *I-don't-care-you're-my-boss* self.

"Wow, it's really coming along in here." Hayes marveled at Quinn's mess of a remodel. Since he'd last seen it, Quinn had added a new mantle around the fireplace, stained the log beams on the ceiling, and slapped a fresh coat of paint on the slats in between.

"You didn't come here to check out my house, and you didn't come here to small talk." Quinn crossed his arms over his chest. "What's going on?"

Hayes shifted his weight and Quinn's body tensed from head-to-toe. Whatever it was, Hayes was nervous as hell about it. Whatever it was, it was big.

"You tasked me with lighting a fire under the crime lab's ass to get stuff pushed through..."

"Yeah..."

"Well, we got the first piece of evidence back."

"What?"

"The bedsheets."

Excitement mixed with the apprehension vibrating through his body.

"They found semen and were able to pull DNA from it."

Bingo. "Name?"

Hayes rubbed the back of his neck. "Look, I know we haven't exactly gotten off on the right foot... but I came here to tell you this because I believe there's some things that just need a certain amount of respect. Especially anything involving a fellow officer's family..."

"Give me the name, Hayes."

The officer looked at Quinn square in the eyes.

"Landon Colson."

16

*L*IGHTNING LIT THE sky as Quinn barreled down the dirt road clutching the steering wheel so tight his knuckles turned white.

What the FUCK?

Hayes had promised he'd had the lab triple check the results. There was no mistake. Hayes also promised he hadn't told anyone about the results, which had instantly earned Quinn's utmost respect. Regardless, Quinn knew it wouldn't be long until the chief found out.

His damn brother's DNA was found on the bed of a woman who was raped and murdered.

Christ.

His heart hammered, his mind racing with thoughts he'd never thought would ever enter his brain. He realized he didn't care if Landon did it. He was Landon's only family, and he'd die before watching his brother return to prison.

Maybe he could buy Landon a false identity and help his brother escape the country? Maybe they'd just skip town tonight and head to Mexico? He'd always liked the beach. Or maybe just take him somewhere where he could hide and live the rest of his life in the mountains somewhere.

After that string of thoughts, Quinn reminded himself that his brother probably didn't murder Hannah, and in which case, his life just took on an entirely new focus— proving his brother's innocence.

But he was no fool. He knew the system was corrupt, and even if someone didn't pin it on Landon, there'd be a witch hunt for him. Everyone would know soon, and everyone in Berry Springs would assume he did it—the ex-con outsider. The gossip would spread, the pressure would triple to find whoever killed Hannah. He and his brother would never be accepted in this small town.

He didn't give a fucking shit.

They'd move as soon as he proved his brother's innocence, or got thrown in jail himself for tampering with evidence to frame someone else. And if anyone stepped in his way or convicted his brother just to ease the gossip and prove to the hillbilly citizens that they were on top of things, well, they'd spend the rest of that night in the hospital.

He couldn't believe the thoughts that were running through him. And it was that moment he realized he'd do anything for his brother. *Anything.*

Hell, he'd kill for his little brother.

Quinn hit a pothole and his truck went airborne as he barreled into his brother's driveway. His heart froze— Landon's truck wasn't there.

Quinn slammed the brakes, shoved the truck into park and jumped out. Rain pounded his shoulders. The front door was locked so he used his key and barged inside. He flicked the lights and his stomach dropped. Three empty cans of Busch beer and a bottle of Wild Turkey sat on the coffee table.

His brother was drinking again.

He clenched his jaw so hard pain shot through his head as he checked the house. Not a single soul.

He knew exactly where the bastard had gone.

Five minutes later—a drive that should have taken him ten—he skidded to a stop behind his brother's beat up Chevy and had to fight from ramming into it.

Quinn left the truck running and burst through the front doors of Frank's Bar.

The bar fell silent as all eyes turned to him.

He didn't notice.

He zeroed in on the guy at the end of the bar nursing a beer with a baseball cap pulled low. The baseball cap he'd gotten for Landon when he took him to a Cowboy's game after he'd been released from prison.

Prison. The same fucking place he could end up in. *Again.*

Hands clenched in fists, Quinn stalked across the bar, emotions boiling like fire inside him.

As if sensing him, Landon turned and froze, his eyes slowly widening in shock—and a hint of terror.

Not a word was spoken as Quinn grabbed his brother by the shirt collar, pulled him off the chair, and dragged him into the rain outside.

The bar door slapped closed behind them. Thunder bellowed though the air. Landon didn't say a word, didn't argue, didn't fight. Although Quinn wasn't sure if it was because Landon had been caught drinking, or because he'd been caught murdering Hannah Winchester.

He spun Landon around and slammed his body up against the side of his truck. Based on the look in his brother's eyes, he was sporting a decent buzz but was far from belligerent. Well, that didn't make him feel any fucking better. Landon had started drinking again, after *everything.*

He had to stop himself from taking a punch.

"I can't even fucking look at you right now." Quinn seethed. "Get the fuck in my truck."

He watched his brother get in and then slid behind the wheel as an ounce of weight lifted off his shoulders. His brother was with him now, in his care. Safe.

He could handle this.

Quinn peeled out of the parking lot and headed up the mountain.

They didn't speak and Quinn took the time to try to calm his insane ass down.

After a few silent minutes, Quinn glanced over at his brother, staring out the side window. His expression was blank.

Goddammit.

"Inside. Now." Quinn snapped as they parked in front of Landon's house.

Quinn followed Landon to the front door, paying attention to every step, every wobble, the way his shoulders slumped forward.

Once inside, he slammed the door and pointed to the booze on the coffee table.

"What. *The fuck.* Is that?"

Landon shamefully looked down and blew out a breath, showing the first sign of emotion.

"Look at me." Quinn demanded.

His little brother's gaze met his and Quinn shut his mouth, his defenses crumbling as he looked into the pain screaming from Landon's eyes.

"She's dead." Landon said, his voice small, weak.

Hannah. Hannah was the mystery woman Landon had fallen for.

Quinn gritted his teeth and scrubbed his hands over his face, then took a deep breath. "I'm going to put on some coffee and you're going to talk."

He walked into the kitchen, scanning for more signs of liquor, or worse, drugs.

Landon slumped into a chair at the dining table and Quinn set the coffee to brew.

The pitter-patter of the rain hitting the window was the only sound in the room, the tension like a five thousand pound weight.

A minute ticked by. Finally, he walked over to his brother, kneeled down so he was face to face.

"I'm going to ask you a question, Landon. And you're going to tell me the truth. Do you understand?"

Landon nodded.

"The *truth,* Landon."

"Okay."

Quinn inhaled and had to force the words out, bracing himself for what the answer might be.

"Are you using again?"

Landon's eyes shot open. *"No."* He vehemently shook his head. "No, Quinn, brother, I swear to you."

The relief was almost as overwhelming as if he told him he didn't murder Hannah.

"But you started drinking again."

Landon glanced at the clock. "Exactly three hours and twenty-seven minutes ago. Yes."

"Why?" Frustration lit his veins. "After everything! *Shit,* Landon, you might as well walk back to prison yourself!" He surged to his feet. "Drinking leads to bad decisions, poor judgment... and you can't fucking afford that. What the *hell,* man?" Blood roared in his ears. He forced himself to shut up as he walked to the coffee pot, taking a silent deep breath as he poured two cups.

Quinn set one cup in front of his brother and leaned against the counter, holding his. He couldn't sit.

"Talk, Landon."

Landon sipped his coffee, closed his eyes, then took another sip. Finally, he started talking.

"That chair in the living room... You were right. I was making it for a girl. I was making it for Hannah." His brother paused, tears forming in his eyes. Landon took another sip. His hand was unsteady.

Quinn stared at his grieving brother. If it weren't for the rain outside, he'd probably be able to hear his own heart breaking.

"We met about a month ago."

"Where?"

"The furniture store. I was in there talking to the owner about my pieces, and she'd just bought a new coffee table. I helped her carry it out to her car, and we ended up talking for an hour in the parking lot." His shoulders slumped even more. "I was making the chair to match her coffee table."

Quinn knew that Landon didn't know he knew they'd been intimate, so he just let him talk, wondering if Landon was going to lie to him.

"We ended up exchanging numbers after I told her I made furniture, and one thing led to another."

"What, exactly?"

"I took her to Gino's for dinner. A date I guess." He looked up, as if he were embarrassed. "And then, a few days ago, she invited me over for dinner."

"A few days ago?"

Landon's watery eyes slitted with anger. "The day before yesterday, Quinn. The day before she was fucking killed."

Shit. Quinn almost wanted to laugh at the irony of the timing. He didn't know much about the forensics side of uncovering semen off a bedspread, but he assumed they could tell if it had been transferred recently.

Dammit. He set down his coffee and began pacing.

"And is that why you started drinking?"

Landon nodded, the shame evident. "When I heard she'd been murdered..."

"Where did you get the booze?" Not that it mattered, but he wondered if Landon had kept a secret stash somewhere.

"The liquor store at the bottom of the mountain. I kept my sunglasses on and everything."

Quinn stopped in his tracks. "Oh, great fucking work, Sherlock. The magic sunglasses were sure to blind the camera that recorded every inch of your uncovered face, your rusted red Chevy, license plate, and the name on your debit card... *dammit,* Landon." He shook his head and started pacing again. "How did you know she was killed?"

Landon heaved out a breath. "The whole town is talking about it. Heard it directly from my landlord. He came over to check on the house and told me as casually as if he was telling me what he'd had for breakfast." He shook his head. "I couldn't believe it."

"Where were you last night?"

"Here." Landon frowned. "Why?"

Apparently, Landon hadn't even considered he'd be a suspect.

"Did you go anywhere?" Quinn stopped pacing. *Please say yes, please say yes.*

"No, man. You know me, I never go out."

"Did you talk to anyone on the phone?"

"No..."

Fuck. Landon Colson's DNA was all over Hannah's sheets and he had no alibi for the night she was murdered.

Quinn looked out the window, his mind reeling. *Make a plan.*

"Okay, here's what we're going to do." Quinn began rubbing his hands together. "I was here last night, do you understand? For dinner. From... six to.... I left at seven-thirty, went to B's Bullseye to shoot some rounds before I went to work for the night."

It still didn't cover the estimated time of Hannah's murder, but it gave Landon an alibi for a portion of the evening. Someone to vouch for him. And if they could prove that perhaps the suspect had been watching Hannah beforehand, then he would be covered.

He continued, "Then, you went back to work on your furniture and didn't leave again, got it?"

"Dude, no one even knows I was there, Quinn. No one knows Hannah and I were hanging out. What're you freaking out about?"

Quinn dead-panned his brother.

Landon's eyes began to widen, his face began to pale. "Whoa. *Wait.* You don't think... you're not saying..."

"They found your semen in her bed, Landon."

Quinn watched the blood drain from his brother's face. Landon's hand shook as he set down his coffee.

"Did you kill her, Landon?"

No response as Landon stared at the table. His brother was paralyzed by shock as the realization of the consequences began to sink in.

"Did you kill her, brother?" Quinn repeated.

"No," the answer came out in a breathy whisper. "Jesus, Quinn, no."

"I didn't think so. But everyone else will." He walked over and squatted down in front of Landon, feeling like a father instead of a brother. A weird paternal instinct took him over.

"I'll handle all this, okay? Until then, I need you to lay low. They'll question you." A lump caught in his throat. He swallowed, feeling like a steel ball rolled down his insides. "But I'll be there. And you can do it, okay? Just tell them I was here for dinner. We'll go over it in detail. You'll be ready. Okay?" He paused. "And if they chase us out of town, so be it. Who gives a shit? We'll blow this hillbilly town and they'll never fucking find us."

Landon nodded but Quinn wasn't sure if anything was sinking in. He grabbed his brother's chin and in a tone as cold as ice said, "And if I ever catch you drinking again, Landon, so fucking help me God..."

17

*B*OBBI CLICKED ON her high beams as she drove through the mountains. The relentless rain pounded her Jeep, pooling on the sides of the road. Her journey home was taking double the time it should. She was tired—*exhausted*—hungry, and had a headache like a jack-hammer. The swelling around her stitches was at an all-time high, and now, various shades of green added to the purple bruising surrounding the bandage. Her face looked like a tie-dye lollipop. She felt like shit.

She'd spent longer than expected going through paper-work at the range after closing and now it was pushing ten o'clock and all she wanted was a glass of wine and a steaming hot bath. The bath to help her relax, and the wine to ease the thoughts of a certain lieutenant that had been racing through her stitched head all day.

It was ridiculous. *She* was ridiculous. Bobbi hadn't been so consumed by someone of the opposite sex since Benny Bucci had winked at her across the lunchroom in seventh grade.

And Benny Bucci had nothing on Quinn Colson.

After their trek through the woods, Bobbi had gone home and changed into dry clothes, then a trip to the resort to do a few things for the retreat, then to the range, where she'd struggled to focus the remainder of the day.

Quinn simply did it for her, in a way that no man had before. Was it the impossibly handsome face? Those dark, brooding eyes? That body that rivaled the cover of any romance novel? Or, was it that confidence, that gleam in his eye when he spoke to her?

It was the way her stomach dipped every time he looked at her.

Quinn Colson was a solid, strong, alpha male.

Quinn Colson could put Bobbi in her place, and that made her hot as hell.

Bobbi knew she was known around town as being a rough and tumble kind of gal. But what she hadn't known was that was exactly how every guy was going to treat her. She was never surprised with flowers, never wined and dined or held during a scary movie. The men around town didn't think she was that kind of chick. Bobbi Cross feminine? No way. Hell, she'd spent half of her last relationship teaching the guy how to shoot.

Yes, Bobbi was strong and independent, but she was a *woman*. And apparently, Quinn had already nailed her rather unstable emotional side, which no guy had done thus far. Bobbi wanted to be held, wanted to be treated softly, wanted to be taken care of emotionally. She didn't want men to be intimidated by her. She wanted to be swept off her feet, like any other woman.

She wanted to be saved.

Like Quinn had done twice already.

Bobbi needed a strong man in her life. If nothing else, Quinn had proven that to her.

She drove up the dark driveway to her house, noticing the lights that lined the driveway were off. Her brother had installed them as an extra security measure last year when someone from his past had threatened everyone he'd loved, including her.

She made a mental note to get them fixed first thing in the morning. She clicked her garage door opener, but it didn't budge.

What the hell?

Bobbi glanced up at the rain pouring from the black sky. Lightning must've taken out the electricity at some point during the afternoon.

Dammit.

She was taking a mental inventory of all the candles she had as she walked through the front door.

She froze instantly. The hair on the back of her neck stood up.

Before her eyes could adjust to the darkness, movement shifted beside her, followed by a *whoosh* of air. Fear shot like electricity through her and she ducked down, missing a blow to the head by a mere inch.

Holy. SHIT.

Bobbi lunged forward, buying a moment while her hand desperately searched her purse for the gun she always kept in the side pocket. The house was pitch-black. No moon-light through the windows tonight.

Two hands gripped her waist and she slipped belly-first to the ground, scrambling against the hardwood floor, her wet shoes squeaking against the silence.

Whoever this was, they meant business.

Survival-mode kicked in and she twisted onto her back kicking and swinging. Her shin connected between her attacker's legs, causing a painful exhale and a split-second of release. Bobbi pulled her legs to her stomach and kicked like a donkey, connecting again.

Her attacker stumbled back, and based on what sounded like a sack of potatoes hitting the floor, he'd tripped and gone down. Bobbi wildly searched for her purse as she scrambled up, but was blinded when a boot connected with her jaw. Pain exploded through her head. She'd be shocked if her stitches hadn't busted open. She fell back, hitting the wall.

The pain brought a fury of adrenaline. She was not going to die like this.

Her attacker was standing, so she stayed low, her hand searching for her purse. She had the darkness to her advantage—her finger felt the strap of her purse—and now she'd have a gun to her advantage. She threw her body toward the door as he jumped forward, missing her by an inch. She yanked the small Ruger from her bag, and while scrambling backward, took a shot.

And another.

The gunshots boomed through the silence, jarring her senses.

A body hit the wall.

Bobbi jumped up, gun aimed toward the sound. She wasn't sure if she'd hit him or stunned him.

A quick shuffle, then the front door flung open and she watched the silhouette of her attacker disappear into the darkness.

Rage clouded her common sense and she ran outside after him, gun up. This was her damn house. No one was going to attack her in her space. No one was going to violate her sanctuary, her peace, her safety.

Who the hell did this guy think he was?

Her boot hit a puddle and she slipped, throwing her off balance and pulling her back to reality.

Stop, Bobbi. Go back inside.

She sent a scowling glance in the direction he'd run and considered taking a few more shots.

Go back inside, Bobbi. Call the cops.

Chest heaving, Bobbi turned and limped back inside. Once she crossed the threshold, she fell to her knees, found her purse again and took out her cell phone.

The adrenaline was dissipating, her whole body throbbing in pain as she felt tears well in her eyes.

Someone had just freaking *attacked* her.

Bobbi sank to the floor and called the man who had saved her life twice already.

Quinn's phone lit on the coffee table. He didn't move. Didn't care. He glanced at his brother asleep on the couch. Not used to the booze, apparently.

That was good. He remembered a time before Landon had gone to prison, his brother would drink from the moment he woke up to the moment he passed out, and could still function.

Not now.

The fire Quinn had started was going full speed, crackling and hissing against the silence. The lights in the house were off.

He watched the call come and go, the bright light eventually turning off. It was sometime past ten, and it if were work, that usually meant some sort of emergency. Another dead body, perhaps? He didn't give a damn. He probably wasn't going to be around much longer, anyway.

The phone lit again, this time with a text message.

Quinn frowned, something in his gut telling him to check it. Even then, another minute passed as he stared at the spotlight shining from the coffee table, contemplating.

Dammit.

He leaned forward, keeping an eye on his brother, and grabbed the cell from the table.

Quinn shot to his feet, his heart lodging in his throat. His head spun to look at his brother, then back to the phone, then back to his brother.

Shit!

He quickly covered Landon with a blanket, did a quick scan of the house to make sure the doors and windows were locked, then bolted out the front door. Quinn jumped into his truck and barreled down the driveway. Rocks kicked up from his tires as he spun around a tight corner on the dirt road.

Someone had attacked Bobbi.

His pulse pounded. He called her back—no answer.

If she could call and text, she was at least conscious and able. He kept telling himself that as he fishtailed his way down the dirt roads that snaked around the mountain.

As Quinn neared Bobbi's house, he looked for anyone lurking in the woods or any sign of a vehicle.

He took a left onto her driveway. The first thing he noticed was the darkness. Not a single light on in the house. Not good. Quinn skidded to a stop, sprinted across the driveway and burst through the front door. He zeroed in on the lighted cell phone illuminating a flushed, panic-stricken beautiful face. Bobbi was on the floor, knees pulled to her chest in a way that reminded him of a child. He fell to his knees next to her.

She'd been crying.

"Are you okay?" Quinn frantically looked her over, freezing on the red bump on her jaw. She'd been knocked around. Anger flashed like fire through him.

Bobbi nodded, obviously shaken.

"Bobbi, I need to know if you're hurt." He angled himself in front of her.

"No, I'm not hurt." Her voice was weak. "He got me in the jaw, but that's it."

He wasn't sure he believed her, so he looked her over again. When he was confident she didn't need immediate medical attention, he put his hand on her knee. "Tell me what happened."

Bobbi took a shaky breath and told him the story as they sat in the dark, on the hardwood of her entryway.

"It was the same guy, I'm sure of it," she said.

"What makes you so sure?"

"My gut." Her eyes dared him to challenge her. "It was like I recognized him from the other night. The height, weight, even the way he ran. Everything was the same."

A cold-blooded, raping, murdering necrophiliac was now after Bobbi Cross. The thought sent his blood boiling.

"And you don't know if you shot him?"

"No."

He needed to search for blood, but he couldn't see a thing. Hopefully she'd hit the son of a bitch and they'd have a name within twelve hours.

"Can you stand?" Quinn held out his hands.

"Yes."

Bobbi gripped him and he guided her to her feet. "He must've cut the electricity."

"Where's the box?"

"Laundry room, down the hall, to the right."

"Stay here, I'll get the lights back on. You've got your gun?"

"Yes."

"I'll be right back." Using his cell phone as light, Quinn walked down the hall, hyper aware of everything around him. He shined the light as he walked. The hallway was parallel to an open, airy floorplan with a cozy living room and massive fireplace, a large stone kitchen and dining room. He'd never seen so many plants and flowers in a house before. Family pictures hung along the hallway—her father in military uniform, standing next to a very mean-looking brother. That picture hung beside a framed target with the center blown out. He had no doubt Bobbi was the one to destroy that bullseye. No pictures of her mother, or friends, he noted.

Quinn walked into the laundry, which was a total mess. It made him smirk—not perfect. He grabbed a clothespin, and using the tip so not to smear potential fingerprints, he flicked the breaker and the house buzzed and beeped to life.

When he walked back to the entryway, Bobbi was nose to nose with a bullet hole in the wall.

"Here's one, and there's the other. I freakin' missed. Both shells are on the ground, there."

She turned to him, the light washing over her face—*holy shit.* Everything else immediately took a backseat to the mess that was Bobbi's face.

"Come here." Quinn gently took her hand although fury was tensing every muscle in his body. The fucker had hurt her—*bad.* Killed an innocent woman and hurt another.

But he knew this woman. He cared about this one. A lot.

Quinn led Bobbi to the kitchen and eased her onto the stool.

"Where's your first aid kit?"

"Under the sink." She didn't fight him. She must be a little loopy.

He poured her a glass of water and grabbed the kit. After handing her the drink, Quinn pulled out his cell phone, dialed the station and requested all available units. They needed to scan the entire house for prints, and quite possibly take Bobbi in for an X-Ray.

She chugged the water. "Thank you."

Quinn carefully turned her chin to the side. He could practically see the boot print on her skin. Half her face was going to be bruised, from her forehead to her neck. And that was on top of the gnarly bruising from her other wound.

"Do you taste blood?"

"No."

"Can you open your mouth all the way?"

He lightly pressed his finger to her jaw joint. She winced in pain but smoothly opened and closed her mouth.

"Go as wide as you can."

She did it again. Her jaw definitely wasn't broken or dislocated, but Quinn had been punched enough to know that it hurt like a bitch.

"I need to check your stitches."

"You read my mind."

Quinn peeled back the bandage and his heart broke at how strong Bobbi was forcing herself to be. It made him even angrier inside. She did not deserve this.

The bandage pulled away, and luck was on their side— the stitches were still intact. He grabbed a cotton ball and dabbed a bit of blood away.

"It needs to air out. You okay if we leave this thing off?" He asked, referring to the bandage.

Bobbi blinked and looked up at him blankly, as if suddenly not registering a word that was coming out of his mouth. She stood, crossed the living room and checked the door that led out to a patio. Then, she disappeared down the opposite hallway.

He followed her and watched as she checked the door to the garage. "Don't touch anything, Bobbi."

Bobbi turned, eyes narrowed. "He had a key, Quinn. All three doors were locked. I had to unlock the front door to get in, so he must've locked it back so he could be ready as soon as he heard me." Her eyes rounded. "Oh, my God. How long had he been here, I wonder? Did he go through my stuff? Take anything? I have to..." she tried to step past him but he grabbed her arm.

"Take a deep breath, Bobbi. You can look around, but don't touch anything, okay? Your entire house is a crime scene."

Just then, headlights from outside bounced off the walls.

Quinn's hand instinctively slid to his gun as he walked to the front door. "It's Hayes."

He opened the door as the young officer jogged across the driveway, his face tight with concern.

"You think it's the same guy?" Hayes asked as he stepped inside.

"Bobbi seems to think so." Quinn quickly rehashed Bobbi's story while she interjected several times.

"We need to look for prints in the house, and boot prints outside. Plenty of mud out there."

"Which direction did he run?"

"Southeast, into the woods." Bobbi said.

"This dude's got to be a local. He slips away far too easily in these woods. Knows where to park..."

"I agree." Quinn said.

"Willard's on his way, too."

"Good." His gaze lingered on Hayes's for a moment.

In an unspoken understanding, Hayes shook his head—
No, no one knows about Landon's DNA... yet.

Thank God. He needed to deal with one catastrophe at a time.

He turned to Bobbi. "Why don't you wait in the kitchen..."

She shot him a *yeah-right* look. "I'm going to look around. I'll know if something's out of place quicker than you guys will."

Quinn noticed Hayes's eyes lingering on her beaten face.

Yeah, she looked like she'd been to hell and back, and it made him sick to his stomach.

Two hours later, Quinn watched as Hayes's and Willard's patrol cars disappeared down the driveway. He turned to see Bobbi standing in the living room, her back to him, gazing out the sweeping windows. He walked over to her, his footsteps loud against the silence.

"Not a damn thing," she shook her head and muttered.

"Nothing in the house, but we got prints outside. Looks like the same size. We'll get him, Bobbi."

He put his hand on her shoulders and she turned, her green eyes pinning him.

"Soon, Quinn. I want this guy caught soon."

She had no idea how badly he wanted this guy caught. For his brother, for her.

Quinn swept a piece of hair behind her ear, his finger lingering on the bruise forming along her jaw. He looked into her eyes, so bright and full of emotion. His heart gave a little kick. Before he could catch himself, he leaned down and kissed her.

Every sensor in Quinn's body exploded with fireworks. She tasted warm and sweet. Her tongue met his and he wrapped his arms around her, devouring the full pink lips he'd been fantasizing about all day.

She kissed perfectly.

Powerless against her, his hands caressed her back, sliding down as if they had a mind of their own.

Bobbi released a soft groan, then pulled away from his mouth, tucked her head into his chest and pressed her body against his. He held her tightly, her little body molding into his, and rested his chin on the top of her head. He was sure she could hear his heart pounding in his chest.

"You can't stay here tonight, you know." He whispered.

She remained nestled against him for a moment, then stepped away.

"I'm not letting anyone chase me out of my house, Quinn."

"Whoever did this has a key to your house. You said it yourself." He glanced at the clock. "And no locksmith is coming out here right now."

Anger flashed in her eyes. Stubbornness. She didn't like to be handled, that much was obvious.

"Fine." Bobbi exhaled deeply. "I can go to my brother's or dad's house. They're both gone—"

He took a step forward. "You're not staying alone."

She looked at him, so small and vulnerable.

"Get a bag packed. I have a place we can go."

18

*I*T WAS JUST past one o'clock in the morning by the time Quinn and Bobbi pulled up to his cabin at the peak of Summit Mountain. The rain had stopped. Temporary flashes of moonlight shone between the clouds that were shifting east. The cabin sat on a cliff, spotlighted under the moon beams, nestled in the middle of the forest. The closest house was a half-mile away, only reachable by dirt road. It was the perfect place to get lost... or hide.

He'd made a quick stop at his brother's house first to check on him—Bobbi hadn't asked why and he appreciated that. Landon was still asleep on the couch, where Quinn imagined he'd remain until morning. He threw another log on the fire and left a note for Landon to call him immediately when he woke. He probably wouldn't, but Quinn would stop by again first thing in the morning.

He parked by the front porch and cut the engine.

"Where are we?" Bobbi asked, barely visible in the passenger seat.

"My side project."

She looked out the window. "I don't think I've ever stayed in a *side project* before."

The corner of his lip curled up. He pushed out of the truck and met her at the passenger door.

"I bought it recently. I have a real house, down the mountain." He took the bag from her hands. "I'm planning to fix this up and either sell it, or move into it. No one knows I own it, or would even assume you'd be with me. You're safe here."

Quinn led Bobbi up the walkway to the wraparound porch. The eerie silence of nighttime in the middle of nowhere engulfed them. Not a critter scurrying around, not a bird swooping overhead, just the occasional drop of rain and light breeze through the trees.

A cloud drifted and moonlight washed over the mountain.

"Wow," Bobbi said as she looked at the view.

"Just wait..."

Quinn unlocked the thick door and they stepped inside.

The moonlight was just enough to illuminate the tiny one-bedroom, one-bathroom cabin. He had a couch, a bed, a few chairs, a rug, and that was about it. Lumber and tools speckled the floor. Unfazed by the mess, Quinn watched Bobbi walk to the floor-to-ceiling windows, soaking in the way the light outlined her curvy body.

"Oh, my... Quinn. *This view...*" she said almost breathlessly.

It *was* beautiful. Bobbi Cross standing in front of moon-light-blanketed mountain peaks—absolutely beautiful. She opened the door that led to the deck.

Quinn followed her.

Bobbi gripped the railing, took a deep breath and closed her eyes. She seemed to be having a moment, so he stood next to her, not so close to intrude, but close enough to let her know he was there.

Finally her eyes opened. "Mind if I sit out here a minute?"

"Not at all." The fact that she liked his place had him swelling with pride. "I'll get a fire going. I don't have the electricity turned on, but we've got running water."

It didn't faze her. Good.

He wanted to kiss her again, to hold her and tell her everything was going to be okay, but he didn't feel like that was what she needed at that moment. She needed to be alone, to process what had happened. He left her standing on the porch and went inside to get a fire going.

The fire was roaring by the time Bobbi walked back inside.

"No electricity, but you've got the water going, you said?"

"Yep. I come out here a lot to work. Sometimes stay the night. Can do without electricity, but not water."

Bobbi kneeled down in front of the fire, next to Quinn. They watched the flickering flames in silence for a moment.

"You're single, then?"

The question caught him off guard. "Yes."

She nodded, keeping her gaze on the fire. She wanted to make sure she wasn't intruding on another woman's space. Didn't want to cause problems for him.

"You?" He asked.

"Yes."

Okay, so they got that out of the way quicker than he'd anticipated. It also opened the door for something he'd been thinking about on the drive over.

Quinn grabbed a flannel blanket from the couch and wrapped it around her shoulders.

"I'll be right back."

He walked into the kitchen and opened the cooler where he kept a stash of food. The cupboards weren't an option, not only because they were a mess, but he didn't want to come home to a black bear rooting through his house.

Quinn frowned at the selection, then grabbed a Snickers bar and a white candle from the countertop. Candle lit, he shoved it in the middle of the candy bar.

He twisted his lips as he looked down at it. Unimpressive, at best. It was going to have to do.

Quinn turned and hesitated at the second cooler. *Hell yeah,* he thought, then yanked out two Coronas.

Legs crossed at her side, Bobbi sat gazing into the fire.

He sat down next to her and raised the paper plate.

"Happy birthday."

Bobbi's eyes flashed as she looked at the candy bar. A slow smile spread across her face—a full blown ear-to-ear grin—and he couldn't fight his in return.

She looked at him, eyes bright with excitement. "I totally forgot. We're one hour into my thirtieth birthday." She took the plate, still smiling. "Thank you," then she laughed. "Wow, getting my ass kicked and turning thirty... what an evening."

"Some say thirties are your best years. Make a wish."

Quinn watched her close her eyes, smile, then blow out the candle. He liked seeing her happy. More than that, he liked that he was the source of it.

She looked at him. "Are yours your best years?"

He gazed into her eyes, reached up, and lightly ran his finger down her cheek. "It's looking up."

Bobbi smiled, then looked down, her cheeks flushing. The smile only lasted a minute before her face dropped and turned to darkness again.

"Quinn, we've got to find this guy."

He put his arm around her and pulled her close. He thought of his brother and clenched his jaw. "I will. I'll find him."

With that promise, she snuggled in the little crevice between his arm and chest and he stroked her hair until she fell asleep.

~

Quinn tiptoed into the bedroom where he'd carried Bobbi sometime after three in the morning. She'd fallen asleep in his arms and he'd held her for hours while his mind drifted from fantasies about ripping her clothes off, to what it would be like to have an actual relationship with her, then to thoughts of his brother, and finally, to thoughts of murder. He'd put her in bed, took his place on the couch, and forced himself to sleep.

His heart squeezed as he looked down at her, her black hair tangled around the pillow, the blankets hugging her curvy body.

A thin beam of sunlight cut through the curtains, sparkling on her face.

She was the most stunning woman he'd ever seen in his life. Bruises and all. Edges and all. He wanted her to continue sleeping and keep the angelic, relaxed expression on her face. He wanted to keep her safe. He wanted to keep her in his arms.

Quinn quietly tugged the curtain closed. The room went dark. After taking one last look at the woman who was making him unsteady, he left a note on the kitchen counter and slipped out the front door.

6:57 a.m.

He wanted to drive straight to his brother's house, but

needed to check on something first. He'd heard that Jessica Heathrow was a workaholic who rarely slept. He was about to find out if that was true.

Quinn rolled into town, glancing suspiciously at every car that passed as if they were the person who murdered Hannah Winchester and attacked Bobbi. His stomach was knotted and bags puffed his bloodshot eyes—a hangover from the stress of the day before.

He took a deep breath. Nothing good came from desperation, and desperate to find the bastard was exactly what he was feeling.

Quinn whipped into a drive-through coffee stand, then pulled into a small parking lot next to a sign that read *County Coroner*. A new, blacked-out Tahoe was parked by the front door, sporting a Rosie the Riveter bumper sticker that said *Made in the Ozarks*.

He'd bet a year's salary that the vehicle belonged to Jessica.

Quinn rapped on the door, waited a beat, then rapped again. He pressed the doorbell, then knocked again. Finally the door swung open.

He lifted a cup of steaming coffee.

The redhead eyed him skeptically, a look that he was used to by now.

"What kind?" Jessica said, blocking the doorway.

"Well, usually I'd go with a skim milk, no sugar, no foam cappuccino for a woman, but you don't seem like the average gal, so I got Grande mocha, extra shot of espresso, extra chocolate drizzle. And sprinkles."

She cocked a brow, then snatched the coffee from his hand. *Victory.*

Jessica stepped back and opened the door wide. That

was as much of a hello as he was going to get and that was good enough for him.

The front room was an office, the lab was the entire back half of the building. He glanced through the window at the blonde on a silver table under a blinding fluorescent light. Her intestines lay next to her body, beside bloody tools. It was Hannah.

His stomach soured, and he refocused on Jessica who was staring at him with narrowed eyes. She sipped slowly, allowing the silence to drag out.

Quinn nodded to the lab. "I thought you completed the autopsy yesterday."

"I did, but just wanted to take a look at a few more things."

"Such as?"

"If anything changes from my official report, I'll let you know, Lieutenant. Now, what brings you to my office at seven in the morning?"

"You said the suspect wore a condom, right?"

"Didn't you read the report?"

He arched a brow. Her attitude had nothing on his mood and he wasn't afraid to show it.

She huffed out a breath. "That's right. He wore a condom."

"And you tested for DNA inside her, anyway?"

"Of course."

"Nothing?"

"No."

This blew his hopes that maybe the suspect's condom had broken, but it also confirmed that his brother must've used a condom as well, otherwise Jessica would have found his DNA inside of Hannah. And he guessed Landon must've removed it immediately after, spreading his damn DNA on the sheets.

"What about around the area... did you check her inner thighs..." The suspect had to have gotten some trace of himself *somewhere*.

"Lieutenant,—"

"Quinn."

"Quinn, I don't mess around with rape victims. I searched her entire body. As I said, her skin was wiped down with bleach, but that's not necessarily a failsafe. Bleach definitely can kill DNA, but not all of it, and not all the time. The thing bleach did for this guy was remove fingerprints and skin cells from her body."

Then, he wiped down the door handles.

"So," he said, "two options: our suspect never removed the condom at the scene, or maybe he did and possibly semen got onto the bed..." He hesitated, eyeing her. By her blank expression he assumed she hadn't heard that the crime lab had found his brother's semen on the sheets... yet.

He continued, "How solid is pulling a DNA profile from bed sheets?"

"I work with dead bodies not bed sheets, you know that."

"I also know that you worked at the crime lab before becoming a medical examiner."

Jessica cocked an eyebrow, then sighed. "Well, there's a lot of factors at play with that scenario. If the sheets had been washed the semen would still be traceable, but—"

"Wait. Semen can be detected after washing?"

"Oh, absolutely. Not only can it still be detected, the semen could have transferred to whatever other items it was washed with. It takes several washes in hot water for semen on clothes, or sheets, to fade to an undetectable level." She grinned. "Don't worry, a woman can't get pregnant from semen on sheets."

"Good thing." Quinn said, ignoring her shot at him. Jessica had no idea how long it'd been since he'd been in any woman's sheets, let alone leaving DNA behind. "How do they pull the DNA from the sheets?"

"Again, it's very situation specific, but first, they'd use a special light to determine if it is some sort of bodily fluid. If so, they determine what kind of fluid it is through certain dye tests that confirm that its either saliva, urine, or semen. Once they determine that it's semen, they look for the highest concentration of sperm under a microscope, and from there, they can trace the DNA inside the sperm."

"Okay, so, then what? They read the DNA, but how do they connect it to an actual person? Wouldn't they need a sample for comparison to pull a name?"

"Not necessarily. If the dude's DNA is in CODIS, the national database, then they can get a potential match."

Quinn's gut clenched.

As if reading his thoughts, she said, "So, if our boy's in prison, or an ex-con, his DNA profile would be in the system already." She eyed him for a minute.

"You said they get a *potential* match?"

"That's right. CODIS doesn't store whole DNA sequence data. Only a portion of the person's DNA. So, if there was a hit, it would not be conclusive, but obviously worth pursuing a full DNA comparison."

So, they'd need a sample of Landon's DNA to officially make him a suspect.

Jessica continued, "If the suspect was unwilling to offer a sample, they could go a few routes, including a warrant or the controversial dig into the person's ancestry. Maybe get a sample from a brother, or something, which can indefinitely link back to the suspect."

She paused again and her eyes said it all—Jessica knew about Landon.

She continued, "Several cold cases have been solved that way recently. Anyway, if they get the control sample from the suspect, and compare that to the DNA from the bed sheet sperm, that's when they'd get a solid yes or no."

"Let's say—hypothetically—it is a 'yes.' Can they determine how old the sperm was?"

"You mean, to prove that the sperm was not left on the sheets during an act of sexual assault or rape, perhaps? To prove that the person who smeared their shit all over the sheets was not the same person who raped and murdered the woman?"

Quinn wanted to make a snide remark to her cold, heartless tone, but the truth was, he was hanging onto her every word. The woman could've spit in his face and he wouldn't have moved until she answered his question.

Jessica took a long sip of coffee, eyeing him over the rim, then finally said, "No, Quinn, they cannot determine the exact time the sperm was ejaculated. Only if it was recent, or not. And my advice to you is this: get your brother a damn good lawyer."

19

*B*OBBI OPENED HER eyes to an unfamiliar room. Panic zinged through her—where the hell was she?

She sat up and looked around.

Quinn's cabin.

The pain registered.

Holy crap.

Bobbi ran her finger along the bump on the side of her face as the memories of being attacked the evening before came screaming back like a freight train to the face. But then, her heart gave a little flutter as the second biggest memory came to life.

The kiss.

Shit, he'd kissed her. They'd *kissed.*

And it was H-O-T.

Her finger trailed to her lips and she couldn't fight the soft smile that crossed her face... and that's when she realized it.

She was *toast.*

A goner. A schoolgirl with a crush the size of Texas.

Her stomach tickled with nerves.

Bobbi had been physically attracted to Quinn the moment she saw him in the woods months earlier, but now, over the last few days she'd become emotionally attracted to him. The snickers birthday cake being the cherry on top. And now, the kiss... the fireworks.

Dammit. She had it *bad.*

Bobbi looked at the empty space next to her. The blankets weren't ruffled and the pillow was gone. Quinn had slept on the couch.

A gentleman.

The sound of birds chirping outside her window made Bobbi realize how silent the house was. She glanced at the clock—7:11 a.m.

Frowning, she pushed the covers back.

Where was Quinn?

Bobbi swung her legs over and slid into the flip-flops he'd laid next to the bed. She walked into the living room. The early morning light streaming in through the windows warmed the room. The smell of freshly burned wood hung in the air, reminding her of their moment in front of the fireplace. She looked past the deck at the picturesque view. A light fog danced around the mountains, bright rays of orange, yellow, and pink shooting out from the peaks. What she would give to wake up to that every day.

Bobbi glanced out the front door—no truck. No Quinn.

After double checking the locks, she walked to the kitchen where a loaded pistol sat next to a battery-powered coffee pot, along with all the fixings to make a cup, and a bottle of ibuprofen. She picked up the handwritten note.

Good morning, beautiful. The ibuprofen is for the pain, coffee is for your morning meditation on the deck, and the gun is for any bastard who comes snooping around. I'll be back later. Will see what I can do about electricity. -Quinn

She smiled and shook her head. Yep, she was a goner.

Bobbi set the coffee to brew, then walked to the bathroom.

Her jaw dropped in pure terror as she looked back at her reflection in the mirror. She didn't recognize herself. It was jarring. The entire left side of her face was swollen and bruised. Tiny red scabs speckled the purple shading where the force of the guy's boot had broken her skin. Her black hair was a knotted mess, the color comparable to the circles under her red-rimmed eyes. She slowly opened and closed her mouth, wincing at the pain.

As she stared at herself, one thing became certain— whoever attacked her had meant to kill her.

The coffee pot beeped, pulling her out of the horrifying thought. Bobbi padded back to the kitchen, the peaceful happiness she'd felt moments earlier long gone. Frowning, she poured a cup and leaned against the counter.

Who had done this to her? Was it the same guy who killed Hannah?

It *had* to be. Way too much of a coincidence. But why?

Her gut told her it was because the guy likely thought she'd gotten a good look at his face. Or, maybe it was because she was helping with Hannah's investigation... which made her wonder if she was being watched? The thought was unsettling.

Bobbi slid the pistol closer and took a sip of coffee. The gun was bigger and meaner than the one she had hidden in her purse. Either Quinn was playing dumb—he knew she carried—or he left the gun for her as added protection. Probably the latter. This thing could put down a grizzly bear.

She sipped again and looked outside where the sun was just beginning to peek over the mountain, shining like a spotlight on the deck. It was a perfect place to meditate.

Although, maybe this morning, she'd do it with one eye open.

~

Payton opened her eyes and a wave of nausea washed over her. She gagged, then panicked as she realized *she* was gagged. Her eyes flew open, the blurry space around her coming in and out in waves.

A cotton gag was wrapped around her head, cutting into the sides of her mouth. She lay on a floor, bound by the ankles and wrists. A carpeted floor, so she must be in a house.

The last thing Payton remembered was being hit on the head—then nothing.

He had her.

Panic sped through her veins, and a cold sweat beaded down her back. Hannah's killer had her.

She was next.

Payton's eyes darted around the small room. Not a stitch of furniture. Beige walls, and... she craned her neck, one small window behind a ratted cream-colored curtain. The air was chilly, too, and musty she noted. She strained to listen, but heard nothing but silence.

Her heart started racing.

Payton bucked onto her back, eyeing the window. She'd have to somehow stand up, which was going to be tough, then find something to cut her binds. After that, she could jump out.

She wiggled her toes, her feet, trying to loosen the binds.

Footsteps sounded outside the room.

Payton froze and closed her eyes, pretending to be unconscious. The door opened and the footsteps stopped.

Her heart thudded in her ears.

"Waking up, huh?"

Her eyes shot open at the recognition of the voice. She was right. It *was* him.

The bastard tapped a baseball bat against the palm of his hand.

Payton tried to talk, but only a gurgle escaped the gag. She would not show fear. Not to this lying bastard.

He stared back at her, his lips pressed into a thin line.

"I had no choice, Payton. I saw you in the woods outside of Hannah's that night. You started sticking your nose around in my business. I know about the medical records."

Maryanne.

He continued, "I *loved* Hannah. But she *made* me do it. She... was unwilling." He enunciated the word with venom, his face distorting with anger. "She screamed so loud. So loud." His gaze slowly slid down the curves of Payton's body. Something flashed in his eyes. Something wild, feral. Desire.

Her stomach rolled. *Oh my God, no.* She'd rather be killed than raped. Tears threatened to sting her eyes but she blinked them away.

He released a throaty moan and leaned the baseball bat against the wall, keeping his eyes on hers. A sick, evil smile cracked his face as he dropped a hand to the bulge between his legs.

Sheer terror gripped her so tightly she felt like her chest was going to cave in.

He stared at her as he rubbed himself through his jeans.

A flush slowly worked its way up his neck. Payton tore her eyes away, and couldn't fight the tears any longer.

He slowly crossed the dim room, his boots stopping inches from her face.

"I had no choice..." His voice was gruff, hungry. "But that doesn't mean it can't be fun this time."

Tears rolled down her face. *No...* she began sobbing. *No, no, no.*

She heard the zipper of his pants. She squeezed her eyes shut.

"Keep your eyes open," he demanded.

When she didn't, he sent a boot into her side with such force she thought she was going to throw up.

"Open your eyes!" He screamed.

Her whole body quivered as she forced her eyes open. He folded his swollen erection out of his pants and stood above her, slowly stroking.

The smell of him made her want to vomit.

He groaned, stroking harder. Then, he lowered to his knees, an inch from her face.

Tears ran down her neck.

He grabbed her hair, yanked her forward and rubbed himself on her face. She felt the hair rip from her scalp as he smeared the wetness of his tip on her cheek. She bit down on the gag with such force she thought she cracked a tooth.

He shoved her back to the floor, pulled a pair of scissors out of his back pocket.

Payton wept like a little girl and squeezed her eyes shut, knowing that whether she made it out of there alive, or not, her life was about to change forever.

20

Q UINN SKIDDED AROUND the corner that led to the station. After his visit with Jessica, he'd gone straight to his brother's house. Landon's truck was there, but he wasn't. And Quinn knew exactly where he'd been taken.

He slid into a parking spot and sprinted across the lot. He burst through the front door.

"Morning Lieu..." Behind the front desk, Janice's eyes widened and her voice trailed off. She quickly buzzed open the door.

His gaze skittered around the bullpen, and for the first time he looked at the station as an enemy, not a place where he wanted to dedicate his life. A few heads bobbed up from behind the tiny cubicles, then sank back down as he strode past.

Quinn breezed past low voices in McCord's office and stopped at Interview Room One.

His heart sank.

He gritted his teeth and walked through the door. His

brother's face lit the moment he saw him. He was alone in the room.

"Who picked you up," Quinn fumed. He didn't have time or patience for *how-are-yous.*

"McCord and some kid."

"Willard or Hayes?"

"Willard."

"Have they officially interviewed you yet?"

Landon avoided eye contact. Quinn's heart raced like an addict on speed. He slammed his palms down on the table and leaned in.

"Landon, have they interviewed you?"

Landon slowly nodded, the fear in his eyes palpable as he looked up.

"*Shit,*" Quinn straightened. "Why the fuck didn't you call me?"

"They didn't let me. They freakin' woke me up," Landon said, showing a spark of anger. "Told me I needed to come in for questioning and before I knew it, they were guiding me into the back of a police car."

Quinn's gaze darted to his brother's wrists. They hadn't cuffed him, and that was a good thing because he didn't know what he'd have done if they had. He might've spent the afternoon in a cage in the back.

"I didn't know what the fuck to do, man."

The desperation in his brother's face made Quinn's fury double. He'd seen that expression before—the first time he visited Landon in prison. Landon was terrified, and rightly so.

"I told them I needed to call you and they said I could when I got here, but then they shuffled me in here and started asking questions."

Quinn looked at the recorder on the table. *Shit.*

"Have they had someone take your blood?"

Landon's brow furrowed. "No."

"Do *not* agree to a DNA test, do you understand?"

"Why? Quinn, I didn't do it!"

"Because, Landon," Frustration had him pacing. "They can't determine the exact time the semen was transferred..." Quinn ripped the cord out of the recorder. "You had sex with her the night *before* she was killed, right?"

Landon nodded. "Where're you going with this?"

"The lab can only determine that the semen was left *recently,* which means there's no way to prove that it didn't happen when Hannah was raped and murdered. But the good news is that the current sample they have isn't conclusive enough to hold up in court. That's why you can't submit to a test right now."

It'll match, and his brother will be screwed. He knew that McCord would push for a court ordered DNA test, but that would take some time. And it better be enough time to find the real bastard who killed Hannah and attacked Bobbi.

Quinn lowered his voice. "Did you stick with our story?" Just then—

"Lieutenant." A tone of warning in McCord's deep voice sounded from the doorway.

Quinn kept his gaze locked on Landon as if he didn't hear the chief. He raised his eyebrows, questioning—*did you stick to the fucking story?*

Landon gave a subtle, quick nod—*yeah, I stuck to the story.*

Quinn inhaled quickly with relief, nodded back, then turned to the doorway.

"I need to see you in my office." McCord's arms crossed tightly over his chest.

Quinn narrowed his eyes and it took every bit of

strength not to pummel the balding, overweight chief. McCord was his boss yesterday, his enemy today.

He turned back to his brother. "Don't say another word."

Landon nodded and Quinn followed McCord down the hall, his heart a steady pounding in his chest. He turned into the office, locked eyes with Willard and pinned him with a fiery gaze that had the young officer shifting in his seat. Quinn's jaw clenched as he stared him down. Bastard should've called or texted him to let him know they were on their way to his freakin' brother's house.

The smell of Old Spice had him looking at the other man sitting in the room—Larry Buchanan, the fucking assistant district attorney.

McCord walked around his desk, but stayed standing, eyeing Quinn, knowing he was a loose cannon.

"Quinn, you know Mr. Buchanan. Larry, Lieutenant Quinn Colson."

He'd only met the attorney a few times but knew they'd work together in the future, which meant he should establish a decent relationship. But not today.

Quinn nodded at the ADA, then turned back to the chief. "Why wasn't I called?"

"It was before your shift started." McCord answered coolly.

"It's my *brother*," he seethed back, then shot another look of death to Willard, who was avoiding eye contact.

"You don't have enough to hold him, McCord."

"I've got his DNA at the scene of a homicide. I've got more than enough to hold him."

"Because he's an ex-con."

McCord eyebrow's tipped. "Yes, Quinn. You know how this works."

Quinn flexed his fingers and had to stop himself from pacing the small room. "I was with him Sunday night."

"That's what he said. But unfortunately, not while Miss Winchester was murdered. You were at the shooting range."

"Right, but he was settling in for the night when I left. He didn't go back out. The kid's a hermit, McCord." The adrenaline burst and he slammed his fists on the desk. "He didn't *fucking* do it, McCord!"

Willard shot to his feet. Ready to take him down? Quinn shot him a look over his shoulder that warned if he touched him, he'd be in a cast by the end of the day. Buchanan remained sitting as if he'd seen this a million times. He probably had.

McCord's gaze leveled on his. "I didn't say that, but the facts are the facts, and we have a job to do."

"You're wasting your time with him while the real killer is out there. Laughing at us."

"Even if he didn't do it, the fact is that Landon had a recent sexual relationship with the victim. If nothing else, questioning him might help us uncover more details and give us more insight into her life."

Yeah fucking right. "So, that's why Buchanan is here, then?" He asked sarcastically.

"This thing's already grown legs, Lieutenant. I'm doing my job," Buchanan said.

"He's just here asking questions. Relax." This from McCord.

Quinn pushed off the desk and ran his fingers through his hair. He looked at Willard, then at Buchanan—the team that could take his brother down.

He needed a lawyer. *Fast.*

"What about Chad Kudrow?" Quinn asked. "He had a recent relationship with the vic, too. Why isn't he here?"

"His DNA wasn't found at the scene."

"Her damn bath towel is sitting in his damn dumpster. Did you get the warrant?"

McCord nodded, glancing at his computer. "Just came through. Hayes should be on his way there, now. And, we don't know if it's hers yet."

He needed to get his hands on that towel. Quinn started to turn, but McCord stopped him.

"Lieutenant, considering the conflict of interest, you need to step back from this case."

Quinn froze, snorted. "My brother's being held for questioning for first degree murder. You really think I'm going to sit this one out?"

"I'm not asking, Colson."

"Landon will not agree to a DNA test right now, so don't even ask. I've also advised him not to say another word until he has a lawyer present."

McCord shook his head, frustrated.

Yeah, that's right, Chief, I'm doing everything officers hate during an investigation—stalling the hell out of it.

"Who's Mr. Colson's lawyer?"

"You'll see," he said as he strode out of the room. But the truth was, he had no fucking idea.

Five minutes later, Quinn pushed through the glass doors of Donny's Diner.

"Howdy, Lieutenant." Mrs. Booth glanced up from the cash register. The waitress's gray hair was pulled back in a bun with her signature yellow number two pencil. Her apron was starched and bleach-white, ready for another day filled with coffee, grits, and gossip. The legendary waitress hadn't warmed to him yet, but he'd heard she was a walking Berry Springs history book, knowing everything about everyone in town. Past and present. So he'd better get on her good side.

"Morning," he said as he strode past the bar.

"Sit where you'd like," she said with a hint of annoyance in her voice.

Quinn ignored the side-long glances from the locals as he passed by the red leather booths. Screw this small town.

He slid into the booth where Hayes was scrolling on his phone with a plate the size of a hubcap in front of him.

"Hayes."

The officer looked up, surprised. "Morning, Lieutenant."

Quinn stared at the young officer for a moment. "I want to thank you for your discretion about my brother. I might not know small-town politics but you should know that I repay my debts, and I owe you one. A big one. No matter what—right or wrong—I've got your back. You need something, you call me."

Hayes's eyes slightly rounded as he nodded. A relationship formed.

"Good. No more of that girly bullshit. Now, why aren't you at Kudrow's?"

"Did we get the warrant?"

McCord hadn't even told him yet. Which meant he also hadn't told Hayes that Quinn had been pulled from the case.

"Yep, it just came through." Quinn glanced at the half-eaten platter of pancakes, sausage, fried eggs, grits, and toast. "You ready?"

"Well, I..." Hayes eyed him suspiciously. "They picked up your brother, didn't they?"

Quinn nodded.

Hayes looked down at his breakfast. "Then, yep, I'm done I guess."

Quinn slapped a twenty on the table.

234 | AMANDA MCKINNEY

"How'd you know I was here?"

"It's eight o'clock in the morning. Everyone in town is here." And, he'd seen his truck outside.

Hayes laughed. "See? You're learning the ropes already." They stepped outside. "Just a few more years until everyone quits eyeing you like a rattlesnake."

If he was still there.

They jumped into Hayes's extended cab truck.

"Who's the best lawyer in town?" Quinn asked.

"Ah, that'd be Clara White. Crazy smart and a bulldog in the courtroom. We all have a great relationship with her. She's been around for decades. Other than that, there's ol' Boris Hempstead, but, uh, let's just say that mansion of his wasn't built on an honest man's paycheck."

"He's crooked?"

"Takes bribes. That's the rumor."

"Why haven't you arrested him? That's corruption."

"Can't pin it."

"Just like you can't pin Kudrow's drug business on him? By the way, maybe if you had, Hannah Winchester wouldn't be dead."

Hayes sat silent a moment. "Lieutenant—"

"Quinn."

"Quinn, we're stretched thin as is, and when tourist season hits, we're all working our asses off. We can't go after everything, especially when an initial investigation shows nothing nefarious."

Quinn heaved out a breath and glanced out the window. He knew small-town officers wore a hundred different hats and usually didn't get the resources they needed. He just never expected it to impact him personally.

"Clara and Boris must be busy, then. Who else?"

"That's it."

Quinn shook his head and rolled his eyes. Two options to save his brother from death row. Well, that was going to have to work because he didn't have time to look for anyone else. He needed someone now... more like an hour ago.

"Does she have an office in town?"

"Right down the road."

"Swing by first, then we'll hit Kudrow's."

"You got it." Hayes glanced at him. "They lock your brother up?"

His fists clenched on his thighs. "They're questioning him now, but they'll hold him for at least forty-eight hours."

"I'm sorry, man."

"He didn't do it."

Hayes nodded, then turned into a small building just off Main Street where a woman with a slicked-back ponytail and power suit was stepping out of a Lexus.

"That's her."

After ten minutes, a hefty retainer, and a promise that he'd have someone patrol her house at least once a day— apparently being the best lawyer in a small town didn't keep you from getting death threats—Quinn got his brother the "best lawyer in town."

As he walked out of her office, a blacked-out truck pulled up behind Hayes. Quinn's hand went to his gun.

"Hold on there, hot shot." Hayes hollered out the window. "That's Jonas. Relax. I called him to deal with the electronics at Kudrow's. Assuming you want all that copied, of course."

Quinn watched Jonas get out of his expensive truck and wink at Clara—who winked back. He cocked a brow and made a mental note to add Jonas to the list of Clara's patrollers, and maybe even conduct an occasional drop in.

"Hello, ladies." Jonas slid in the backseat of Hayes's truck, never looking up from the cell phone in his hand.

"Hey, princess."

"Where're we going?"

"Chad Kudrow's."

Jonas snickered. "My pleasure to raid that asshole's place." He shifted his attention to Quinn. "Sorry about your brother, man."

"Is he in a cage?" Quinn asked.

"Yeah. But I gave him a protein bar."

"Oh, well, that makes everything better."

"What kind of protein bar?" Hayes asked.

"Blueberry."

Hayes wrinkled his nose. "Gross. Should've given him strawberry."

"Hey, I like blueberry. Has a nice tart to it."

"Tart?"

"Yeah. You should be familiar with tart tasting biscuits."

"Leave Eve out of this."

Quinn scrolled through his phone, trying to ignore the tit-for-tat.

Hayes continued, cocking his head to the side. "Tart, as in, agreeably sharp on the tongue? Or a cream filled pastry? Because if we're talking about delicious cream filling...."

Jesus. "Enough kids, what are you guys, eight?"

"Sorry." Jonas grinned. "Anyway, I also gave him a pack of habanero flavored peanuts. So he should be good."

Why Jonas thought vending-machine snacks made everything better, Quinn had no idea.

"Way to give a recovering addict a snack reserved for happy hour," Hayes said. "I hope you gave him a water, at least."

"Nope."

"You gave the man a tart blueberry protein bar and habanero peanuts and didn't give him anything to wash it down? Might as well handed the guy a razor blade."

Quinn looked up from his phone, leveling Hayes with a single look, then glanced in the rearview mirror at Jonas. "Did McCord press him to submit a DNA test?"

"Not sure."

Hayes pulled into the gravel parking lot of Kudrow's garage and Quinn noted the same black low-rider as when he'd dropped in the day before. Interesting.

"Keep your head on a swivel, guys."

Hayes looked at Quinn. "This ain't my first rodeo with Chad, Quinn. And my head is always on a swivel."

Quinn cocked an eyebrow. He liked the kid's spunk, and the fact that he stood up to authority.

"Mine's only on a swivel when I'm enjoying a cream filled tart." Jonas quipped from the backseat. "And it's not my first rodeo with this guy either," he said with a wink, flexing his fingers in the backseat.

Quinn got down to business. "I'm going to go straight to the dumpster for that towel," he said as he slid on a latex glove and pulled an evidence bag from the back. "Hayes you go talk to Kudrow, then search the place. Ask him again what he did Sunday night. Jonas, I'm going to want everything—his entire computer on a hard drive, emails, bank accounts checked, everything. And everything cross referenced with Hannah's."

Jonas nodded, and after checking their guns they got out.

Quinn scanned the woods surrounding the garage as he walked up to the dumpster. Kudrow had tossed in two more bags of trash since yesterday.

Great.

He hadn't been dumpster diving in over a year and he didn't miss it. He rolled up his sleeves, gripped the sides, and hurled himself over.

Quinn picked his way through the moldy bags of fast food, empty beer cans, plastic bottles, and a few very suspicious looking small aluminum foil trays. He narrowed his eyes and leaned closer, noticing the burned edges. Heroin. Unfortunately, he was all too familiar with every way heroin could be smoked.

Fucking heroin.

He shot a look at the garage. Kudrow wasn't some small-town drug dealer peddling pot. He was dealing heroin. At that moment, Quinn made a promise to himself that he was going to get the kid off the streets, with or without charging him for Hannah's murder.

He carefully placed the pans in an evidence bag and kept digging. More cans, more nasty-ass food, and finally he found the blue paisley-print towel. He looked it over for the obvious—blood, bodily fluids—but saw nothing. He tucked it into a bag, and just as he was about to jump out, his phone rang.

"Colson."

"Lieutenant, this is Ellen from dispatch. We've got a report of a missing woman."

"Who?"

"Payton Chase from NAR News."

21

*I*T WAS JUST past seven-thirty in the evening by the time Quinn pulled up to the cabin. He noticed a dim light on in the kitchen. Apparently, Carl at Carl's Electric had come through and got the power turned on—the only positive in a shit-filled day. He grabbed the bag of takeout from the passenger seat and walked to the porch. His feet, his back, everything seemed to ache with each step.

As he walked inside, he was met with silence and a tickle of panic slid up his spine. His gaze darted around the house, landing on movement on the deck outside.

Rays of dusk speared out of gray clouds like spotlights over Bobbi's body, her curves outlined by a background of soaring mountains. His tired eyes widened as he stepped across the living room, watching her.

With her long, dark hair knotted in a messy bun on top of her head, Bobbi wore black leggings and one of those little-to-the-imagination tank tops. She was inverted, head down, on a bright orange yoga mat, one bare foot in the air, the other firmly planted on the ground. His eyes soaked in the tight curves of her ass as she switched positions, fluidly as if she were in water. Her breasts rose and fell with each breath, with each movement, as she moved through some sort of yoga routine.

Like a siren, her movements called out to him, hypnotizing him as he stood frozen watching her through the window. It was like some erotic dance, and before he knew it, he had a full-blown erection in his pants.

She turned, met his gaze, and a soft smile crossed her lips.

He smiled automatically, then concentrated on calming the raging hard-on between his legs as he stepped outside.

"Hi," her smile widened, excitement to see him in her eyes.

God, what he would do to come home to that every day.

"Hi, there. You put on quite a show."

A breeze tousled the strands of hair that had fallen around her face, still horribly bruised, and still stunningly beautiful. He wanted to kiss her. Right there, on the deck, under the trees and setting sun.

"Thank you for getting the electricity going."

"Figured it would help with your imprisonment." As the words slipped out, his gut clenched. *Prison. His brother.*

She must've noticed the instant change in his demeanor because her face fell. "What's going on?"

Quinn walked to the railing and looked out at the mountains. "It's been a long day."

"By the tone of your voice, I'm assuming that doesn't mean you caught the bad guy."

He inhaled deeply and shook his head.

"Sounds like we need a beer to go with this conversation."

Bobbi disappeared and came back with two ice-cold

longnecks. He was officially in love. He took a long sip, then rested his elbows on the rail.

Bobbi hiked a hip onto it and looked at him. "Tell me," she said softly.

"They pulled my brother in for questioning... about Hannah's murder."

"What?"

For some reason, her shock made him feel better. Like she understood. Like she automatically knew Landon didn't do it, which was crazy because she didn't even know him. He wanted to say it was insane that they considered him a suspect, but in his gut, he understood. Hell, he'd have done the same thing.

She placed her hand on his arm as he launched into the story.

It felt good to talk about it. To talk to *someone* about it. As the words tumbled out, he realized he didn't have a single person in his life to talk to about *things*. Bobbi listened, giving him her undivided attention as he unloaded his anger and frustration on her and bared his whole damn heart.

"I'm so sorry," she said when he'd finished.

Quinn nodded, grinding his teeth. "I'll find this fucker and get Landon out. I'll get it done."

"I know you will. How long will it take for them to test the towel you found in Kudrow's dumpster?"

"It better be done tomorrow morning." And it would be. If he had to drive to the crime lab himself, it would be.

He glanced through the house at his truck in the driveway, already planning out his morning for the next day.

Bobbi noticed. "Look, if I weren't here, you'd be still at the station working the case. I know that. I don't need to be babysat, Quinn, I can just go home..."

He turned fully toward her. "There's something else, Bobbi."

She stilled at the tone in his voice.

"Payton Chase is missing."

Her mouth dropped.

"I spent the afternoon at her house, her office, and speaking with her friends and family. Last someone had heard from her was around eight last night—the janitor at NAR News and a reporter named Jax. She was at the office, getting some work done and said she was going home after. Know him?"

"Jax, the sports guy?"

"Yeah."

Bobbi frowned, then shook her head. "No, not personally." She pushed off the rail and began pacing. "*Shit,* Quinn. We freaking know she was lurking around Hannah's house and that someone had been watching her from behind a tree. It's *him.* The same guy who killed Hannah and tried to kill me. We're stupid to think he doesn't have her. Have you tracked her cell?"

"Her last location bounced off a local tower, but that's all we know. It's turned off now. Best we can tell she left work, and disappeared. It didn't appear that she made it home."

"Can't you turn the cell back on, or something? Remotely?"

Jonas had already tried, a hundred times. "We think the SIM card's been removed."

She stared at him. "So that's not good, then."

"No."

"What about her car? Anyone seen it?"

"No, but the plates and description have been passed around the station. Everyone knows to keep an eye out for it."

"What about Kudrow?"

Something flashed in her eyes—the same spark of something every time she said his name. What was she holding back from him? Had she dated the asshole?

"He has a legitimate alibi for last night. He was at some hole-in-the-wall bar until midnight, then on camera getting gas, then took two girls home with him, both have vouched."

"They could be lying."

"I had someone check their cells, too. Both girls sent multiple texts throughout the night from his house. Sure, he could've left them there and snuck out to go kidnap Payton, but it's not likely. I've put together a search party with the local SAR team, K-9 trackers, and a handful of volunteers to search the woods around her house at first light tomorrow morning. Jonas is going to monitor her social media, email, and keep checking her phone through the night."

"What about putting it on the news? Plastering her photo all over?"

"It hasn't even been twenty-four hours, yet. If nothing comes through tonight, we'll do that tomorrow."

Bobbi took a swig of beer, her mind racing. "It's connected."

"Of course it is."

"For whatever reason, Payton was watching Hannah's house, and the bad guy knew it. She got too close."

"That's what my gut's telling me too, and, Bobbi," he took a step forward. "You got too close, too. You actually saw the guy, and you've been helping with the investigation. That's why you were attacked. This guy doesn't want to get caught and will do anything in his power to prevent it from happening."

"Even kill."

Quinn slowly nodded, ran a finger down her bare arm.

Goosebumps prickled her skin. "Which is why I don't want you to leave here."

Her green eyes slowly searched his face. In a small voice, she said, "I don't want to leave, either."

Their eyes locked and it was the moment they both acknowledged something big was happening between them. More than just a kiss.

Something stirred deep inside him.

Bobbi tore her gaze away and blushed. He stroked her hair. Yes, something was happening between them, and dammit if it didn't make him feel excited as hell. She took a small step back, and he took that as a sign—too much. She was overwhelmed. Everything was just too much.

He dropped his hand. "I brought food."

Her face gleamed like a kid on Christmas morning. "I'm starving."

"Sorry there's no room service in this palace."

Bobbi laughed and he slid a hand on her lower back as she walked inside. Damn, she felt good.

Two beers and two bags of Mexican food later, Quinn worked on getting a fire started as Bobbi kneeled next to him handing him kindling.

"I think that'll do it."

He wiped his hands on his pants, and sat back, next to Bobbi.

The sun had set, the woods were dark. The glow of the fire danced across her face. Her bruising was at an all-time high, but she was still sexy as hell to him. More so, as if the marks were a badge of honor that showed her strength. His gaze scanned each one, anger beginning to bubble up. Yes, Bobbi was tough, and yeah, she could take her hits, but he'd die before he let another man lay a finger on her again.

Her lips pressed tightly together, a line of worry running across her forehead.

"I'm worried about Payton, Quinn." She bit her lip. "First Hannah, now Payton..."

He nodded, his thoughts turning to his brother.

She sniffed and he noticed tears in her eyes.

"You remember when you asked me if I liked being called ma'am, and Miss?" She stared into the fire.

He scooted closer to her, laser-focused on every word, movement, breath. He hated to see her cry.

"Yes, I remember." He hadn't forgotten a single second of that walk in the woods.

"I do like it. I like it when you say it. I like the way it sounds when it comes out of your mouth. I like the way it makes me feel; like you're the type of man to respect and honor a woman."

A tear rolled down her face, and he swept it away, then kissed her cheek.

Bobbi continued, keeping her gaze on the fire. "And remember when you said I wasn't as strong as everyone thinks I am?" She looked at him now. "I'm not. I'm a mess inside, Quinn." The tears rolled down her cheeks. "And tonight..." her chin quivered. "I'm *scared*. I'm crushed about Hannah and I'm scared for Payton, and I'm scared what will happen if this guy isn't caught."

"Bobbi..." Quinn whispered as he stroked her arm, wanting to pick her up and curl her into his lap.

"I'm scared," she interrupted and said again, as if it felt good to admit it. She looked at him, emotions pouring from her eyes. "And I want you to keep me safe tonight."

His heart skittered, breaking at the vulnerability she was showing him. Her guard was down. She'd stripped herself bare for him.

Quinn wiped the tears from her cheeks and cupped her face in his hands. "I will not let anything happen to you, Bobbi Cross."

He had two people to save now.... His brother, and the woman who was slowly stealing his heart.

With that thought, he leaned forward and kissed her.

She inhaled deeply and wrapped her arms around his neck, pulling him to her as if she'd been waiting for that kiss her whole life.

A shiver swept over his skin, a frantic desire, a need to have her that suddenly outweighed all else.

Bobbi melted into his kiss. Her head swam, her limbs felt shaky. She gave in, totally and completely to him. She'd shown him her vulnerable side, and now she felt raw, naked, and overwhelmingly free.

His kiss intensified and she knew what was next. Excitement sent renewed energy through her. It felt right—everything about this man felt right.

And safe.

The fire crackled and popped next to her as she swept her hands over his chest, her lips never leaving his.

He gently laid her onto her back, his hands greedily running over her body, her curves, and settling on her breast. His kiss deepened, more frenzied.

He slid his hand under her tank top. Goosebumps flew over her skin as he gently gripped her bare breast.

"Dammit, Bobbi." He whispered in her ear, his warm breath on her lobe sending a quiver over her body. As he softly kissed her ear, she felt a rush of wetness below—her body responding to his touch, the passion radiating from him. Her body preparing for what her brain was already screaming in need.

She tugged off his shirt and he leaned up, his eyes locked on hers, the fire flickering in his dark, penetrating gaze. The golden light danced over his chiseled, thick body. Wide shoulders, a massive chest that faded to that perfect V. She kissed him as he kicked off his boots and slid out of his pants. His boxers hit the floor...

Oh, dear Lord.

Quinn was long, thick, and rock-hard, and everything inside her turned to liquid.

"Your turn," his voice was low and husky.

Bobbi sat up and with a shy smile whispered, "This might take a minute." And she wasn't joking—removing spandex usually had her bouncing on her toes and tugging for five minutes.

"You have one minute, or I'm cutting them off," he said with a small smile, but his eyes were completely serious.

She grinned, watching him watch her as she ripped off the top. His eyes locked on her bare breasts, the coolness and passion in the air sent her nipples prickling. Next, the leggings—which was impossible to do in a sexy way, but he didn't seem to care.

And finally she was naked. She'd bared herself emotionally to him, and now, physically.

"Lay back," he demanded, his eyes never leaving her body.

He started with her neck, his tongue slowly licking, caressing her skin. Then, her breasts. His mouth worked one nipple, his hand on the other.

Her breath picked up, every touch making her more and more desperate.

Lips on her stomach, hands sweeping over her sides.

Next, her inner thighs.

Bobbi bit her lip and squirmed underneath him. He slowly kissed the crevice of her inner thigh, then his tongue glided closer, closer, until his warmth fell over her.

Her breath caught.

She closed her eyes and inhaled deeply as his tongue explored her folds, sliding around the creases and finally, over her clit. He slowly circled the tiny, swollen bud. Sensation exploded through her body.

"Oh, my God, Quinn."

She wanted to move, buck into him, but he had her pinned. His tongue flicked over her and when he inserted a finger she almost lost it. She gripped the rug, opened her eyes and looked into the fire, the scorching heat reflecting the animalistic lust she was feeling inside.

His mouth pressed harder into her, he added another finger. The tingles, the warmth and wetness intensifying. She began to throb, her body getting so close to letting go.

"*Quinn...*" desperation filled her voice, the words faded by the euphoric lightheadedness gripping her.

The orgasm tore through her, from the tip of her toes to the top of her head. He kissed, sucked, riding the wave of explicit pleasure with her.

She went limp, her entire body feeling like it had melted into the floor. Bobbi opened her eyes and stilled at Quinn's expression staring back at her. It was more than just lust. Eyes locked, he crawled over her, the wet tip of him dangling above her abdomen.

"You're the sexiest fucking woman I've ever seen in my life, Bobbi," he whispered.

He lowered, staring into her soul, and speared into her wetness. A soft gasp escaped her lips. He filled her up, every inch of her. She squeezed around him, the rawness of her orgasm increasing her sensitivity.

He groaned, lowered into her ear, kissed.

She released a long exhale as he slid out, which was cut off when he thrust back inside her. She wrapped her arms around him and gripped the tight skin of his back, grinding her teeth and pressing her hips forward. He couldn't get any deeper inside her, but she couldn't get enough. He hit all the right places—places she never even knew existed.

"Quinn..."

He pumped into her, harder, faster. She wrapped her legs around him and he lifted her torso, hugging her against his chest as he pushed even deeper, hitting new depths of her, awakening a new pleasure she'd never felt before.

His breath became heavy, a sheen of sweat slicked his skin as they rocked back and forth, passionately kissing.

She closed her eyes. Her world began to spin again.

"Bobbi..."

She felt him explode inside her, warm, wet passion.

She came undone again and rode the pleasure until the wave finally stopped and she was left breathless.

22

QUINN AWOKE TO the buzzing of his cell phone. He rolled onto his side, fumbling over the nightstand until his hand hit the evil noise maker. He clicked it on and with one eye, looked at the clock—2:47 a.m.

Shit. A text or call at three in the morning was never good. He opened up his messages—one new text from Jonas.

Hey, been digging into the hydrocodone angle and found something interesting. Hannah had no RX for it, but I looked at everyone who'd filled that drug over the last week and noticed Bobbi Cross did—filled it the day before Hannah was killed. This didn't necessarily raise any red flags for me until I looked at who the doctor wrote her RX was. It's a fake. Written by a doctor from another town who died thirteen years ago. Definitely worth checking into this. -Jonas

Quinn sat up in bed, blinked and re-read the message three times. Bobbi? On hydrocodone? No. It didn't make sense. He typed a response:

Buckley gave Bobbi a painkiller RX two nights ago. Did she fill it?

A second ticked by.

Nope. She has no other RX's to her name.

He frowned. So Bobbi fills a fake prescription that could get her thrown into jail, but doesn't bother to fill a bottle of pain pills legally prescribed to her? He looked over at her sleeping soundly next to him. She was keeping something from him. He knew it—he'd known it since he first interviewed her in the hospital room.

His attention was pulled to a sound outside the window —a low rumble and gravel crunching beneath tires.

What the hell? The only thing worse than a call at three in the morning was a visitor.

Quinn clicked off the cell and grabbed his Glock as a truck door opened and slammed shut.

He looked at Bobbi, sleeping naked under the covers, curled with her knees hugging her chest.

Boots on the gravel outside.

Shit.

Quinn quietly slid out of bed, yanked on his boxers, and leaving the lights off, silently padded across the room to the doorway.

The heavy steps stomped onto the porch.

He raised the gun and peered around the corner. A large —*make that massive*—silhouette loomed in front of the door.

Adrenaline awoke in his veins.

Alright, mother fucker, let's go.

He watched the man raise his hand to the door.

Bang, bang, bang! The sound of the knocks boomed through the silence.

"*Quinn!*" Bobbi whispered loudly from bed, now sitting up. "What's... who's?"

"Stay *there*. Do *not* get up."

Another knock, but this time, the knob jiggled. He watched, weighing his options... until a *click*, and the door cracked open. The bastard just popped his lock—in record time, he might add. This guy knew what he was doing. He'd never seen someone pop a lock that quick in his life.

Gun raised, Quinn stepped into the hall as the door opened. He couldn't see a face, just a large silhouette against the dark night.

"Turn around, walk the fuck out and I'll let you live." His finger slid over the trigger.

The figure lunged forward and Quinn took the shot a split-second before the gun was knocked from his hand. He heard Bobbi scream, and everything turned to a buzz in his ears. He swung a right hook, connecting with the man's jaw, then was knocked back by a thunderous punch to his own. He shook it off, lunged forward, knocking the man back a few steps. Quinn got him in a headlock, until a boot connected with his shin sending a blow of pain up his leg.

"Wesley! *Stop!*"

An uppercut to the guy's chin, and then a perfectly timed headbutt had his attacker momentarily blacking out.

"*Stop,* Wesley! Stop!"

Bobbi's shrill screams faded in and out. Who the hell was Wesley?

Quinn staggered backward and opened his eyes. Someone had turned on the lights.

Blood was everywhere—the wall, the floor, in his mouth.

He swiped the blood dripping from his nose and looked at his attacker—his face also covered in blood—staring at him with a savage look he'd seen in serial killers' faces. Their chests heaved, breath wheezing with fury as they stared at each other.

Bobbi jumped between them, wearing nothing but his T-shirt, and began beating the dude in the chest with her fists.

Quinn instinctively stepped forward, and then so did the guy, but Bobbi flew her arms out.

"*Stop!* Both of you!" She turned back to the guy. "Wesley, this is Quinn—*Lieutenant* Colson, with the *police department.*"

Wesley—apparently—wiped the blood from his face and eyed him suspiciously.

"And Quinn, this is my *insane,* overprotective brother, Wesley."

Ah, the former Marine. Now everything was coming together.

She continued, "What are you doing here?"

Quinn watched Wesley finally tear his eyes away from him and looked down at his sister.

"Why the *hell* didn't you call me, B?" Wesley asked.

Bobbi blew out a breath. "I knew you were on an important business trip and didn't want you to worry."

"You were *fucking* attacked!" Wesley shot Quinn a look as if it was Quinn's fault. Quinn's blood began to boil. He didn't need this bullshit. Especially now.

Wesley looked back at Bobbi. "Jesus, B. Walker called me about it and I was on the first flight out. I've called you like a hundred times."

"My phone died."

Wesley threw his hands up. "Oh, okay, so that's fine

then." His eyes skimmed over Bobbi's almost-naked body, then narrowed and focused on Quinn again.

Quinn widened his stance and flexed his fingers, actually wanting to go another round with this jacked-up jarhead.

"Is this the kind of fucking police protection you offer, Lieutenant?"

Quinn bowed up, ground his teeth.

"Stop, Wesley. *Please.* That's enough," Bobbi said in a calm, rational voice.

Shockingly, Wesley stood down and Quinn realized how close they must be.

Wesley stared at him, obviously waiting to hear his side of the story. Well, Bobbi's bulldog brother could go to hell for all he cared. He didn't owe him a damned thing except maybe a few more right hooks and a bill to replace his front door.

Bobbi sighed. "After I was attacked, he brought me here. No one knows about this place, and no one would think to look for me here. I'm safe; I've been safe here. Thanks to Quinn."

Wesley looked at Quinn. "She's not safe until you find this piece of shit. Have you?"

Quinn pressed his lips in a thin line and narrowed his eyes making it clear he didn't answer to him.

Wesley rolled his eyes and looked back at his sister. "Get your stuff. You're coming to my house."

A moment of silence weighed down the room, and finally Bobbi opened her palms as if to surrender. She rolled her eyes and shook her head as she walked into the bedroom.

Quinn flexed his fingers, but looked away as Wesley stared at him like a piece of meat. He didn't need to lose his cool. He had much more important things to worry about than all this fucking drama.

Bobbi came out with a bag slung over her shoulder. She paused beside him but it was obvious that the muscled-up goon wasn't going to give them a second of privacy.

"Thank you," she said softly.

Quinn's aw twitched as he looked down at her. Anger boiled. "When were you going to tell me about the prescription, Bobbi?"

Her eyes flashed and her mouth dropped open. "It's not what you think," she stammered.

"What prescription?" The brother asked.

Quinn kept his eyes locked on Bobbi. "Are you on drugs, Bobbi? Or were you giving them to Hannah? Feeding an addiction?"

"Quinn, it's not what you think..."

Wesley grabbed her arm. "It's time to go."

Desperation screamed from her face as Wesley pulled her out the door.

He didn't give a shit. There were few things that were unforgivable to him, and enabling a drug addict was one of them.

Quinn clenched his fists and looked away from Bobbi's watering eyes as she was escorted out the door by her real protector.

23

*B*OBBI PARKED HER Jeep under a canopy of trees next to a *Shadow Creek Resort* sign, pulled the keys from the ignition and blew out a breath.

She was tired—*exhausted.*

It was only eight-thirty in the morning, and even though her body was screaming at her to go back to bed and not come out until this whole freaking mess was over, she had a sold-out yoga retreat starting in exactly two days.

Two days—and she had a ton left to do.

The bleak, depressing morning she'd awoken to had gotten even darker, with thick, menacing clouds rapidly moving across the sky. Out to the west, they were almost black-gray with the promise of rain. *Fantastic.* She'd be working in the rain. As if her twenty-four hours couldn't get any worse.

Bobbi checked her phone one more time, her stomach sinking at the blank screen. Nothing from Quinn.

When she'd arrived at her brother's house sometime after three in the morning, he'd insisted that she tell him the entire story surrounding her attack. She'd had to revisit the burning house and Hannah's beaten, raped body. After persuading him not to leave and start searching for the *"piece of shit"* on his own—because BSPD apparently didn't have the skills necessary to get it done—Wesley went to his bedroom and Bobbi retreated to one of the guest rooms in his three-thousand square foot ranch house.

She didn't sleep. Visions of her brother and the man she was falling for bloodying each other up kept flashing through her head. The blood had sprayed everywhere—the walls, the floors, their faces. Her stomach sank every time she'd thought about it. The sinking she could handle, but the knots from knowing that Quinn had figured out she'd kept something from him was even worse. Maybe he'd understand, but the fact that it was about drugs—a thing that had single handedly ripped his world and family apart—she knew he'd consider it unforgivable.

He was *pissed.*

How had he found out? She'd slipped the pill bottle that had fallen from the nightstand in her pocket before carrying Hannah's dead body out of the burning house, and tossed it later that night. And she hadn't seen any more pills when she glanced through the drawers with Quinn later that night.

She'd only filled the prescription once—one fake prescription that was ridiculously easy to get. One prescription to help her friend who'd come to her admitting she was addicted and wanting to turn her life around. Hannah had been getting drugs from Kudrow, and Bobbi had promised to help Hannah as long as she cut ties with him. Hannah did, and Bobbi got the drugs to help taper off her addiction. When she saw the bottle by Hannah's bed, she'd taken it without hesitation. Sure, not only to cover her own ass, but because she didn't want Hannah's reputation to be tarnished. She was getting clean, and Hannah's parents would've been devastated to learn that their only child died as an addict.

Yes, she'd withheld information from Quinn, but it was innocent information.

And that innocent information just destroyed the budding relationship between them.

The thought that he potentially regretted their night together made her sick to her stomach. No amount of fire-works-inducing kisses or toe-curling sex was going to make up for the drama she'd brought into his life. She'd pushed herself into his investigation, pushed herself into his sacred cabin, and then her damn over-protective brother had pushed his fist into Quinn's face.

What a mess.

No wonder he hadn't begged her to stay. She'd caused nothing but trouble in his life, and he had enough trouble already with his brother being questioned for murder.

She'd laid in bed wanting to text him a million times, but didn't because if he was anything like her, he needed space. The last time she'd looked at the clock it was five in the morning, and then she'd awoken to her brother making coffee at seven. Two hours of sleep.

Wesley had demanded that she stay at his house until the guy was caught.

Hell, no.

Bobbi was done sitting around doing nothing. After promising to carry her gun with her at all times and check in through the day telling him exactly where she was and where she was going, Wesley had conceded. Her brother knew if she set her mind to something, it was happening, no matter what. And she was not hiding anymore.

Around seven-thirty, she'd broken down and sent Quinn

a text, explaining everything in one rambling, epically long message.

He hadn't responded.

Since then, she'd checked her phone a million times, and now, she was forcing herself to spend the day decorating the cabins and getting everything ready for the retreat.

A sick feeling waved over her as she threw on her backpack and grabbed a box.

She'd ruined *everything*. She'd finally opened up to a guy only to get everything thrown back in her face.

Well, she'd make it through it. She was better off alone, anyway, right?

Bobbi gritted her teeth and began walking down the pebbled path that led to the cabins.

She didn't need a man in her life—she'd get along just fine without one, as she'd always done.

Like Quinn, *she* didn't need this drama in her life, either.

Sprinkles of rain dotted the box in her arms. She rolled her eyes and shook her head. Of course it would start raining.

Bobbi pressed on, listening to the rain falling on the leaves above her and the sound of her boots crunching on the path.

Over the years, she'd visited the resort countless times and it was always bustling with happy, excited tourists or local joggers filling the trails.

Not today—today it was desolate, dreary, and silent.

A feeling of unease swept over her and she looked into the dark woods that surrounded the trail.

Bobbi glanced over her shoulder then picked up her pace, focusing on the sound of rushing water from Shadow Creek just ahead. She was almost there.

Snick.

The sound of a twig breaking had her heart leaping into her throat. Keeping her pace, she glanced behind her again, but saw nothing.

Probably just a squirrel.

A chill slowly snaked up her spine, an acute awareness of her surroundings gripping her.

Another faint sound behind her had her whipping around just as Rocco emerged from the woods.

"Hey, there, need some help?" The outdoorsman's shaggy, dark hair was wet, along with his swim trunks and a *Shadow Creek Resort* T-shirt.

She eyed him, her heightened instincts making her wary.

"I've got it. Thanks."

He slowly walked toward her. "You should take a dip while you're here. The creek's up. The water might be the highest I've seen."

"I might do that." She said, watching his every movement. As he drew closer, she realized both her hands were occupied holding the box. Her gun was strapped to her belt. Her brother would kill her for not having her gun hand freed up.

"Sure you don't need help?" Rocco stopped in front of her.

"No, thanks."

He stared at her for a moment and the world fell silent —except for her heart pounding in her ears. Finally, Rocco nodded and stepped into the woods.

She watched him disappear past the trees.

Rocco was a local who definitely knew his way around the mountains... Rocco was also athletic and into outdoor sports. Rocco was reclusive, and a bit odd by everyone's standards. Did Rocco own a pair of five finger shoes?

She started toward the creek again, recalling the night she'd seen Hannah's killer bolt out of the house.

Could it have been Rocco?

Quinn stepped out of the tree line as a group of volunteers wearing yellow raincoats and holding mugs of coffee walked past him. The rising sun was dimmed by thick cloud cover. It was just beginning to sprinkle and the ominous clouds promised storms were on their way, which would hamper their search efforts. The local SAR Team was headed up by two former Berry Springs police officers, and were the real deal—or so he'd been told.

He'd been at the base site since five-thirty in the morning memorizing the maps and laying out paths for each group to take. He had Payton's clothes for the K-9 trackers to sniff and hopefully guide them to her. They still hadn't found her car, and there had been no sign of her on social media.

He'd already searched the area by himself for an hour, with only a flashlight guiding his way. Why? Because thanks to his little run-in with Bobbi's brother, Quinn hadn't been able to sleep a wink. He needed to get his brother out of jail, and get the hell out of town. Those had become his two top priorities ever since Bobbi had left with her brother after lying to him and getting his ass kicked.

Quinn was on zero sleep, zero food, and all adrenaline. His impatience was almost as thin as his temper.

His phone rang as he walked through the field to his truck. He glanced at the clock before answering—7:14 a.m.

"Colson." His name came out in more of a grumble than a welcome.

"Hey, you sound like shit."

Jonas. "Please have something for me other than your trademark witty banter."

"The towel found in Kudrow's dumpster—it's clean."

"You're fucking kidding." Quinn gripped the phone and gritted his teeth.

"Nope. That blue paisley-print towel set is sold at Betty's Gifts and More. According to Betty, it's a popular item and a lot of locals bought it, including Kudrow, apparently."

Shit. *Fuck, fuck, fuck.* The towel was Quinn's ace in the hole to make Kudrow their main suspect.

Jonas continued, "So regardless of the fact he doesn't have an alibi for the few hours around Hannah's murder, we've got absolutely nothing to pursue him on... for that, anyway."

"What do you mean, *for that?*"

"Well, I'd pat you on the back if you were here. Congrats, Lieutenant, not only did the foil trays you found in the dumpster come back with traces of heroin, a deep dive into his bank accounts show that Kudrow has been laundering money for an extensive drug dealing ring for the last seven years. The DEA's involved and everything; there's potentially dozens of dealers in the surrounding states involved. They're on their way to arrest him now."

Quinn nodded. Silver lining. "Anything else?"

"The lab has determined that the candle holder was the murder weapon. Traces of Hannah's hair, skin and blood were found on the tip. Hell of a way to go."

"Prints?"

"Nope, and same result with the tiki fluid container. He must've wiped them down, too."

Quinn's pulse picked up with frustration. "So Kudrow's out, and other than knowing the suspect's shoe size and presumed height and weight, we have absolutely nothing. Not a fucking thing. No DNA, nothing."

Pause. "Well, no DNA found on the scene other than Hannah's and your brother's."

He began pacing like a lion in a cage. "What about the five finger shoe angle? Did you compare the list of everyone who's bought a pair with criminal records?"

"The lists that I have, yes, and no hits. I'm waiting on one more store to pull together their list. They promised to have it by lunchtime today."

"What's the store's name?"

"Uh, hang on...."

Quinn listened to the shuffling of papers in the background.

"Summit Trail Outdoors."

He knew that store. He'd purchased new running shoes for himself and his brother there a few weeks earlier. He jogged to his truck.

"Text me the address."

"You got it..."

"You in the office?"

"Yep. Been here since six, like always."

"Tell my brother I'm going to get him out today. And get him a *strawberry* protein bar."

"Strawberry. Geez, okay. And a water, too, I get it. Just sent the text with the address."

"Thanks, Jonas."

24

*B*OBBI STEPPED OFF the path and onto the rocky beach, relieved to be out of the woods.

A gust of wind scented with rain sent a shiver over her skin. The temperature had dropped a few degrees since she'd parked.

She set down the box and removed her backpack to pull out her hoodie. The box flap flipped open in the breeze, revealing a handwritten note of to-dos for the retreat, in Hannah's handwriting.

Her face dropped. *Poor Hannah.*

Her finger trailed the cursive letters, and flashbacks of that moment had her knees feeling unsteady.

The oozing flesh wound on Hannah's head.

The blood.

Bobbi took a deep breath and stepped to the edge of the creek. White caps rippled the flowing water. A waterfall had formed between two massive rocks on the far side.

A rumble of thunder sounded in the distance. An ice-cold chill slipped up her spine.

Her hand slid to her gun.

"Don't even think about it."

Her eyes rounded as she recognized the voice. Goosebumps flew over her skin as she finally put a face to the silhouette she'd seen sprinting out of Hannah's bedroom.

Quinn knocked on the glass door that read *Summit Trail Outdoors.* He cupped his hands and looked inside. The lights were on, but the doors were locked. He impatiently looked at his watch—8:03 a.m.

He knocked again, louder, then walked to another window to peer inside.

The front door opened.

"Mornin', there, Lieutenant."

It was the same woman with short silver hair and leisure suit that had sold him his shoes. In fact, he was certain it was the exact same powder blue leisure suit as well.

"Good morning, ma'am."

"Oh, dear, call me Eleanor."

He stepped inside. "Okay, Eleanor. Are you the owner of the store?"

"Yes, sir. Owned it for over twenty years now." Pride shone from her wrinkled eyes.

Quinn smiled. "Good for you, and you're just the person I'm looking for. One of my officers stopped by here yesterday requesting a list of folks who'd purchased..." his gaze slid to the shoe rack behind her. "This shoe."

"Oh, yes, sorry. It's top of my to-do list this morning, sir." She grabbed the black five finger shoe and rolled her eyes. "These things are ugly, aren't they?"

"Ugly as sin, ma'am."

She grinned. "My grandson bought a pair a few days

ago." She shook her head. "I told him that the woman he's been obsessing over..." she frowned. "Never would tell me her name. Anyway, I told him there was no way she'd fall for him wearing a pair of those things. But he promised they were just for yoga."

A tickle grabbed Quinn's stomach. "Did you say yoga?"

"Yes. These ugly things aren't just for water sports, you know. We sell a lot."

"What's your grandson's name?"

"Grady Messick."

25

*G*RADY.

Quinn frowned. "I didn't realize that was your grandson. He was hurt in a bike accident on trails a few months back, if I recall. Doesn't he use a cane?"

Eleanor tipped her head back and laughed. "That silly cane. I think he's addicted to it. Enjoys the attention, if you ask me. He doesn't need it anymore. Grady is as healthy as a horse now. Runs several miles a day on the treadmill I got for him."

Quinn's heart started to race. "Can you give me his address, Eleanor?"

"Oh, sure, he's got a little house on the mountain. I'll write down the directions for you."

Quinn blew through a yellow light and called Bobbi for the third time. No answer.

His thumbs pounded the steering wheel. Where was she and why the hell wasn't she answering her phone?

He tried one more time, then dialed Jonas.

"Hey, Lieutenant."

"Hey can you get me Wesley Cross's number?"

"Yeah, hang on."

Jonas rattled off the number, and Bobbi's brother answered on the first ring.

"Wesley, it's Lieutenant Quinn Colson." He sucked in a breath, along with his pride. "Is Bobbi with you?"

"No." There was an edge to the former Marine's voice. "Why?"

"I tried to reach her on her cell. Couldn't get through. Just wanted to make sure she was good."

There was a pause and then car keys jingling. "She was headed to the range this morning, then to the resort to get ready for the retreat she has coming up."

So, why the hell wasn't she answering her phone, then?

"Will you let me know when you hear from her?"

"Yes."

Click.

Bobbi had texted him about the pills earlier, so she obviously wasn't mad at him. Why wouldn't she answer his call? A faint warning that something was wrong had him pressing the gas as he wound his way through the mountains. He checked the directions Eleanor had written down and flicked on his turn signal. His truck rolled to a stop in front of Grady's house, not three miles from Hannah's, on the other side of the mountain. Dense woods surrounded the home, with plenty of trails to take to—and from—her house.

He should've seen this.

Quinn banged on the front door, with no answer.

Again, louder.

A faint *thud... thud, thud* drummed from the side of the house.

Quinn drew his gun and followed the noise, tracing his hand along the siding until the noise grew louder. Something was banging against the wall. He stretched his neck and looked in the window, which was blocked by curtains. Something was in that room, and something wanted out.

He jogged to the front door and knocked again. When no one answered, he picked the lock—not nearly as fast as the former Marine—and with this gun raised, he stepped inside.

Grady's house was an absolute pig-sty with trash, laundry, and empty food containers strung all over. The coffee table was stacked with adult magazines.

Thud, thud.

Quinn turned toward the banging and walked to the closed door just off the living room. He pressed his ear to the wood and listened to shuffling, and then more thuds. His finger wrapped around the trigger and he took a quick inhale before busting open the door.

His gaze landed on Payton Chase, bound and gagged on the floor, her head up against the wall. He holstered his gun, jogged over and cut the gag from her mouth. Blood smeared her swollen face and tears filled in her bloodshot eyes.

"Payton Chase?"

"Yes," she said breathlessly, licking her lips. "Oh, my God," she croaked out.

"You're safe now. Are you hurt?" He cut her binds.

"No. It's Grady Messick. He took me and he killed Hannah Winchester. He hid my car in the woods behind his house."

Quinn called for reinforcements then asked, "Where is Grady now?"

"I overheard him on the phone a few minutes ago talking to someone about going to work on some retreat."

Bobbi.

~

Bobbi's pulse spiked as she felt Grady step closer behind her.

Grady! What the hell?!

Her friend and fellow yogi had killed Hannah, kidnapped Payton, and attacked her.

And he wasn't finished. Grady intended to kill her, too.

Her heart skipped wildly, her eyes darting around the creek ahead of her. The sprinkles had turned into a steady rainfall, bouncing off the rushing water.

"I'm going to pull the gun from your belt, Bobbi, and if you make a single move I'll slice you open."

She felt the prick of a knife through her T-shirt.

Freaking *Grady*.

She'd trusted the bastard. Pulled him into her inner circle after the crippling guilt from the accident. And he'd milked it, faking his injuries while plotting to kill Hannah. Son of a bitch.

Her lip curled to a snarl as he moved closer, his arm brushing past hers.

Grady. Unbelievable. A burst of adrenaline combined with the fearless military genes she'd inherited from her father sent rage spinning up inside her.

She wasn't going to get justice for Hannah and Payton if she was dead.

It was time to fight.

The moment Grady's hand slid into her belt, Bobbi jammed her elbow into his stomach, sending him doubling over and the gun flying out of his hands. She spun around, gripped his head in her hands and rammed her knee into his face. Blood sprayed with a simultaneous *pop!*

Bobbi lunged for the gun, but Grady caught her arm, yanked, and slammed his fist into her kidney.

She heaved, doubling over, the pain felt like her insides were exploding.

Before she could straighten, a boot slammed into her side, sending her stumbling into the creek. Water splashed her face. She slipped on a moss-covered rock and went down. The ice-cold water rushed over her body as she scrambled to get up, her feet sliding on the slick rocks.

Another shove sent her deeper into the creek, the water hitting mid-thigh.

Swim. Let the water take you, then run like hell.

Bobbi dove blindly but a hand gripped her ankle. She bucked, twisted onto her back, the water rushing over her face, into her eyes, in her nose, her mouth. She choked, trying to blink away the blinding water. This had to be what waterboarding felt like. She coughed, spat. Sheer panic replacing the rage.

Grady threw his body over hers, straddling her torso. Her eyes met his wild, rounded gaze. *Crazy.* The guy was absolutely crazy.

"Grady, *stop...*" she sputtered out as the water washed over her face.

His feral expression didn't waver at her plea. He gripped her head and shoved her under the water.

A fear she'd never felt before shot through her body like electricity. She was about to die.

No. No, this cannot be happening.

The human instinct for survival took over and even with her head under water, she thrashed her arms and legs trying to connect with any body part she could. She hit something and his grip loosened just long enough for her to pull her head up and gasp for air. She sucked in a breath, but was shoved under again, kicking, punching, until a lightheaded-ness took over. Her limbs began to feel rubbery.

Keep holding your breath, Bobbi, do not give up.

Her arms felt like they were attached to lead weights.

Don't give up...

Her head began to spin.

No...

Her body fell limp, her mouth opened and breath escaped her.

QUINN SPRINTED DOWN the trail, the rain pounding his shoulders.

Grady had Bobbi, he knew it.

Panic had his heart racing as he burst through the tree line onto the rocky beach, where he saw Grady straddling Bobbi, holding her head under water. Terror lodged in his throat.

He raised his gun and sprinted to the creek.

"Police! Let her go!"

Grady's head whipped toward him, his hands still holding Bobbi under.

"Let her *go!"*

When Grady didn't let up, Quinn paused at the edge of the water, narrowed his sights, and aimed for Grady's arm.

Pop!

Grady slumped off of Bobbi's body as Quinn ran into the rushing water. Bobbi's black hair snaked to the surface, but no face. Quinn dropped to his knees, digging his heels into the rocks against the rushing water.

"Bobbi!" He grabbed her head and yanked her forward, her limp body turned with the current. *"Bobbi!"*

Her face was pale, lips blue.

Oh, God, no.

He lifted her out of the water and laid her on the beach.

He began CPR.

One, two, three, breathe.

One, two, three, breathe.

"Come on, baby, come on."

Tears of desperation swam in his eyes. He couldn't lose her.

One, two, three, breathe.

He'd promised her he wouldn't let anything happen to her.

One, two—

Bobbi's eyes fluttered open as she coughed up water. Relief flooded him and he quickly turned her head to the side, then lifted her enough to spit out the water she'd swallowed.

Just then, a flash of movement to his side.

Quinn turned to see Wesley Cross mid-air, leaping onto Grady's back like a cheetah attacking its prey.

Six days later...

Bobbi stumbled on a rock and reached up to her face.

"Hand *down,*" Quinn warned as he tightened his grip on her arm.

"Why do I need to wear a blindfold, anyway?"

"Shhh..."

She grinned and shook her head. They were in the woods, that much was obvious. The fresh smell of spring, the birds chirping overhead, no voices or cars nearby. Nothing but the calming sounds of nature around her. The setting sun warmed her bare legs, and a mild breeze felt like silk against her skin.

When Quinn had shown up to her house thirty minutes earlier and demanded she come with him, she'd pulled on a simple cotton dress, not knowing where the evening was going to take her. No questions allowed, he'd said.

But then she'd had plenty when he'd strapped a blindfold over her eyes. Bobbi didn't like surprises, but Quinn had remained silent during the short mystery drive, and she hadn't expected less.

"Step," he said as he guided her. "Another. Okay, don't move."

Bobbi heard a screen door creak open and suddenly, she knew. They were at his cabin on top of Summit Mountain.

A smile spread over her face as the familiar scent of burned wood and sawdust swept past her nose, reminding her of the incredible night they shared together there. But there was something else in the air, too... spices. Something that made her mouth water.

"Stay here."

She heard him shuffling around the room, and then felt him move behind her.

"Ready?"

She could practically hear the smile on his face.

"Yes!" She laughed.

The blindfold fell to the floor and she gasped.

The setting sun crested the mountains in the distance, its golden beams shining onto three dozen roses and a birthday cake that sat on a makeshift dining table, surrounded by hundreds of balloons dancing around a massive *Happy Birthday, Bobbi* sign.

Plates, a fresh garden salad, a loaf of French bread, a bottle of Champagne on ice, and two long stemmed glasses filled the kitchen counter. In front of a crackling fire was a blanket and stacks of pillows.

"Oh, *Quinn!*" She turned to him, butterflies bursting in her stomach.

"I figured we could replay your thirtieth birthday."

"I would love that." Tears threatened to sting her eyes.

"Dinner's in the oven. I actually made it... I mean, literally it's homemade. So, my apologies in advance."

"You *cooked* for me?" Heart officially melted.

"Trust me, I had Gino's on hold."

She wrapped her hands around his neck and pulled him close. "You really are something else, Lieutenant."

He smiled, a hint of pride in his brown eyes. "You like it?"

"Of course!" The truth was that no one had ever done anything like this for her, in her entire life.

"Good," he nodded out to the deck. "Come here." He grabbed her hand and led her across the living room to the window. A yoga mat, towel, and bubbling glass of champagne were laid in the middle of the deck facing the mountains.

"Didn't want you to miss this sunset."

Her mouth gaped open. "That is... you are the sweetest."

Quinn took a deep breath and turned her to him. His smile faded, his face grew serious. "I've been doing a lot of thinking since everything happened."

Since everything happened—he said it as if he'd simply had a tooth pulled, when in reality, the last six days had been a total whirlwind. Grady was treated at the hospital for the gunshot to his arm, then taken into custody, moments before Quinn's brother was released. They'd found the condom Grady had used with Hannah in his trash, right next to a massive shrine of her—pictures, most taken from his hiding spot in the woods. Grady had been stalking her for months. Her screams when he'd snuck up on her in the shower had led to a scuffle, and Grady had hit her over the head, not intending to kill her. And the rest was necrophilia history.

Quinn's instinct about the fire had been correct, Grady was too obsessed and emotional about killing Hannah that he couldn't directly light her on fire. Grady had also confessed to breaking into Bobbi's yoga studio and stealing the spare key to her house she kept there—information that she'd entrusted to her "core yogis" while they were helping to get everything packed up for the retreat.

Payton had given her statement, and had been unharmed and untouched during her entrapment thanks to a well-timed visit from Grady's grandmother moments before he'd intended to make Payton his next sexual assault victim. Payton then joined Bobbi in pulling off her first ever yoga retreat, a success by all counts.

Quinn had forgiven Bobbi about the pills, understanding the lengths someone would go to help an addict stay clean.

Quinn Colson had saved Payton's life, hers, and proven his brother's innocence, and gained the respect and admiration of every single citizen in Berry Springs.

And through all this, he'd managed to pull together a birthday party for her.

Quinn continued, staring down at her, the look in his eyes making her stomach flip flop. "A lot of thinking about you—about me, and about us." He swept a lock of hair behind her ear. "I'd like to see where this thing can go... if you'll have me."

Tears filled her eyes as a smile crossed her face. "Are you asking me to be your girlfriend, Lieutenant Colson?"

"Yes, ma'am."

She leaned up on her tiptoes. "It would be my honor to be yours."

He blew out a breath and smiled. "Mine. I like that."

She kissed him, then said, "And, Quinn... I *am* the type of woman to stick around when things get tough."

Tears twinkled in his eyes, a moment passed between them. He smiled and whispered, "Nothing bad will ever happen to you again, as long as I live."

And with that promise, he wrapped his arms around her and carried her to the blanket in front of the fire.

The cake could wait.

~

SNEAK PEEK

THE SHADOW (A BERRY SPRINGS NOVEL)

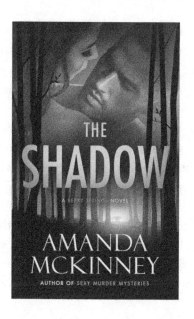

A gruesome murder linking to a famous painting sends

FBI Criminal Profiler Eli Archer down a path of lies, deceit… and infatuation.

Eli Archer has been called many things at the Bureau, but carefree and light-hearted aren't two of them. As one of the FBI's top criminal profilers, Eli spends his days inside the minds of sadistic serial killers, and he's got the brooding eyes and permanently packed suitcase to prove it. Days, murderers, and dead bodies blend together until he gets a call about a homicide that's shockingly similar to a case that haunts him. He catches the next flight to the small, southern town of Berry Springs even though there's no way the cases are connected because he already caught the killer… unless he didn't.

Payton Chase grew up in a family rich in money, dysfunction, and secrets, leaving her with a mountain of cash and emotional brick wall to match. Determined to gain independence from her past, Payton buries herself in work, chasing her dream of becoming a network news anchor. When a young woman is found tortured to death, Payton is certain that this is the opportunity to catapult her into the spotlight… she just has to figure out how to work with the secretive—and incredibly sexy—federal agent who's on the case.

As Payton's and Eli's chemistry steams hotter than the heat wave blazing through the mountains, another victim is found that looks eerily like Payton, and Eli fears she may just get her lead story… with her name as the headline.

THE SHADOW is a standalone romantic suspense novel.

❧

PROLOGUE

ELI SWATTED AT the mosquito buzzing incessantly around his head. It had been a while since he'd had the pleasure of being in the presence of so many aggressive blood-suckers. Then again, he'd never been this deep in the Ozark Mountains at dusk—in the middle of the damn summer.

The humidity was suffocating, like being in a sauna with ten middle-aged country-clubbers just off of a round of golf. Although this was no country club. Country clubs didn't come with mutilated corpses.

He ignored the bead of sweat that trickled down his back as he paced the small clearing at the base of the mountain. Nothing but miles and miles of woods surrounded him, thick and wilting. He'd chucked his suit jacket the moment he'd stepped out of the postage stamp-sized building they called an airport and the heat had hit him like a slap in the face. Berry Springs was in the middle of a brutal heat wave, typical for August, according to the local weatherman. He'd rolled up the sleeves of his blue button-up, but the fabric was still sticking to him like papier-mâché. His black slacks and black wingtips were already dusty. He'd worked plenty of homicide cases in the Deep South in the summer, but this scorcher was unprecedented—about as unprecedented as the amount of time the BSPD lieutenant was making him wait.

Normally, he'd be inclined to say a big "screw you" and hightail it out of there—God knows he had a million other things that needed his undivided attention at that moment —but hell on earth couldn't keep him from visiting this particular crime scene. The moment he'd received the call from the Police Chief David McCord, he booked the next flight out.

They had to have something wrong. There was no way the cases were connected... right?

Eli circled his rental car for what seemed like the hundredth time. A normal person would be sitting in the driver's seat with the AC on blast, but he had too much energy to sit. His mind was racing already, wondering what hell lay before him on this mountain. The directions had been shoddy, but homicide scenes in the middle of the woods usually were. He'd driven straight from the airport and the road he had to take to get to the specified meeting spot was more like a jogging trail... and his rental had the scratch marks to prove it. Not that he gave a shit. The red, eco-friendly sardine box they'd rented him had about as much power, speed, and agility as an eighty-year-old hooker on a Sunday morning. The damn thing belonged on a toy train track leading matchbox cars around a bunch of preschoolers—not that he knew much about that... toys, or children for that matter.

God, he was hot.

He glanced up at the sky where beams of red and orange fused together, fading into the mountains. He guessed they had about an hour before they lost the light.

He was just about to head into the woods by himself when he heard the low rumble of an engine in the distance.

Finally.

A blacked-out truck bumped over the ruts and rolled to a stop behind his rental.

"Sorry 'bout the wait." The moment the lieutenant stepped out of the door, he sized Eli up, no doubt noticing the wrinkled button-up and dusty shoes. Hell, the guy was lucky Eli hadn't stripped down to his boxer briefs. In train-ing, they'd been told to always wear a full suit—jacket and tie—during initial meetings. First impressions weren't just everything, they were the first pissing match with local authorities. Suits projected professionalism, and in some cases, intimidation.

But Eli didn't give a shit. Never had. And as one of the top criminal profilers at the FBI, he didn't need to.

Next out of the truck came a tall, jacked-up dude with short, buzzed hair wearing a perfectly-starched uniform. A newbie, by all counts. But, the guy had a look of steel in his eyes and the squared shoulders of pent-up testosterone that reminded Eli of a loose cannon. Note to self.

"Lieutenant Quinn Colson, nice to see you," they shook hands. "And this is Officer Owen Grayson, former search and rescue swimmer with the Coast Guard." Well that explained the brick wall demeanor.

"Agent Eli Archer." Another handshake.

"Special Agent," Quinn corrected. "Thanks for coming out so quick." He grabbed a bag from the back of his truck. "After we saw her, we were directed to you immediately." He paused. "Your reputation at the BAU precedes you. Hope-fully you're as good as they say you are."

Eli stared back. He hoped he was, too.

"Anyway, sorry about the wait. We had a domestic on the way out. My officer needed a hand."

"Not a problem." Eli knew all about the lack of resources and staff in small-town police departments, but the lieu-tenant was here now, and he wanted to get a move on.

"Call me Quinn."

"Head's up." Grayson launched a yellow spray can and Quinn caught it mid-air. "You're gonna want to spray this on." He handed Eli a can of DEET, and instantly became his best friend.

"Thanks." He shook, sprayed. "Aggressive bastards."

Grayson snorted.

"How far out is the scene?"

"'Bout a quarter mile through the woods. Bugs'll get worse. Especially at dusk, and we're not too far from the lake."

Lucky him.

Quinn sprayed down his T-shirt, tactical pants, and ATAC boots—attire much more equipped to handle a hike through the mountains—and Grayson followed suit. After Eli grabbed his bag from the car, they fell into step together, descending into the woods, which were darkening with each passing minute. He made a mental note to come back out at first light.

"Has the scene been released yet?"

"A few hours ago."

Dammit.

"Run me through everything again." Although he'd read the report in addition to the phone call with the chief of police, he still always made a point to get the story from as many people as possible. Perception was a huge hurdle when hearing a story second-hand. Small details that one person missed would be exaggerated by another. Biases—whether realized or not—were always injected into a replay of events. Especially in small towns.

"Vic's name is Mary Freeman." The buzz of the heat bugs was so loud around them, Quinn raised his voice. "Twenty-three, single, works as a tech at the local vet's office. Animal lover, apparently. Straight A's in high school, member of FFA. All around good girl, or so her friends and family say. Rents an apartment with a girl she works with."

"Roommate's name?"

"Cami Whittle. Works the front desk at the vet clinic. Same age, best friends since babies."

"Cami got an alibi?"

"Iron-clad. She was working the overnight shift at the clinic. Went in at four, was there until five the next morning. When she got home and realized Mary wasn't there, and hadn't appeared to sleep in her bed, she called everyone she knew asking if they'd seen her. Nothing turned up. She finally called us around noon, 'bout four hours before Mary's body was found."

"Mary's folks live here?" Eli stepped over a rotted, fallen log crawling with ants.

Quinn nodded, swatting a fly. "Raise chickens. Homebodies. Church-goers. Donate half their income to the church. Typical Berry Springs family. Not much to talk about. Mom says she talked to her at seven-fifteen yesterday morning, while Mary was on her way to work. Folks at the vet says she left when her shift ended at four o'clock."

Exactly twenty-four hours unaccounted for—a lifetime in a homicide.

"Did her co-workers know where she was going when she left? Any plans for the evening?"

"No. One thinks she remembers her saying she needed to go to the grocery store at some point, although that was it."

"You check the store cameras?"

"Yes—nothing."

Eli knew that BSPD still didn't have any solid leads, let alone a suspect. According to the thin file, they'd checked Mary's email, bank account, and had already received the phone dump for her cell. No secret internet love luring her to meet. No communication with anyone from her past that raised a red flag. No angry emails or text messages. No suspicious calls to, or from, unidentified numbers. Mary Freeman had no crazy boyfriends, past or present, wasn't into drugs or alcohol, and walked the straight line as far as anyone was concerned. Mary Freeman didn't live a high-risk life. It was as if she'd disappeared into the thin air... and then been guided into the deepest depths of hell.

Just like the other two.

The chief had been quick to call him in, chomping at the bit for Eli's help to solve the case, although Eli got the feeling it wasn't to help the grieving family get justice, it was to keep him from looking bad. One day down, and not one solid lead.

Nothing, nada. Zip. Thin air.

Just like the other two.

Quinn continued. "The owner of the land found her yesterday afternoon. Man named Gary Powell. Called dispatch about sixteen hundred. We were out here maybe twenty minutes later and closed off the scene immediately." He paused, shaking his head. "I've got to be honest with you, I haven't seen anything like this in my career."

Eli wished he could say the same.

"You saw the pictures, right?"

Eli nodded. They were burned into his brain.

"Sick son of a bitch, man. There's the start to your criminal profile right there. Anyone who could do that to a woman... a girl... shit, anyone."

Sick son of a bitch. Unfortunately, Quinn couldn't be more wrong. But there'd be time to discuss that. For now, he wanted to start from square one and check out the crime scene.

"Take me through when you arrived on scene."

"It was obvious she was fresh—"

"How so?"

"A few things, her clothes weren't dirty, soiled, wet. Hell, they looked like they'd just come out of the dryer. She was dressed in scrubs—blue—the kind they issue at the vet's office. Her skin was pale, grey, but not scavenged, which made me think she'd been recently dumped." He paused. "She looked good, so to speak, considering the heat."

Eli nodded. Heat sped up decomposition significantly, especially this firebox.

"I checked her neck for a pulse, anyway. And that's when I noticed the burn marks on her arms. Before I even kneeled. Cigarette burns."

"How are you sure?"

"I actually wasn't at first. Owen was."

Eli glanced at the mountain of a man walking next to him who had been silent so far. The guy carried a certain edge—akin to most military guys, in his experience—that made Eli a bit uneasy.

"I've seen more female victims with cigarette burns on their bodies than I can count overseas." Owen said. "It's a very common branding practice with gangs, terrorist groups. Sometimes the burns are symbols, like branding a cow, other times it's plain torture."

He believed that. Burning a woman with a cigarette in violent cases was common. It almost always signified the man exuding dominance over the female.

"In this case, there's no pattern to the burns indicating a symbol of any kind."

Eli watched him while he talked. Wasn't a big talker, but confident, smart, with eyes that said he'd seen a hell of a lot. Eli guessed he had some sort of special ops in his background.

Quinn nodded. "I had a hunch it was foul play at that

point but when I noticed the slices on her wrist..." He paused and shook his head again. "I thought maybe it was suicide. She burns herself—I've seen that before—all leading up to the grand finale of ending her own life. Finally, one day just did it. Something she'd probably been contemplating a long time. But, there was no blood on the ground around her. Nothing. Not a single drop. No way in hell she cut herself that deep then walked out into the woods."

"You canvass the area?"

Quinn nodded. "Walked almost a mile radius around this spot. Got nothing. No blood, no drag marks, tracks, nothing. Called in our K9 trackers, too. Nothing."

Eli looked down at the ground where his shoes were crunching against dust-covered rocks. The environment was perfect for finding trace evidence—dry as a bone, and low winds over the last few days. He narrowed his eyes and looked around the dense forest as Quinn continued.

"I didn't see her face initially, her head was cocked to the side with her hair covering it, but when I noticed the matted blood, I turned her chin." Pause. "The face was unrecognizable." Something in his tone had shifted now. Deeper, darker. "Mary had been beaten so badly I wouldn't have even been able to tell if it was someone I'd talked to the day before." Another pause. "Then, I noticed the eyes."

Eli looked over and watched the six-foot-two lieutenant shudder. He knew exactly what that moment was like. He knew exactly the gut squeezing moment of looking at two hollow holes in a woman's head where her eyes had been ripped out. He'd seen it twice now.

"At that point, I backed away and waited for Jess."

"Jess?"

"The medical examiner. Oh, that reminds me, I chatted with her on the way over. She's expecting you after this. Anyway, at that point the team started slowly moving in and we started taking pictures." He looked over at him. "I read Miller's file."

Eli felt his body begin to tense.

"I spoke with the warden where Miller's locked up, too. No way he could've gotten out, killed Mary, then snuck back in prison..."

The lieutenant trailed off, leaving the implication hanging in the air like a dead weight—a weight that had settled onto his shoulders since the moment he'd received the call about the mutilated twenty-three-year-old.

Grayson pointed ahead. "It's just past that thicket of bushes."

Eli looked around as they walked through the thick underbrush. He'd expected a clearing, maybe a biking trail at the very least. As if reading his thoughts, Quinn said—

"Whoever dumped her had to carry her body out this far, so he's got to be strong."

"Not necessarily. The strength could've been drug induced."

"Considered that too, but that's a long damn walk."

"He'd have to have parked somewhere, too. You're sure you didn't see any tire tracks."

"I'm sure. But that doesn't mean there aren't any. There's plenty of places around here. The entire mountain's covered in hiking and biking trails, which makes it surprising that no one saw him."

It made it risky, too.

"I'm guessing he dropped her during the night, or early morning."

"The ME give a TOD?"

"Her estimate at the scene was that Mary had been dead less than twenty-four hours. We haven't received Jess's full report, yet. She might have it completed by the time you get there. Here we are."

Quinn motioned to a small patch of ground beneath an oak tree. The grass was bent from where the body had laid. Bent grass, nothing else—no blood or bodily fluids from the beginning stages of decomposition, nothing. He kneeled down, peering at the patch of dirt as his mind reeled.

Why here?

Why that day?

Why her?

Everything had a purpose, a reason. Everything added together, and it was his job to put together the psychological piece of the puzzle that would lead back to the suspect.

It was his job to predict the killer's next steps. His job to prevent another victim from turning cold.

A few minutes ticked in silence as they surveyed the scene.

"So, what's your take so far? A copycat?" Grayson asked, getting straight to the point.

A copycat killer was the obvious go-to, but the ball in Quinn's gut was telling him there was much more to this than a copycat. When he didn't respond, Quinn said, "I'd like to read your report on Miller. If it is a copycat, that'll give us a few things to go on."

Eli tore his gaze away from the tree he'd been analyzing and turned to the lieutenant. "I'd like to talk to the ME first, then I'll have more of an idea of what we're looking it."

Quinn shifted his weight, an impatient tick Eli had seen plenty times before when officers expected him to immediately draw a full picture of their suspect for him.

He glanced up at the thick canopy of trees absorbing the last of the day's light. "I'll have something for you first thing tomorrow morning."

Quinn nodded as his cell phone rang. He stepped away and answered as Eli did a three-sixty scan of the woods. Miles and miles of dense forest, miles and miles of secrets.

Quinn clicked off the phone and nodded at Grayson, "We've got to get on..." He turned to Eli.

"You go," Eli urged. "I know my way back." He looked over his shoulder in the direction of the clearing where they'd parked. He needed to get back soon, too. He had about a hundred calls to make, and return. This was going to cause a media firestorm. Careers would be destroyed, fingers pointed.

Plenty of fingers pointed directly at him.

Quinn glanced up at the sky. "You've got about thirty minutes until these woods'll be black as ink. You got a light?"

Eli nodded to his bag.

"Alright then, I'll talk to you first thing tomorrow morning."

As Eli watched Quinn and Grayson disappear into the woods, the words, *copycat* echoed through his head.

No, this was no copycat. Arnie Miller, sentenced to life without parole for the first-degree murders of Courtney Howard and Pam Robertson, didn't inspire someone else to imitate him and kill another innocent woman by extreme torture and mutilation.

Why?

Because Arnie Miller didn't do it in the first place.

～

THE SHADOW

ABOUT THE AUTHOR

Amanda McKinney is the bestselling and multi-award-winning author of more than twenty romantic suspense and mystery novels. Her book, Rattlesnake Road, was named one of *POPSUGAR's 12 Best Romance Books,* and was featured on the *Today Show.* The fifth book in her Steele Shadows series was recently nominated for the prestigious *Daphne du Maurier Award for Excellence in Mystery/Suspense.* Amanda's books have received over fifteen literary awards and nominations.

Text **AMANDABOOKS to 66866** to sign up for Amanda's

Newsletter and get the latest on new releases, promos, and freebies!

www.amandamckinneyauthor.com

If you enjoyed The Creek, please write a review!

Made in the USA
Monee, IL
22 February 2025

12744853R00184